Tattoos and Baby Food— A Boy's Guide To Life

By

Nescher Pyscher

W & B Publishers
USA

W & B Publishers

For information:
W & B Publishers
Post Office Box 193
Colfax, NC 27235
www.a-argusbooks.com

ISBN: 978-0-6159370-5-2
ISBN: 0-6159370-5-5

Book Cover designed by Dubya

Cover Photograph by **Kate Bokas**

Printed in the United States of America

For Geir and every little boy who has looked with adoring eyes on the man they call "Daddy."

Man Quotes:

"I think a man's duty is to find out where the truth is, or if he cannot, at least to take the best possible human doctrine and the hardest to disprove, and to ride on this like a raft over the waters of life." ~Plato

Part I - First Steps:

Okay. Let's start at the beginning. Yes. It's *really* 'Nescher Pyscher.' It's not a pen name. I'm not in witness protection, and I couldn't tell you why my German-Irish-maybe-Jewish parents thought doing that to me would be a good idea.

Believe it or not, I got off easy. Of the four of us, my name is probably the least difficult. It rhymes and that makes it user friendly. One of my brothers has a hyphen in his first name, the other has a 'Z.' My sister has a double-vowel-hyphenation. When you see her name in print it makes you think of *Star Trek*.[1]

If you believe them, my parents[2] met in something they called "A Jesus-Freak, dope-smoking, hippie commune." As near as I have been able to ascertain from their loose and wobbly recollections of the place, it was basically a church where everyone had sex and got high *all the time*.

---

[1] I call her "JAPhead": Jewish American Princess . . . head. One of those stupid nicknames that only a big brother can invent. And despite the fact that she's in her mid-thirties and can kick a hole in the side of my face from four feet away, she'll always be "JAPhead" to me.

[2] Neh-sure Pie-sure, but long experience has taught me to respond to anything that remotely sounds like it. I perk up when people sneeze in my direction. Okay, the way it works is, you hold on to the power of your name. You protect it. My name is Hebrew for "Eagle." My father explains that it's a reference to Isaiah 40:31. But that explanation is for *me*. When you grow up in America with a name that rhymes you learn to deal with it using humor. Because people are too busy coming up with other stupid rhymes to listen to the majestic explanation you were given when you were five. My personal favorite has always been "Nestle Nescher. "

They[3] have given us a couple of different reasons for their experiments in child-naming, but I've decided the whole thing is the direct result of long nights in poorly ventilated tee-pees, exposure to unlimited after-sex hormones, and readily available pharmaceuticals during the heady days of the 1970s.

For some reason Dad went directly from smoke-filled, sexed-out yurts to the Army. With, like, zero transition time in-between. They gave him a pair of boots, scraped the barnacles off, detoxed him, and shoved him behind the controls of a tank.[4]

This kind of spontaneous, life-changing decision making should give you some ground-work on which to build the consistently dichotomous edifice of my life.

My parents weren't very good at what they did and I had a pretty miserable childhood. I won't belabor it, but I had a difficult childhood, a difficult young-adulthood, and was well on my way to making my life a perfect trifecta of misery when I met my wife.[5]

Our relationship was built on one firm understanding: We. Were. Going. To. Have. Children. It was one of the first things your mother asked me when we were dating. "Hi! I'm Christine. What's your name? That's nice. Do you want to have children, Nescher?"

---

[3] Dale and Dana. I mean, c'mon! "Hey. We've got normal, whitebread names. Wanna do that to our kids, Dana?"
"No, Dale. Let's sit up all night watching the lava lamp, having sex and taking hits out of Gandalf's head until we come up with something better."
"Sounds good to me!"
[4] I think it's fair to admit at this point that there will be a bit of exaggeration in the pages to follow. This anecdote, however, is completely and totally true; a matter of verifiable public record.
[5] Of course, she wasn't my wife when I met her. At least, not yet. But she soon succumbed to my sawed-off, furry, Viking-Jew charm.

It took us a little while to get there,[6] and there were some speed bumps along the way, but eventually we got the news that we were pregnant. We were going to have a baby,[7] and all of a sudden, we had decisions to make. One of the very first was an appropriate name.

See, I came from a family where "Nescher Edsel Pyscher" was considered a good name choice. Your Mom came from a family where "Bob" was. I wanted to give you the same amount of heavy, spiritual power my parents had. I wanted something like "Holy Soldier Power-Warrior-Rainbow-Scout Pyscher." Your Mom wanted "Henry."

We went back and forth about it, shouted a lot, and didn't talk to each other for long stretches. Compounding the problem was the fact that we didn't know if you were going to be a boy or a girl. Despite the advances of medical science, we are basically two old-fashioned people. We wanted to get to know you over time, not be bombarded with all of your vital statistics before you were born.

I wanted to inflict a family tradition on you; your mother wanted you to grow up "normal and well-adjusted." When I pointed out that normal and well-adjusted was boring, your mother pointed out that my childhood was nothing to be proud of.

After long arguments, tears, a few threats of direct violence and a couple of head-slaps from your mother, we finally narrowed it to a small handful of names—for both genders—that we could live with.[8]

---

[6] Mostly because your mother had to finish raising me. I wasn't anywhere near her level of emotional maturity yet.

[7] That'd be you, son. You know, just in case your focus shifted.

[8] She might *seem* to be all cuteness and light, but I wouldn't bet money against your mother in a fight with *anybody*. Her skull-punches can break a donkey's neck. She *scares* me.

And then you were born. I held you in my arms, bawling like a nine-year-old-girl who'd just skinned both knees, when the nurse asked me what your name was.

I will never forget that moment, son. The world held its breath. Your mother, drugged out of her skull on pain meds, still had the presence of mind to look at me. I was given the priceless gift of telling God and the universe what your name was.

"His name is Geir,"[9] I sobbed out.

The world came back. The medical staff went back to what they had been doing, and despite all of her earlier protestations, your mother smiled.

Then she passed out.

Raising you was another hurdle we had to jump together. We faced a different set of challenges than our parents did. Your mom is what my father would call "an emancipated woman,"[10] and I'm what my mother would call "a kept man."[11]

We enjoyed a lifestyle that was pretty self-centered.

We took the child-rearing classes, and asked for advice and help, and we did the best we could within the limitations of our abilities. One thing I have learned is that fatherhood is almost impossible to be satisfied with. You're never going to look in the mirror and say "Hey, I did a

---

[9] I had the honor of naming you, but the name was your mother's idea. It's Scandinavian and it means "spear." You are the spear we are throwing into the future, the strong weapon of our right hands. And when you tell your first girlfriend what your name means, remember to spare a moment of thanks for your mother.

[10] I don't know what that means. It's a term from an earlier, less enlightened era. I *think* it means she went to college, but Dad says it means she gets to wear her shoes in the kitchen.

[11] An enviable state of affairs, my son, most especially for the artistically inclined. It basically means your mother felt obligated to take care of me as a way of expressing her modern, liberated femininity. As a modern, enlightened man, I was only too happy to let her. And we *love* each other, too!

great job as Dad today!" It's a constant struggle not to screw up.

I don't have the slightest clue what I'm doing as a father, and it hasn't gone anything at all like I planned. I'm *not* the cool dad who plays lullabies on a Fender. I *don't* make French meals for dinner every night, and I have *yet* to build a single piece of furniture.

I used to tell myself that it can't be that hard. Parents have been successfully raising kids for thousands of years.

I've worked construction. I've worked as a gravedigger. I've delivered furniture; driven, loaded and unloaded trucks; folded cardboard; manufactured armored wire, tossed boxes and had every awful third shift job you can name, and nothing I've done has *ever* been as hard as Daddy-ing. I don't know how the human race has survived this long.

My parenting goal is to get through each day without you losing a body part, catching on fire, suffering some phobia-inducing-emotional-collapse brought on by my ham-handed parenting technique, or other general calamity.

An outside observer watching my learning curve would probably be laughing his head off.

Man Quotes:

"My heroes are the ones who survived doing it wrong, who made mistakes, but recovered from them." ~ Bono

A Father's Daily Prayer For His Son:

"Dear Lord Jesus, I humbly ask and pray that you please allow my son to grow up to be better than I am in every conceivable way. In Jesus' Name I pray, Amen."

I love you, son. If I never do anything else with the rest of my life, if I never accomplish anything more than the continued grind of daily existence, having been your Father, I can die content.

You are my single greatest triumph and the pinnacle of my existence. You. Are. My. Son. And I love you, I believe in you, I'm proud of you and you have my approval.

Man Quotes:

"Sometimes it's only madness that makes us what we are." ~ Batman

Part II - Definitions & Clarifications:

Dear Son . . .

Nope.

That isn't going to work.

It reads like I'm writing you a letter from beyond the grave or something. And while doing that to you has a certain appeal[12] I actually want you to listen to me. This is important stuff I'm laying down. I figure if I talk to you like your Coach or a Drill Sergeant instead of "the beloved ghost Dad speaking from the grave of years" you might actually put down your futuristic gaming device— something involving lasers and alien technology from our new, and hopefully benevolent, overlords who landed after the sun exploded on the 12th of December, 2012. How'd that work out for us, by the way?[13]—and listen.

Admit it: You didn't think I could pull that sentence off. Well, I did. Know why? 'Cause I'm a *Man*; a Man with dirt under his fingernails, beer on his breath, a beautiful woman in his bed[14] and money in the bank. A scotch-swilling, red-blooded, meat-burning-and-eating-with-

---

[12] Don't deny it. You know you're thinking about doing the same thing to your kids. We're men and we're genetically creepy.

[13] He asked, from beyond the grave of years. Bwah-hah-hah-hah-hahhh.

[14] Yes, that's your mother I'm talking about.

nicely-prepared-au-gratin-potatoes-while-telling-a-hilarious-if-ever-so-slightly-off-color-joke MAN.

Wanna be like me?

Tough.

You've gotta earn it. And it's an uphill slog the whole way. You've got miles of dust, sweat, blood and tears ahead of you.

Here's something you already know. You were born knowing it and every moment of your life brings it further into focus: being a man is hard.

Here's something I sincerely hope you already know. If you don't, you'll have to learn it soon: being a *good* man is even harder. The difference is profound. A man just goes through the motions. But a Man, a Good Man, will kill himself, every day, trying to be better than he was the day before.

Men on one side of the line cannot perceive the difference, while men on the other side find it all too obvious. If you aren't sure which one you are, then you're ready to begin the journey to becoming a Good Man.

Men like things easily defined. We like rigid, immovable boxes that describe What a thing is, What it does, and What it means.[15] To that end, I present, for the first time anywhere, The Man's Glossary, or *The Manossary.*

---

[15] Yes, I know that *most* things in the Universe can be identified as "Food Item," "Sex Item," or "Other." I'm trying to expand your consciousness a little here. Work with me! Plus, learning these words will make reading this *tons* easier.

Chapter 1 - The Manossary:

I have a real talent for offending people. When I was younger I did it on purpose and without conscious thought. I was a jerk.

I try to overcome that these days, having achieved a level of maturity that makes being a jerk noisome. The problem is compounded by the fact that I'm a Gen-Xer.[16]

My generation, Generation-X, did some truly stupid things. We re-invented "body modification" by shoving surgical metal in places that forced people to deal with the fact that you had a fishing lure hanging from your bottom lip. We've gotten brands and tattoos; smoked a broad range of textiles; drank beer by the barrel, and other things that qualify as toxins; eaten items no one can identify and given our children names like "Apple Rose," "Bus Pilot," and "Hammer Toad."

My generation has done everything it could to prove it was as stupid as it could get. Like, tattooing a huge domino over our left eye, and then trying to get a job.[17]

---

[16] Classically defined, Gen-X is the group of people born after the Baby Boomers: the generation after World War II. We were called "Gen-X" because we were "The Unknown Generation." A better name might've been "Entitled, Smoked-out, Brainless Sex-Monkeys." But that might've been a mouthful. Gen-Xers were taught from a young age that the world was our oyster. We were *entitled* to everything we wanted, and as a consequence an entire generation of Americans grew up believing the world *owed* them everything. We bred like cold sores and the next generation grew up thinking the same thing. While I hesitate to suggest that *all* the world's problems are my generation's fault, it's not entirely untrue, either.

[17] Here's a tip: don't be that guy.

But one of our more serious infarctions is what we have done to the language.

To begin, you should be aware that every generation of humanity builds its language on the bones of previous generations. As I write this I am in my late thirties. And already, I find I need to have things defined for me by the eighteen-year-olds I work with. In another thirty years I will have the same kind of trouble talking to your children as I have talking to my grandmother. We'll all—hopefully—still be speaking the same language, but the sense of the words will have migrated enough to make the occasional translation necessary. It's a defining characteristic of humanity. Some words, however, never really change. They become bulwarks of the lexicon, and I present a few here.

Chick (*Chik.* One syllable.) An American Woman; a totally happening babe.

Thirty or forty years ago, if you called a young lady a "Chick," you would have to be prepared to reap the whirlwind of fury you had sown. I mean, like, break out the surgical sponges and tourniquets. There wasn't a woman alive back then who would want to be called "Chick." It was sexist and demeaning, and women were just beginning to pull themselves up to a plateau of equality with men.

And then Gen-X was ascendant. We decided that it was *feminine* for women to be re-objectified, as long as it was the woman allowing and permitting that choice. It was suddenly not only okay to be a stripper, it was considered sexy and daring. It was a woman's personal choice to be treated like a sex object. Thus the word "chick" came back into the vernacular and a generation of women who *fought* to make life better for their daughters probably still wonders what happened.

Proper usage might look like this: "Dude. I was like, at this rave, and this chick comes up to me and says, "Dude, are you Hammer Toad?" And I was all like, "Dude! How'd you know my name?"

Dude – (*Doo-duh.* One syllable.) Prior to writing this definition I googled the word "dude." There's a surprising amount of information about the definition and history of the word. The general gist seems to be that the word "dude" originated in the Victorian era as a way to describe gentlemen who were ridiculously stupid about fashion. Apparently guys who had more money than sense didn't know their knickers from a knapsack and were royally belittled for it.

But I don't like that definition or etiology. So it's wrong.

Take note, son. That's how a Man deals with information he doesn't like.

Here, then, is your Father's "historically accurate" definition of the word "dude." The word "dude" originated from a usage by the author/poet and general *raconteur,* Oscar Wilde. Oscar was hanging out with his homies— defined later—at a ranch back in the day. They were watching cowboys work when one of them remarked that the cowboys wore their *duds* with a swaggering *attitude.* Oscar, being the kind of guy who did twisted and naughty things to words, jumped on the unspoken concept being expressed and christened those cowboys as "dudes" on the spot.

The word is — in general, contemporary parlance — an asexual term, applying to either men or women. I use it in conversation with women I'm not married to in order to put some distance between them and my overwhelming sexual power.

Nothing cools a woman's ardor like being called a "dude."

A good usage of the word "dude" has already been illustrated above, but Gen-X took this word and made it a catchall. It's a greeting as in, "Dude! I totally saw you puking in the corner last night! All right!"

It's a way to determine identity, as in, "No, dude. It was that dude with the spike through his left eyelid. Remember? That guy with the pink dreads."

It's also a term of affection and respect, as in, "Dude! You, totally rawk, dude!"

It is, as already alluded to above, perfectly acceptable to call a chick "dude." Proper usage might look like this: "Dude. You are like, one smokin', scorchin' hottie, yo'! I wanna get them digits, and like, (Insert inappropriate sexual innuendo here.)"

Rawk (*Rok.* One syllable.) I've yet to figure this out, but Gen-X *loooooves* to contort the spelling of words. It's yet another example of some of the horrors we've inflicted on the language. "To rawk" would be, in another age, "to Rock And Roll." It means you are so indescribably awesome that you "just totally rawk."

Homeboy Variations: "homie"; "home-skillet, -brew, -slice, -loaf (*Hoe-muh-boyee.* Two syllables.) – The word "homeboy" is basically an increasingly archaic urbanization of the word "dude." A "homie" is a "dude" you love; usually someone you're not related to, but someone you'd nevertheless jump in front of a speeding Peterbilt for. You *like* your friends, and your buddies are important to you, but you'd only faceplant the bumper of a dump truck for family or a "homie."

Anyone can be a "dude," but unless you're speaking of them in a sarcastic and low way, you *never* refer to someone as a "homie" unless you love them. Again, anyone who says anything different about this definition is lying to you.

You don't hear the word "homie" being used much anymore. This breaks my heart. It encapsulates an idea of heterosexual, masculine love that is so perfect it can only be described as transcendent. I believe the dying of the word "homie" is evidence of the continued drying of the milk of human love and compassion. But I tend to think along those lines anyway, so maybe we'll just segue to the next definition.

Bro – (*Broh*. One syllable.) The word "bro" is a singular pronoun for any man you're directly addressing in an affirmative way. "Bro" is generally used as an approbation, but I've also heard it used as a simple form of address for anyone a dude doesn't know well.

"Bro" has largely become the property of frat-boys, keg-masters and gym-monsters.[18] Using "bro" in conversation generally tags one with those labels. This is useful as camouflage for the less fraternally endowed.

It's been suggested by at least one person of my acquaintance that "Bro" is taking the place of "Homie." If this is true then the world has become a colder, dryer place in my opinion.

Manling – (*Man-ling*. Two syllables.) A "manling" is a larval man; a young'un that hasn't yet crossed the psychosocial/spiritoemotional[19] divide between boyhood and manhood. It should be noted that while a dude can be *chronologically* considered an adult, it takes quite a bit

---

[18] A sub-set of manhood self-identifying as "guidos" has recently absconded with "bro." If you spot one using it, feel free to tell him to give it back to you.

[19] **Spiritoemotional** (*Spear-eh-toe-ee-mo-shun-ul*. Seven syllables.) The combined cache of the spiritual and the emotional. Yes, son, I made that word up. No, you won't find it in print anywhere else. You knew what I meant.

more for that adult to become a Man. Conversely, a boy who has made the journey into Manhood despite chronological age should be afforded the respect due a Man. Anyone who hasn't yet completed the journey, regardless of age, is a "manling." You will meet many of these crippled creatures, my son. Most of them don't seem to realize the handicaps they suffer from. You should feel free to pity them.

Man and man – (*Ma-an.* One syllable.) This is a subtle distinction. Almost anyone who has a "y" chromosome is, biologically speaking, "male," or a "man." A "Man" is any male who has fully evolved as a unique, specific individual, into the total package. He understands and accepts the full complement of manly duties, rights and rewards with clear gaze and unflinching vision. You will meet many malformed men, but not many "Men," my son. We are a dying breed.

Brah – (*Brahh.* One syllable; as a breathy inflective.) "Brah" is basically a surfer-dude mutation of the word "bro." It's heard most often on the West Coast. Interestingly, "brah" often picks up harsher connotations then "bro." It almost seems to carry a certain amount of built-in scorn and derision. And while I can't seem to prove this etiology, I'm also certain I'm the only one who has ever lived who cares.

Douche (*Dooshh.* One syllable) A "douche" is, according to *The Urban Dictionary*, "An obnoxious bastard who mooches off of family and friends and is a complete and total ass to everyone."

That pretty much nails it. While certain other components can be glued to the douche, obnoxiousness and selfishness are defining characteristics. This is just about the bottom layer of existence. Beneath a douche is only the schmuck, and nothing on earth is lower than a schmuck.

Guy (*Geye*. One syllable) Singular pronoun for *any* individual, male or female. "Guy" is the least offensive, least descriptive word that can be applied to a person. In a sentence it might look like this:

"Dude. Who was that douche, brah?"

"Him? Oh. Just some guy."

"Guy" is used when one wants to accomplish the highest possible level of dismissiveness without causing direct reason for offense. Calling someone "Guy" to their face says, in a way that nothing else can even approach, "I'm entirely too cool and important to be bothered to learn your name. Admire my masculine daring."[20] "Guy" is useful when you want to establish your superiority over someone without actually banging your chest or mounting them.

Schmuck (*Shh-mukk* or properly *Shh-mokk–* One syllable.) – This is a difficult word to define. The American English spelling of "schmuck" is one you see most often in print, but the word is Yiddish, and spelled "shmock." It is the single most offensive thing to call anyone, male or female, and it doesn't have a very definitive translation into American English. *A* translation, provided by *The Dictionary Of Popular Yiddish Words, Phrases, And Proverbs*, by Fred Kogos, is "a self-made fool; obscene for penis; derisive term for a man."

Reading that definition, it would be easy to translate it as "dork." But that isn't right. It's difficult to translate the cache of offensiveness calling someone a "shmock" conveys if you're not a native speaker of Yiddish.[21] It is a

---

[20] It's also a *great* way to catch one in the beard.

[21] Waiting . . . . Juuuuuuuuust waiting . . ..

label of complete and deeply personal contempt. Calling someone a "shmock" tells them that you firmly believe they are—and always will be—an irredeemable loser. You are telling them that if they killed themselves the entire human race would then be able to evolve. You are telling them that their mother birthed them anally and their father was bovine. You are telling them that you've scraped bits of filth from out of a body cavity that was A. better looking, B. smelled better and C. smarter.

"Shmock" is a word of enormous power and shouldn't be used.

Ever.

Think it if you must, feel it if you can't avoid it, but treat it like the nuclear option of insults and *don't use it.*

Ninja (*Nin-juh* Two syllables.) A "ninja" is, as defined by my main man, Mr. Webster, "a person trained in ancient Japanese martial arts and employed especially for espionage and assassinations." As defined by your old man, a "ninja" is "any man who can do what needs to be done, how and when it needs doing." A "ninja" is a Man at the top of his field; an ace; a first class warrior; the MVP; the All-Star who smiles, shrugs, and does it over and over again, day in and day out, because that's what needs to be done; a Man who doesn't *need* any help, but will accept it if he thinks he can teach you something; a Man with all of his own tools, the ability to use them and the know-how to get the job done right. It's almost the most complimentary thing you can call a Man.[22]

It's often used with a prefix, as in "Word-Ninja," or "Money-Ninja."

---

[22] Please note, son: only a Man—and equally proficient lady-folks--can be a ninja. Are you beginning to see how this works?

Pimp Variations: "pimped out; "pimping." (*P-imp*. One syllable.) A "pimp" as defined by my favorite word ninja, Mr. Webster, is "a man who solicits clients for a prostitute." In modern, or slang usage a "pimp" who isn't actually a "client soliciting entrepreneur" is a Man at the same skill level as a ninja, but he's doing it with a sense of flair and style. "Pimp" is largely the property of the urban set, closely associated with a Hip Hop lifestyle, and should never be carelessly used on lesser men. Proper usage in a sentence might look like this:

"Man! That guy is seriously pimping that ride!"

"Yeah. He's a stone-cold motor-pimp, dude. He pimped out my ride last year."

It should be noted that you c-a-n-n-o-t self-identify as either a pimp or a ninja. Only another Man can award you this label, and only after they've seen you in action.

If you really want to suck up to a ninja or a pimp, label them with the ultimate manhood compliment: a pimp-ninja or a ninja-pimp. If ninjas are rare, and pimps are rarer still, a ninja-pimp is the love child of a unicorn and a roc.

Which would be a beautiful segue for our next definition:

Geek (*Geeek*. One syllable.) A "geek" is, properly defined, "a carnival's side-show attraction, most notably associated with the removal of small animal heads using one's teeth."

Modern usage defines a "geek" as "anyone who expresses an inordinate amount of enthusiasm or demonstrates an excessive amount of ability in any one area, and doesn't give a flying damn about the coolness factor or lack thereof."

A "geek" might be the guy who can name all of the birthmarks on Spock's back, the episodes they appeared in, and the celebrity faces they most resemble.

I am, unapologetically, a knife geek, a coin geek, a rock[23] geek, a D&D geek, a mythology geek and a word geek.

There's nothing wrong with being a geek, assuming you're ready to embrace the mantle of geekdom. Geekdom is a commitment. It's an all-in proposition of manhood and it basically means rejecting every precept of "coolness."

Nerd (*Nurd*. One syllable.) A "nerd" is "any person with an intellect greater than the collective average of any grouping of men; generally known for being a socially awkward creature with ill-fitting clothing and bad manners."

Nerds are generally looked down on and mocked. They tend to congregate in small herds, fearfully taking shelter among the members of their pack as they try to hide from the withering blows of masculine derision. I would strongly caution you, son: don't *ever* earn the enmity of a nerd. If you aren't one, you will be working for one as an adult or owe one money. And they are vindictive creatures. I aspired to be one, but I'm not smart enough. I get a pass on their kill-lists because of my assorted geekeries, but I'm not a member of the nerd herd.

While it's true that Geekdom and Nerdery often overlap, they are distinct and separate creatures. It seems to me that the loneliest man on earth would be the nerdy geek or the geeky nerd who didn't embrace his personality traits.

Gray Collar Stud (*Gray-call-urr-stud*. Three words, four syllables.) There are three kinds of laborers in Modern

---

[23] Igneous, sedimentary, metamorphic: you name it, I rock it.

America: a White Collar Stud, a Blue Collar Stud and a Gray Collar Stud. A White Collar Stud is a skilled, technical worker: a lab rat, a computer geek, consultant, a geologist, et cetera. A Blue Collar Stud is a skilled service worker: a carpenter, a plumber, an electrician, et cetera. A Gray Collar Stud is an unskilled laborer. (They sweat in dirty environments and their shirt collars get filthy.)They get by on the strength of their backs. A guy pulling wire and making armored cable for a little under fourteen dollars an hour is a Gray Collar Stud. So is the guy flipping burgers for minimum wage or the guy loading trucks at a warehouse at three in the morning.

When politicians are talking about "saving the American worker" they're really talking *about* Blue Collar and White Collar Studs, but they are invariably talking *to* Gray Collar Studs. The Gray Collar Stud is the backbone of American manufacturing and industry. If it weren't for guys with strong backs willing to dig graves, make windows and otherwise sacrifice their bodies on the altar of commerce, there wouldn't be a need for the other two.

Man Quotes:

"Talk low, talk slow and don't say too much." ~ John Wayne

The Ten Commandments and The Mancode:

Chapter 2 – How To Start Becoming A Man:

Even if you don't believe in God or the Judeo-Christian ethical system, a good place to start for a moral foundation in masculinity is The Ten Commandments:

Thou Shalt Love The Lord Thy God With All Thy Heart, All Thy Soul, And All Thy Mind – That's pretty cut and dried. God is first. It's harder to follow than you might think, but learning to put God—or, if you are of an atheistic/agnostic bent, *something*—above everything else teaches you how to be a Man faster than anything else ever will.

A Real Man puts his highest priority first.[24] Everything else in his life, no matter how important it might be at the moment, comes *after* he's fulfilled his obligations to his highest priorities.

This is often harder to do than you could ever believe. We get distracted by nonsense. We get enthused about things that don't matter, and we shove things that do into a hole in our lives, expecting them to be there when we're ready for them.

---

[24] My list of life priorities looks like this: God, you, your mom, our family, and everything else.

It doesn't work that way, son. God comes first, everything else comes after. If you grow up without God, then whatever your highest priority in life is, it should be a central, defining pillar of your existence.

Thou Shalt Make No Graven Images – This one was pretty specific to the Israelites trying to carve a civilization out of the desert, but if we use our imaginations a little, and stretch some definitions a bit, we can also use it to cover our lives today.

When God wrote this commandment, He[25] was telling the Israelites that He didn't want them making physical representations of Him or anything else that would be venerated. He was talking about idols.

But we can look at that commandment today as a reminder to not ever treat *things* as objects worthy of love, respect or admiration. That's a really hard lesson to learn, and even harder to apply to your life. It's easy to fall in love with a fifty-seven inch, plasma-screen-TV with Dolby surround and Wi-Fi capability.[26] But realizing that the TV is just a thing is necessary for full-on Manvolution.

Sure, having the fastest, nicest sports car on the block is nice, but once you start treating *things* as being somehow worthy of love, you begin to lose focus on what's important. It starts the process of objectification: treating

---

[25] Alright, let's get this right out in the open: I'm a Christian. I believe in a living, breathing, omnipresent, omniscient, omniloving, omnipatient, omniforgiving, omnicompassionate God. He has a name, He has a face, and He lives in our hearts when we let Him. His ways are so far beyond our ways as to defy understanding. There. I said it. I believe it and I won't apologize for it. I believe His name is Jesus Christ. I'm totally cool with the idea of you not agreeing with me, but I make no apologies for my beliefs, either. Here's how I put it in conversation. "Jesus loves you and so do I. And there's nothing you can do about it. Neener, neener, neeeeeeeeeeeeee-neeeeeeeerrrr!"

[26] I have this mental picture of you reading this in some dim and dark future, wondering why I didn't just spring for the Bloo-Toob implant that everybody else has; providing me with a hundred and fifty-seven channels of on-demand entertainment, twenty-four hours a day. I can only hope that by the time they're able to wire TVs into our heads I'll have been dead for a hundred years.

people like objects; like they don't matter and they aren't important.

Things are not people. Your life *isn't* in any real, measurable, way improved by the acquisition of things. There's nothing wrong with having nice junk, but don't make it a priority.

Thou Shalt Not Take The Name Of The Lord Thy God In Vain – Don't disrespect God. Easy, right?

Okay, apply that to modern life for a modern kid: don't disrespect *anything*.

Treat everyone with a level of basic decency and respect and you'll be surprised at how much easier life is. If you don't have to spend your time running away from people who want to rip your lips off, life is easier. Trust the voice of experience on this.

Respect is hard to find in our modern age, but don't be afraid to buck the trend.

Honor the Sabbath – Take time off, for crying out loud. And I don't mean a three-day immersion in, like, a Reality TV marathon on your Bloo-Tube, either.

Take time every day for personal growth and reflection. Even if it's just an hour or so, take some time for yourself. Life is too farking short to have perfect attendance.

Read a book, watch a movie, take a long walk through the trees or just take a nap.

But don't let your life be a 24/7 slog into oblivion. There's more out there to see and do than can ever be experienced by one person, but you were given a measure of years to at least *try*.

Don't devote your entire life to a job, a career, or making money. Live life to the fullest, my son.

Honor Thy Father And Mother – This one's pretty easy. Note the commandment says "honor," not "love."

The difference is that I have to *teach* you to love me. I have to *earn* your love. And I promise I will spend every day trying to do exactly that. Many parents don't make that effort, and they grow old and bitter, wondering why their children don't call them anymore.

I will not make that mistake.

You will love me and your mother, and we will have earned it, I promise. But you are *obligated* to honor us because you were born our son.

While God was responsible for all the hard work, your mother and I were given the gift and commitment of your conception, rearing and molding. In return, you have to honor us. Respect, obey, and otherwise provide for the appropriate veneration of—that's "honor." Don't like it? Tough noogies. I didn't write the commandment.

Thou Shalt Not Kill – Look, we can have endless arguments about the morality and necessity of death in a modern society; we can dialogue about euthanasia and capital punishment and everything else that goes into being a member of the most advanced civilization the earth has ever seen.

We can argue about self-defense and impossible scenarios involving your unborn child, the woman you love and some deranged maniac with an axe. We can even talk about the occasional necessity of war. All of these arguments have their validity. I've had a conversation with someone who claims the commandment is actually "Thou Shalt Not Murder," covering, I suppose, the fact that a meat-eating society kills constantly.

It's your obligation to determine, for yourself, what the commandment is, but God said "Don't kill nobody, never."

Thou Shalt Not Commit Adultery – If it ain't yours, don't take it home or let it take *you* home. Otherwise somebody else might be forced to break commandment number six.

At some point your significant other is going to cheat on you. It happens to every man at least once, and it's part of the journey into Manhood. It will feel like they pulled your still-beating heart out of your chest, defecated on it and then fed it to pigs.

It will cause you to die a little.

Now think really hard about how that feels and apply it to the poor bastard that you're doing it *to*.

Some people confuse adultery with lust. Lust is *wanting*. Adultery is *taking*.

Being human, your biology has wired you with a certain amount of in-born lust. It's normal, it's healthy, it won't kill you and as long as you don't debase yourself with it, lust—in and of itself—isn't any kind of a sin. Adultery, on the other hand, is letting that lust control you and it *is* a sin

Being a Man means that you're aware of the lust, but you're not an animal that descends into the pit of adultery. There are any number of complicated, theological doctrines regarding adultery, but the basic concept to remember is "If it ain't yours, don't even *look* at it."

Thou Shalt Not Steal – Don't "borrow" it, don't "take it for a test-drive," don't bury it under layers of "high finance" or laundering schemes; don't even *look* at it if it doesn't belong to you.

Real Men don't steal. They've outgrown the need to take what they don't own.

If you didn't buy it, build it, grow it, or breed it, then it ain't yours and you don't need to be touching it.

Thou Shalt Not Lie – This one's contrary to manhood in a lot of ways. Manhood is about popping and flexing, posturing and preening. We tend to tell tall stories about our prowess and victories. But telling something that isn't true is just as bad as killing someone. And to some people, it's even worse.

Don't do it, son. Just don't.

I'll tell you a little story that will help illustrate why you should avoid lying.

I wasn't a happy kid. My parents did what they thought was their best, but your Grandma Pyscher suffered from a life-long mental illness that left her medicated and absent for most of my childhood. She was hospitalized a number of times in various mental-health facilities, but nothing seemed to take.

Your Grandpa Pyscher was only fourteen-or-so years older than I was. Neither one of them was ready for the responsibility of children and they had four of them before hitting thirty. We never had and money for anything and that just made everything harder.

Without trying to sound like Oliver Twist, we were abused and neglected. As the eldest, I was at the top of the manure heap.

I didn't like my life. I was small, I was poor and I was powerless.

Everything I owned was a hand-me-down. Everything I wanted cost money we didn't have, and my parents were too absorbed in the misery of their own lives to notice how much pain they were causing the four of us. I was depressed. I look back on it now and I can say, without reservation, that I was suicidal for the entirety of my teens.

One summer, in between grades, I started wearing a golf glove. I didn't play golf, mind you, I just started wearing the glove. We lived on Fort Knox at the time, smack-bang next to a golf course. I used to wander around in the rough surrounding it,[27] and you could find all kinds of interesting things: golf balls, empty beer bottles, tees or the occasional twisted wreckage of a golf club.

On one of my rambles I found the glove. Something about the way it was designed for one hand and the Velcro closure over the back of it appealed to me. I don't know why.

I liked the way it looked so I wore it all the time. I decided I needed a *reason* to continue wearing it, otherwise my peers would think I was a dork.

So I handled that by telling them that my hand had been horribly injured and was replaced with an advanced prosthetic device. To enhance this illusion, I cut myself with my father's safety razors and stuffed aluminum foil in the glove.

Now, I'm pretty sure that none of my friends believed a word I was saying. If I'd been paying more attention I probably would have realized this meant I had the kinds of friends who loved me enough to fill the emotional holes in my life, but it went right over my head. They wanted to help me, I think, but were probably unsure how to go about doing it.

I got lots of well-meaning, if misguided, sympathy that only enabled me. My fabrications grew daily. At various points I told people I was five years older than I was, that I had an apartment in the city, that I was the father of a Latin baby—this one I proved by showing people a wallet-sized

---

[27] Given all my prefacing it probably doesn't need to be mentioned that I spent as much time as possible away from my house. My sophomore year I was on the swim team, the wrestling team, and two or three different bands. I didn't know how to swim and I've never been to a wrestling match, if that tells you anything.

picture of one of my cousins[28]—that I was a convicted felon, that I wrote all of the songs they were currently hearing on the radio, that I was a thirteenth degree "Black Dragon Ninja," and that I was an uncontested bad-ass.

At one point, a friend of mine, trying to trap me in one of my lies, I think, asked me to beat up a rival for his girl's affections. A few days later I told him I had torn one of his rival's arms off and buried it. He wanted to *see* the arm and I quickly came up with a plan to bury a pound of hamburger in the ground . . . and on and on. I was putting more effort into being this *thing* I'd created than anything else in my life, and my lies were taking on the dimension of delusion.

God, in His great mercy, took pity on me and I got caught. Like a house of cards, all my stories fell apart around my ears.

Yes, I was a miserable kid and I wanted to be living a different life than the one I had. But that doesn't excuse anything. It cost me a number of dear friendships and I'm still deeply ashamed of myself, twenty-some-odd years later. I've apologized, I think, to everyone I affected, but you can never rebuild or completely repair relationships affected by lies. My friends are still deeply suspicious whenever I say anything that veers into the improbable. As a direct consequence of this period in my life, I am a neurotic truth-teller.

Don't lie, son. You will always be caught, and when you are, life is a cold, miserable place.[29]

---

[28] Don't ask which one. I'll never tell.

[29] To quote one of my favorite authors "All Storytellers Are Liars." It's important to note that there is a difference between "storytelling" and "truth." I am a storyteller. As a result, many of the things I say carry a certain amount of built-in exaggeration. I justify this to myself as I **genuinely** believe that most people can see right through my exaggerations to the truth and enjoy the story for what it is: my attempt to entertain or

Thou Shalt Not Covet – If it ain't yours, don't pine for it. Then you won't want to kill the man who owns it, steal it, lie to the police about it, and commit all kinds of horrifying adultery when you get caught and thrown in jail.

I can't improve on these very basic rules for a moral life in any way. Any man who wanted to be upstanding would follow these guidelines without reservation. I add my own humble list merely as an addition. I call these injunctions The Mancode. Every Real Man will eventually write his own Mancode and follow it to the letter, adding subparagraphs and addendums as necessary. Wisdom, age, and experience provide further amendments, but here are the basic foundations of mine.

---

enlighten them. When I see that something I say that was intended as story is taken as truth, I clarify and correct. And if you ask me, directly, if something is true or not, I will always tell you the truth, regardless of what kind of a light it puts me in.

Chapter 3 - The Mancode:

A Real Man Is Not A Douche – Thou. Shalt. Not. Be. A. Douche.

This is the first and most important commandment of Manhood.

Overcoming our biological tendency towards selfish bastardy is the very beginning of the journey to successful Manhood. You can't do anything else until you figure this out. If you find yourself, despite our best efforts, becoming a douche, let me know. I will remind you where you come from and try to save you from yourself. I promise.

Your mother and I will provide lots of help, but most of the work has to come from you.

I can't emphasize this enough, son. Douchebaggery is worse than kidnapping puppies or eating kittens.

THOU. SHALT. NOT. BE. A. DOUCHE!

A Real Man Is Honest And Sincere In All Of His Dealings – After my rambling confession about honesty above, this one is probably pretty self-explanatory, but you'd be surprised at the number of men—note the lower-case usage—who never quite figure it out.

Jesus said it best: "Let your 'Yes' mean 'Yes,' and your 'No' mean no. Anything else leads to trouble." Real Men don't lie because real Men don't need to. It sounds trite and horribly clichéd in our modern, "get ahead by any means" era, but honesty really is, like virtue, its own reward. Yes, there may be short-term gains from dishonesty. And if you drop into the all-too-easily-fallen-into sewer of douchbaggery, you will find yourself justifying dishonesty as a matter of course.

The problem with dishonesty is that eventually you'll be caught, and being the guy nobody trusts to put out fires with hot cups of other people's urine is no fun at all.

Sincerity is harder to master, but it falls under the same basic category as honesty. Be sincere! Treat people with the very best representation of who you really are. If they're honest and sincere people themselves, they'll respect you for it. If they're not, who needs them around anyhow?

A Real Man Is Always Kind – Always. No exceptions. A Real Man is *always* a kind man to everyone.

Anyone can pull the wings off flies. Anyone can call people names and push them around and make them feel weak. Anyone can be mean. It's easy, but it diminishes the race as a whole.

Being kind is much harder, but every act of random, no-reason-but-that-it's-right-kindness lifts the entire populace up by a few degrees. Strive to be better than the herd, my son, and practice kindness.

As Dr. Seuss' Horton said, "Every person's a person, no matter how small."

A Real Man Is True To Himself – Don't, for any reason whatsoever, let anyone else tell you who you are.

Don't let your mother or I define you.

Don't let your girlfriend tell you who you are.

Don't let anyone—no matter their motivation or their undying love for you—put you in a box.

If you are a silly dork, be the silly dork you *are* instead of pretending to be something you're *not*. A Real Man knows himself inside and out, and while there may be any number of things about himself that he doesn't like, a Real Man is comfortable inside his own skin.

A Real Man Works - Listen very carefully, son: Real. Men. Have. Jobs.[30] It doesn't matter what your job *is*, only that you *have* one.

If, for some reason, you find yourself living at your girlfriend's house, and you can't find a job, then your job just became taking care of your girlfriend and her house.

A Real Man never mooches off people or lets anyone pay his way. Even if you can't find a job, even if there are no jobs available, even if you're crippled from your eyebrows down, a Real Man *finds* a means of making his own way and contributing to his own welfare.

If he has to, a Real Man *invents* a way.

A man who doesn't is a shmock.

Contribute, pay your own bills, produce something other than carbon dioxide.

A Real Man Does Not Suck – Don't be the guy nobody trusts. Don't be a sore loser, don't take the last slice of anything, don't moan, gripe and bewail; be open-minded to try something new as long as it doesn't hurt anybody and be tolerant of people who maybe deserve to be smacked in the throat.

Don't be the loser who's worked so hard at being disliked that he's succeeded.

Don't be anybody's burden, don't be anybody's tale of suffering and woe.

Don't be willfully ignorant, don't be intolerant, don't be condescending or patronizing; don't be a racist, don't be a misogynist, don't be a sadist, a satanist, a flawed fundamentalist, or any other kind of an –ist.

Don't be afraid of the unknown without at least *trying* to understand it.

---

[30] That's actually worth repeating: Real. Men. Have. Jobs.

Don't be a suck-up or a snitch.

Don't be lazy, don't be a quitter and never say "I can't!" before you've tried. Failure is always an option, but only you've exhausted every attempt at success.

Don't cheat to win. Win graciously, lose graciously, and accept defeat as part of life.

Don't fear-monger.

When a Real Man dies, the only thing he has left is his integrity. If you spend your entire life trying not to suck, you'll have plenty.

Don't suck, son.

A Real Man Is Respectful – A Real Man treats each new scenario, each new person and each new experience with cautious respect until it's proven that respect isn't deserved.

Each man has to decide for himself how much respect is earned and given, but a Real Man treats each initial interaction with cautious respect. Doing this has its own rewards.

I was lucky enough to build one of the most profound relationships of my life with an elderly gentleman named Anthony Byrd. "Birdie," as I called him, was a sixty-ish, stick-thin, black man from Brooklyn with a regal bearing and the temper of a street-fighter.

Birdie weighed all of a hundred and ten pounds, but I'd give good odds on him in a fight with anybody. He was wiry, mean, and smart as a feral cat. I loved him like a father.

Most of what I now call my Mancode was gleaned from conversations we had at work or in the car driving home. He taught me more about Manhood in the few years I worked with him then I had managed from any other source in all the years previous. He was noble and obscene, caring and indifferent.

His stories—masterpieces of truth, fiction and exaggeration—rambled from point to point, digressed and rambled back and made me stop and listen in open-mouthed appreciation.

I couldn't get enough conversation time with Birdie, and one of the very hardest things about leaving Kentucky was knowing I wouldn't be working with Birdie anymore.

He would share his TV dinners with me and yell at me when I was acting a fool. He was, in every possible way, a father figure, a friend and a mentor, and I cried when I shook his hand for the last time.

I will carry the memory of our friendship in my heart forever, and none of it would have been possible if I hadn't had the concept of "Respect your elders" beaten into my head as a small boy.

Don't lose out on your own Birdie, son.

Chapter 4 - Fighting:

I'm not the best person in the world to talk about fighting. I'm a dyed-in-the-wool pacifist.[31] As I like to tell the eighteen-year-olds I work with, "I'm a hugger, not a hitter."

Ninety-nine times out of a hundred I will walk away from a confrontation. I don't like hurting people. Not even accidentally. I make an effort to be nice to insects.[32]

As I define it, a pacifist is a person who doesn't view violence as an acceptable alternative. It is sometimes a *necessity*, but only when everything else has failed. When I find I have to resort to violence, I tend to use the minimum necessary. I don't burn down their village and sow their fields with salt. If I *have* to fight, then my goal is to end the fight as quickly as possible.

You will find, as you migrate your way through boyhood into Manhood, that fighting is sometimes necessary. It can't be avoided, no matter how much you try, so if you're going to get in a fight, here are a few pointers.

1. Never Start A Fight: This is a cliché of the first water but it's also dreadfully important. Always, always, *always* let the other guy be the first one to descend to violence. Don't even start a fight with a bully (more on them later).

---

[31] I'm not sure that's an entirely accurate description. I prefer to work things out in a calm, reasoned fashion with my antagonist, but I understand, intellectually, that there are times when a Man has to fight in order to remain a Man. There really is a time for everything, my son, and sometimes you just gotta spread a guy's nose across his face.
[32] Except for cockroaches. And don't give me any Circle Of Life nonsense. Cockroaches get the hammer.

Yes, the Shihans of the world will tell you that many fights are won by the person who threw the first punch, but many *lawyers* will tell you that they're also the shlub who ended up paying all the punitive costs, too.

If you can't talk your way out of a fight, you don't have to be the one to decide to initiate it.[33] Most people over the age of twelve don't want to be in a fight; most people don't even want to be in a *confrontation*. Provide them with a reasonable escape and the situation will often defuse itself. Keep pushing and you'll find yourself having to put up or shut up.

2. Never Back Down From A Bully: Yes, it looks like I'm contradicting myself, but I'm of the opinion that this will end more fights than it will cause. But before we go any further, let me make a few things perfectly clear: I can't stand bullies. I will never punish you for being in a fight with a bully and I will never punish you for standing up to one. If, however, I find out you *are* the bully, then you've got a worldful of hurt coming your way from your dear, old dad.

A bully's power comes from fear. They know you're afraid of them and they feed off it. They will push you down to make you cry, they will call you names, they will do whatever they can to establish their perceived superiority over you. Standing up to them robs them of this power.

If they call you names, try to reply in a clever, belittling fashion that will embarrass them. Never start anything and don't escalate anything that's already begun if you can avoid it.

---

[33] And like everything else about fighting, this rule is subject to individual interpretation and present situation. Use your best judgment, son. If hitting him over the face with a 2 X 4 before he can stab you with a knife will end the fight, then swing away.

Remember, son: no one has the right to hurt you, but *you* have the responsibility to keep yourself from being a victim. Don't ever let a bully molest you, or you will be his victim forever. If they push you, push back. If they hit you, hit back. Match force with force and eventually your bully will decide you are not a target.

3. Learn How To Fight: I grew up on an Army base. Most of the kids I knew had spent time all over the world, experiencing different cultures and learning different languages. One of the things you learn *really* quickly in that kind of an environment is that many of the kids you go to school with are accomplished Martial Artists.[34] Nothing ends a fight like a fifteen year-old-boy deciding he's had enough, throwing himself into Horse Stance, and plowing his right fist through your spleen.

If I have anything to say about it, you will take a Martial Art just as soon as you're able to focus your attention on something for longer than fifteen seconds at a stretch. I will be there right next to you, groaning, sweating and making all kinds of unpleasant cracking and popping old-man noises. It should be a lot of fun.

Martial Arts are invaluable for not only teaching you how to fight, but how *not* to fight as well.

Your Uncle Christopher was a small, meek kid in high school. We were in band class together. I was a freshman, he was a junior. Something about him being small, meek, and several years older than me flipped all kinds of switches in my head.

---

[34] True Story: I knew more Black Belts in Tae Kwon Do by the time I was sixteen than I've ever met elsewhere in life. Many of them were probably faking the funk, but taking a correctly thrown punch to the esophagus is a pretty convincing argument, too. That's probably what inspired me to start telling people I was a ninja: nothing trumps ninjitsu. Of course, then you've got to worry about meeting the guy who actually *knows* ninjitsu, but I wasn't thinking that far ahead at that point.

Big Boy's Pants/Nescher Pyscher

I wasn't very nice to him.

Don't get me wrong; I've always *liked* your Uncle Christopher, but I used to toss him around like a football. I'm ashamed to admit this, but in high school I was his bully.

He graduated and I lost track of him. Years later your Uncle Christopher looked me up. I was genuinely happy to see him, but he wasn't small or meek anymore.

By that point I'd been through everything the Army could throw at me, I'd been an LPN for a year and, if anything, I was bigger, stronger, and I *thought* I was a fifteen-flavored bad ass.

Christopher looked confident, but I wanted to remind him who the Big Dawg was. He smiled at me in a knowing way and I didn't much like it. I tried to do . . . something. It was probably a bear hug. You know, since I hadn't seen him in so long. Maybe a toss for old times' sake.

I learned something painful that day: I am *not* a bad ass. Your Uncle Christopher? *He's* a bad ass. He's a bad ass mofo and I pity anyone stupid enough to mess with him.

Uncle Christopher did something complicated with my wrist and arm, and before I knew what was happening, I was looking at the floor with an explosive pain in my elbow, wrist, shoulder, and rib cage; I was crying and trying not to throw up.

"Nescher," he said. "I'm a Brown Belt in Aikido now. You don't want to do that anymore."

I gargled out some kind of a reply and Christopher let me up off the floor. *Then* he gave me a hug.

If I live to be a hundred years old, I will never understand why your Uncle Christopher *still* wants to be my friend. I was a jerk to him in high school and when he

- 40 -

could've come back and fed me my own feet, he became one of the best friends I've ever had. I love him for it.

We both know that if he wanted to he could peel the back of my head off and use my spine to floss with. I'm not sure what keeps him from doing that. Maybe just *knowing* he could is enough for him. If it had been *me* who took rides across the band room, I don't think I would have stopped at putting me on the floor.

He got me into Aikido in a big way. I will never be as good as he is—I've lost track of how many Black Belts he has now—but ironically, thanks to a guy I bullied in high school, I know enough to make a bully who's bothering me go away. Learn a Martial Art, my son. Learn one early and learn one well.

4. Know When To Admit It's Too Much: Okay, so you're a third-degree Black Belt in three different Martial Arts. You can put your hand through a brick wall, swallow live coals, and dance across broken glass. You can do ten-thousand push-ups in ten minutes and you can bench-press seven-hundred pounds.

You're a bad-ass. But it might, just *might*, mind you, be a bad idea to kick over the line of motorcycles in front of Ned's Satanic Coffee House to prove it.

Don't walk around with a chip on your shoulder. Somebody'll always come along to knock it off and feed it to you.

Don't mess with the guy with cauliflower ears, a nose like a squashed bread loaf, and nicknames for his knuckles.[35]

Yes, you might think you're the baddest thing on two legs, but there's *always* someone, somewhere who's badder

---

[35] Especially if he's got, like, "PH-LU-F-F-I B-U-N-N-I" tattooed across them.

than you are. Don't go looking for him. Accept your own mortality, son. Ironically it might end up prolonging your life.

5. Choose Your Battles: Every Man has to decide when he will stop talking and start swinging. I recommend you put your "action trigger" it as far out on the ol' Emotional Trauma Curve[36] as you can. Again, don't walk around with a chip on your shoulder or you'll never stop fighting the same battles.

Learn to laugh at yourself, learn to jolly your way out of a fight, and for crying out loud, don't go ballistic every time some idiot says the wrong thing. People will like you more and you'll find that the need to swing on some fool will decrease in proportion to your willingness to let them *be* a fool.

Instead of a line that can't be crossed without you reacting, have an ever-shrinking boundary that states "This is as much as I'm willing to take today. Leave me alone or suffer the consequences."

Knowing when to apologize helps, too. Sometimes it's just easier to swallow your pride and say, "Hey, my bad," than it is to get in a fight, face possible criminal charges and civil damages, and spend the rest of your life with a limp and an empty wallet.

---

[36] The Emotional Trauma Curve is a life-long index that starts you out at the median point of birth. Every point along the curve is self-determined. For me, a high-index reaction would be finding a hairy, moving lump in my coffee. Your response to life is determined by where you set your points on your personal curve. Keep things light and you'll be fine. Set things too high and you'll be a twitching mess by the time you're twenty-five.

Man Quotes:

"We boil at different degrees." ~ Clint Eastwood

Part III - Love, Dating, Sex & Marriage:

Chapter 5 –Women, Woman, Womyn:

Women. The fairer sex; the "weaker" sex. They hold up half the sky and control everything underneath it.

Heaven protect us.

Libraries have been written about the Yin half of humanity, and no one has ever figured them out. So here's a distillation: women are awesome; women *suck*.

There is no "Battle of the Sexes," son. They let us *believe* there is because it makes us happy. The truth is that women won the war at the very beginning of human history and they let us continue to flail along for dark and unholy reasons of their own.

They're smarter than we are. Cunning. They can shut our brains down. I know a woman who can stop work on a five-hundred-million-dollar production floor by playing with her hair.

We hate them, we love them, we despise them, we worship them. They fascinate us and hypnotize us and wrap us around their fingers like jewelry. We can't get enough and there's nothing we can do.

With one well-timed comment, a woman can disembowel your self-esteem for life. They can build you up into a god and cast you down to the deepest pits of human misery. They bound our existences from birth to death. Everything we do, everything we are, and everything we hope to become or achieve is all about impressing them enough to get one fleeting smile. Until you learn to protect yourself from the gender as a whole, you will be a helpless pawn in our never-ending subservience. You may eventually learn enough to *limit* their power over you, but you will never truly be free. After all, every man has a Mother.

If you can, find *one*, love the hell out of her and let the rest of the gender gnash their teeth at you in impotent fury.

You've got some lumps coming your way before you find her, though. It's a fact of human existence: at some point, someone is going to come along and tie your heart into little pink knots. Accept it. There's nothing you can do about it, it happens to everyone at least once, and it will be both the most joyous and painful experience of your entire life. Your friends will try to save you, your family will try to intervene, and you won't listen to anybody. All you'll be seeing is the face of your beloved dancing just beyond your fingertips. Their voice will be music and they'll smell like sunshine. You will spend all your time and energy trying to make them happy; you will elevate them to the highest possible pedestal . . .

. . . and when they come crashing down your world will, briefly, end.

The trick to surviving it is to be aware of it. You won't be able to stop it, but you'll at least have the consolation of knowing that it's happening to *you*.

There are any number of pithy clichés people use to try and understand love. I'm sure you've heard your share of them. I've heard at least one argument suggesting that love is nothing more than a "biochemical response designed to ensure that an organism's genes get passed on."[37] I can't agree fully with this assessment since love has nothing whatsoever to do with breeding. The two often happen in concert, of course, but love flourishes everywhere.

The J Geils Band said it succinctly: "Love Stinks." And it does, but it's also *awesome*.

I'm not sure I'm the best resource to come to for this stuff. Your mother once described me as "A Serial Monogamist." And she's right. I entered every intimate relationship I was ever in with the specific goal of marrying the woman, having kids with her, and dying at a ripe old age by her side. As soon as I realized that wasn't going to happen, the relationship ended. Sometimes I ended it, sometimes she did, but it always ended.

I never dated for *fun*. I didn't know how. All the advice I got about girls when I was a wee nipper was about how to make them marry you. But I like women. I like being around them, I like having them for friends. I like the way women smell, the way they laugh, the way they approach the world. I like swimming around in the piranha-infested

---

[37] There's some truth to that argument. For many people of my acquaintance, *only* love could ensure breeding.

waters of the average woman's brain. Young, old, fat, skinny, rich, poor, black, white, Asian, Latin, and all others: I like women. I always have. I've put some thought into this and I sincerely believe it to be true: if I were born a woman I would be a lesbian.

My father was no help. His advice on dating was to make sure the woman wasn't diseased or would pass on any diseased traits to our children. "Because sometimes you can't tell until you have kids, Nescher. Make sure you find this stuff out *first*."

By the time I was eighteen years old I had been engaged. Twice. I've been there, done that and had my heart ripped open and kicked in the butt. Every one of my romantic relationships has been a failure or a mistake, and sometimes both, with the happy exception of the very last one. I've learned a few things along the way and I share them with you here.

Chapter 6- What They Want You To Know:

I put a hypothetical situation to some people—predominantly women—of my acquaintance. I said "God has given you a pulpit in front of every man who has ever lived, is living and will ever live. They are all sitting in front of you, listening attentively. What do you say to them? What do you want the entire gender to know, learn and absorb?"

These are the responses I got back from women from all walks of life: wives, mothers, successful business women, working professionals, artists, and stay-at-home-housewives; married, single, widowed and divorced.

It's interesting in that after I explained what this hypothetical was for there was some grumbling that I hadn't made it clear that it would be given to a young son. That's a good point to remember: some women are wives, some women are mothers, and some women are wives *and* mothers. It's different for them in a way a man and a father can never fully appreciate. Except for God, no one in your life will ever love you as much or in the same way as your mother. No one can. They didn't carry you for nine months, give birth to you and nurse you. To quote a currently popular meme, "You are the only one who knows what her heartbeat sounds like from the inside."

In every way possible, you are a part of your mother, and the advice a woman would give to a son is often very different from the advice a woman would give to a Man.

Some of this advice seems to me to be along the lines of "Know your place, boy." But I present it here as it was given to me. Listen, son. This is stuff you won't otherwise get from women and it's an invaluable, unvarnished insight into their thinking.

"We can't read your mind." - Christine Gale Huth Pyscher, Happily Married, 40ish, Geologist, Ohio.

"My wife says, and I quote: "It's not that damn hard to put the fucking toilet seat down!" - Eugene Kodadek, Married, 30ish, Musician, Minnesota.

"If you like/love her, tell her and show her in everything you do!" And then she added, "If you can't remember, try sitting down to pee."– Rita L. Smith, In a Relationship, Author, Ohio.

"Be my friend and equal not my daddy or boss." - Dawndra Helton, Married, 30ish, Registered Nurse, Indiana.

"I can think of so many things, but when I condense them all, it comes down to one main idea: all I want and need is to be loved as wholly and freely as I love someone. No bullshit. No shenanigans. With these circumstances, I could handle the toilet seat being left up and hairs in the shower." – Rachael Adamson, 30ish, Tennessee.

"I stand at the pulpit - both palms flat against its slightly sloped surface. I lift my hands, shaking them above my shoulders. "Talk to me!" I yell. "Talk. To. Me!" She then added "One thing women do appreciate are men who don't have strange (homo)phobias."– Laura Kepner, Married, Author, Florida.

"Don't be intimidated that my "internal pair" (*of testicles*) are firmly established! - Plan something and surprise me! - Don't mistake my zeal/passion for X topic as sexual desire! - Love me for me, not my appearance! - Don't be afraid to challenge me to grow!" – Raya Pyscher, Married, 30ish, Soldier.

"Romance isn't sex. We need the daily hugs, the "You look pretty today." or even a hug while we're washing dishes. Unexpected appreciation and attention is everything. That's real romance." – J.M. Powers, Married, Author.

"We all want to be loved and treated as if we are the only woman in the world. It's the gratitude for the small things that you notice that matters most: how hard I work to keep the house for you, the fact I remembered to make your favorite meal or pick up your dry cleaning. Women say "I love you." every day with actions which show care and respect. Notice. Compliment. Do some for her too." – Jennifer Black Georg, Married, English Teacher, Maryland.

"I am going to be serious and my comment has nothing to do with women. It is more like advice I would give my sons. Be steadfast and sure in every decision you make. Do things that would make people proud and make yourself proud. Be yourself and love yourself. Earn respect if you want to be respected. Love and protect your family and friends, never leave someone in their time of need. Anybody can walk away from a difficult situation, but it takes a real man to stick around and help the suffering." – Cynthia Sisco, Married, Author, Minnesota.

"Use the word 'Love' only when you mean it. It's not some fickle thing to be thrown around when you think you'll be forgiven easily by using it." – Kimberly Riggi, Health Care Aide, Arizona.

"You are a spiritual being having a human experience. You have only two choices in life, Love or fear. Choose wisely. You are God incarnate, behave accordingly." - Lisabeth L-"Boogie" Lohmann, Chef, Florida.

"Don't talk to me like my IQ is 80. And if my IQ happens to be higher than yours, don't get bent out of shape if I don't dummy down just for your ego. That's what I would say and probably have to a few." – Barbara Pappan, Married, 40ish, Literary Agent, Oklahoma.

"When I have a bad day and talk to you about it, I'm not asking you to fix it. I just want you to listen, give me a sympathetic look and a hug. Very little effort on your part for a huge return!" - Rachel Annette DeMott Harper, Married, 30ish, Family Resource Director, Michigan.

"It is super sexy and super loving when a man takes the garbage out ... without being asked ... especially when it's his agreed upon job." – Patricia Neumann, In A Domestic Relationship, Freelance Producer, New York.

"Once you win her over, continue to treat her the same way." – Heather Spires, 30ish, Married, Machinist, Ohio.

And then I asked one of my very best friends the same question. Her response filled most of three pages and I present it here:

"Make eye contact with store clerks and waitresses and mechanics, and people you hate and people you love. Notice them, and meet their eyes. Real eye contact. So you can tell the color of their iris. Life gets shallow. Add a moment of human connection.

"Try to write or speak the truth and do no harm. That's harder than it sounds. Chronic honesty can be cruel and some people use it as a weapon, just as sharp as a lie.

"Don't be a Dementor[38], and don't hang with them. Some folks suck the happy out of you. Chronic victims, life shits on them nonstop... and those relationships are exhausting and toxic. *Everyone* gets shit on nonstop. We are all Job. If you can't cry, scream, rage, and move on with a fart joke and joy that at least the boils aren't on your elbow, then you *are* the Dementor and you need to get over yourself.

---

[38] Hopefully, by the time you read this you will have either read or been read the Harry Potter books.

"Chronic victims will suck you in and make you a weak codependent. Learn how to say no with love. Learn how to say no without love. Learn how to say no, and then... *mean* no, don't say no and do whatever you were just asked.

"You need friends. Good ones. With similar values. So you can form meaningful relationships. You need friends. Make shit-ons of them, and love them all, but only hold those who touch you close. Friendship is a little-marriage, sans sex and dishes, and it takes an investment.

"You're going to do stupid shit that might kill you to impress your friends and to impress women. Avoid stunts and drunken dares that might leave you a quadriplegic.

"Girls are pretty, magical creatures. It takes some effort shitting glitter. Once *you* stop trying, don't expect *her* to. What I'm saying is the first time you break wind, you've opened the court and you have no business being offended if your little princess feels comfortable farting in your presence. No double standards.

"Money will bring you down. Or, more importantly, lack of it. Money will make you feel like you're having a heart attack. Money will make you pick fights that don't mean anything. It'll make you irritated. It'll cause worry. The further from the bottom you come, the more losing everything will fuck up your mind. But we all die naked. Really, we do.

"Every day someone dies unexpectedly. Even if you hate her right now, even if you're not speaking, even if you hate your parents, your children, yourself, don't ever walk out the door or hang up the phone without saying "Love you." Even if it tastes like shit on your tongue. One day they'll be your last words to that person.

"Don't iconicize your woman in your mind. She's human. She thinks about sex as much as you do, and, she'd probably surprise you with the kinky thoughts she'd be OK acting out in a safe, nonjudgmental environment. Sex shops are filled with shit for women. Why do you think that is? So you think your angel of purity would die if you wanted her to gag you like Marcus in Pulp Fiction... maybe she would, but you have to give her the chance. You aren't the only person with fantasies, dreams or desire. There shouldn't be shame or sex secrets in a relationship. Not a real one. Sex isn't everything, but it's a damn lie that it's not important. When the door closes, if you aren't hurting anyone, what happens between you and your partner is OK. If it's consensual, it's nobody's business.

"Don't iconicize your woman, continuation: She gets tired and doesn't want to take a shower. She wants to be touched. Like eye contact, humans get stingy with the cheek caresses, the couch snuggles, the hair-petting. Give and ye shall receive. But hey, don't expect sex just because you rubbed her shoulder. Just hope she gets in the mood, or hope she returns the favor in the near future.

"Women remember everything forever. Since they tell their girlfriends about it, they can cross reference their memories. Just know and fear it. You can't stop it. It's beautiful when it comes times to tell stories from back when. It's like a tank taking down an outhouse when it's in a fight.

"Be silly. Not so much you're another child. But enough to make you feel good, because that's contagious.

"If you're arguing, get naked, or start clucking like a chicken.

"Make her laugh. Not because you're so fucking funny, but because you know her well enough to know exactly what line is going to make her giggle.

"Read.

"Volunteer.

"New people and new relationships are like drugs. They get you high. Make you obsess. Hook you. Flush your skin. Yay! But don't get addicted to it. The new wears off. If you can't handle the reality of a real person, you have no business looking for your next fix.

"The most evil form of life on planet Earth is the sixteen-year-old girl. From fourteen to sixteen, freshman and sophomore years, date every girl in your class. Twice. Date at that age means "Wanna go out?" in the hallway and flirting during lunch for three days before breaking up. You have to do this quickly, because once the girls turn sixteen, it's over. You piss off one and you will never date again in your high school.

"In middle school and high school, it's okay to crush on all of them. They're called crushes because that's how it feels. Like you've been dropped off a cliff. You are going to change your mind. Your hormones are going to drive you insane. You're going to like a person for two years and then, when she smiles at you for the first time you're going to realize she's a douche... but her best friend? Wow! And the next week that'll change too. Just ride it.

"Do not speak to a woman like she's a slut. That makes you a tool.

"Nothing wrong with tattoos, but until you have an established career, you may want to make sure they can all be hidden in a polo shirt and pants.[39]

---

[39] "Never get a tattoo where a judge can see it." – Somebody a lot smarter than I am.

"If you can't afford it, you can't have it.

"God said we have to forgive. You can forgive from a distance. You don't have to harbor hate and anger, but you also don't have to harbor the causes of those things and people in your life.

"There will always be that one person who makes you want to quit. There will always be the one personality you can't work with, can't win over. It will feel like that person has nothing to do but make you miserable. Make eye contact and compliment that person. Then just Zen chant in your head. Don't let that a-hole beat you. Don't quit the job, leave the club. It's not about winning, it's about understanding this will happen *everywhere*, and you need to learn to adapt because . . .

You cannot change another person. You cannot. If you're smart, hardworking and lucky, you can change yourself. That's it. It's vanity to think otherwise and it'll make you miserable.

"Have a pet.

"Take care of your body, you only get one.

"We aren't meant to get old. Spartans were in service from age seven to sixty-five. God gave us 120 years. Why aren't we making that? Shit, sixty should be middle life according to the Word. I just wrote a story about a ninety-eight-year-old skydiving for charity. Old, older, is a state of mind. You still dream. You still think. You are still you when the years pass. Once you think "I'm old," you're right, so never think it. It's an affront. Your soul is always sixteen and filled with the vigor and delight of a sixteen-year-old.

"If it moves you, say it aloud. Or stop and silently appreciate it. A sunrise. A cloud. Graffiti on a train car. Make eye contact with the world. It's breathtaking.

"Nobody really gives a shit. Every single person is egocentric and wrapped up in his or her trials and life. People care less about what you do than you think. So be free. And don't posture.

"Do not drink and drive. Ever. For real. Or text.

"Smile." – Jennifer "The Barefoot Sewer Dweller" Horton, 30ish, Author Extraordinaire, Florida.

Chapter 7 - Love:

The first thing to understand about love is that no two people think of it in the same way. It comes in as many flavors as there are people in the world. Deific love, fraternal love, paternal love, maternal love; real love is all the same thing, boiled in different pots.

When someone meets and, presumably, falls in love with someone, they often spend all kinds of time and energy agonizing over whether they really love them or not. They try to tell themselves that they've only known each other for X days; that it won't work; that they're all wrong for each other and that everything they're thinking, feeling and experiencing is just loneliness, hormones or whatever. People try to say things like, "Well, I love her, but I'm not *in* love with her."

You'll do it too, my son, and be aware that when it happens it's just your brain trying to control something that can't *be* controlled. Love comes in like a knife in the back and it hits you whether you're ready for it or not. Luckily there are a few ways to easily determine if what you're feeling is really love. It's called The Love *Is* Rule. It comes, like most of your Father's philosophies, from The Bible.

See, Christians believe that God *embodies* Love.[40] Therefore, Love has certain absolute, God-like properties. The Scripture is as follows: 1 Corinthians 13:4-8: "4: Love is patient, love is kind. It does not envy, it does not boast, it

---

[40] We're talking about *real* love here, not the watered down, adolescent stuff that lets you sleep with her/him because you "love" them, and then, when their breath smells in the morning and they've got a zit in their ear the size of a fist, you decide you're not in love with them anymore, freeing you from further obligation.

is not proud. 5: It does not dishonor others, it is not self-seeking, it is not easily angered, it keeps no record of wrongs. 6: Love does not delight in evil but rejoices with the truth. 7: It always protects, always trusts, always hopes, always perseveres. 8: Love never fails."

Love, like God, is perfect, son. It *never* varies from that perfection. Love—real love—like God, is perfect and holy. Love never causes pain. Love never fails. Love never ends. Anything that doesn't measure up to that isn't love.

And because love is God-like, you *can't* fall out of love with someone once you fall in love with them. You may not actively be in a relationship with them, but some part of you, somewhere, still loves them. As happy as I am being married to your mother, and as joyfully committed as I am to her happiness and well-being, any woman I've been in love with can approach me and expect kindness and gentleness. Because like God, love never fails; like God, it never ends; like God it doesn't cause pain.

I'd expect no less from your mother if any of her exes came around.

Remember that before you commit to loving someone. Love *never* fails. It *never* ends and it *never* dies. It is holy. It's the single most serious thing there is and it should be approached cautiously and carefully.[41]

To belabor a point as only a Dad can, if you subscribe to the philosophy of God being Love, then anything that you're experiencing that doesn't demonstrate absolute, God-like properties *isn't* love. It's something that may look, feel and *act* like love, but it will never be the real thing.

---

[41] In one ear and out the other. But you'll get it.

Boiled down to its absolute essence, you love someone when A: Their happiness and well-being is of paramount importance to you. You want them to be happy and well, *regardless of what this might cost you.* And B: You never want them to be in pain.

See where that's heading? If you feel that way about someone, then you love them. But pain is part of love. Here's an example. You meet Ms. Right. She's everything you dream about. She rocks your world inside out and the two of you are inseparable. And then she comes to you one day and says "I met someone else." If you love her you A: Put her happiness first and B: Don't want to cause her pain *even if she doesn't feel the same way about you.* And that's *haaaaaaaaaaaaaard*, son. It's a loser's choice. If you love her . . . *really* love her, the only thing you can do is let her go be with her new man, even if it kills you.

That's what they mean when they say love hurts, it stinks and it sucks, except for all the times it doesn't.

It's terrifying, son. And it should never be entered into lightly. Date her for a couple of days. If it's working, stretch it out to a couple of weeks. If you find yourself wanting to spend more time with her after that, ask her to be your girlfriend. If you guys make it in a committed, monogamous relationship for a year, then you should probably think about moving on to whatever the next step is for the two of you. If she still wants to be with you after all that—and vice versa—you *might* have a winner on your hands. Take the time to get to know her before you decide you love her. Learn her likes and dislikes, her hopes, dreams and fears. Find out what makes her tick and get to a point where you understand why she thinks the way she does. Fight with her. Disagree with her. Root for the team that's beating hers. Introduce her to your family.

Another thing to remember, son: she's not "The One" until she *is* "The One."

"The One" is an untouchable paragon of feminine virtue. She is beautiful, she is kind, she is smart, funny, articulate and able to shotgun a beer. She farts pure oxygen and can hit a running target with a black-powder .50 revolver from 500 yards away. Her looks inspire sculpture, her voice inspires music, and her body inspires sin.

Some guys genuinely believe that for them to even begin to consider being serious about a woman they need a divine sign that confirms it. It doesn't work that way. You don't get divine signs. You have to listen to your heart. You can't be the kind of guy who isn't willing to marry someone unless she somehow fulfills the nearly impossible obligation of "soul mate." It took me years to figure this out, but *any* woman can be a soul mate if the two of you are willing to put in the work to make that happen. Enter each relationship with a ready heart and an open mind. If it's right, you'll know. If it isn't, you'll know that, too. Even if you spend a couple of years lying to yourself.

One thing I will say about "The One:" Don't let her be "The One That Got Away." Don't spend the rest of your life regretting your cowardice when you can tell yourself, "Hey, at least I was man enough to try."

Chapter 8 - Dating:

I thought about it once, trying to write a Romantic Timeline for myself. Near as I can figure, there was a point in my life when I fell "in love" about once every ten days or so.

I've joined the Army for love, gotten a deeply penetrated "tribal" tattoo of a black rose and a pair of names over my heart for love[42], married, divorced, moved and married again, all for love. I'm a loving kind of guy and hope springs eternal, but I'm not the best source for solid, objective advice about love and dating, either.

Growing up the way I did, "dating" wasn't emphasized as part of adolescence. We were encouraged to meet someone in the same church we were in, fall in love with them, get married as soon as possible to avoid even the possibility of the temptations of the flesh, and then spend the rest of our lives having procreative sex. To my best recollection, no one ever pulled me aside and said, "Hey. You know the way it feels like your pants are on fire about two-thirds of the time? That's normal. The way you feel about girls right now? Normal, too. It'll calm down and

---

[42] I asked the woman to marry me. She said she'd marry me if I brought her a black rose. So I went to the tattooist, told him I wanted a tattoo of a black rose with our names that would last forever. "Go back over it a couple of times! Yeah!" I spent three hours in the chair, something like $200, the tat bled for most of a week, the name she wanted me to use for her ended up being the same one she used for one of *her* ex-boyfriends and two weeks later she broke up with me. This was just about twenty years ago, and your mother says she can read this tattoo on my chest in the dark with her fingertips.

you'll be fine." No, it was all, "Get married before you get sent to hell."

That kind of thing doesn't foster "getting to know your intended paramour" behavior. Our church was all about getting new recruits. This was best accomplished by putting young people from churches in different areas together in rallies and camps and letting them mingle in a heavily chaperoned, religiously-centered sort of way. Every summer we went to Junior Youth Camp and Senior Youth Camp. It was something like a religious concentration . . . camp . . . off in the woods; a compound of barracks, mess hall and church building—the only one that was air-conditioned, by the way—where kids from all over Kentucky got together and got preached at in the dogma of our cult for ten days.

It was ten days of *church*. No fishing, no hiking, no swimming in the pond, no dancing or flying kites or any other normal, summer activity for kids. We sat in our air-conditioned church, singing songs that were a hundred years old and getting yelled at by well-meaning but clueless people who told us over and over we were going to hell if we put one foot wrong. Some of these kids had never been further than twenty miles from their hometowns. They just wanted to breathe air that hadn't been already been processed by five generations of relatives.

We weren't allowed to wear typical summer clothes, either. We belonged to a fundamentalist cult that said women who didn't wear floor-length dresses and cover their arms were going to hell. Men wore pants and button-down shirts. Short sleeves were allowed but uncommon. I spent ten days sweating through Apostolic Adolescent Fury.

Church. Just chuch. Ten days of that would force you into love with *anyone*, son. I couldn't tell you how many people got married as a result of Junior Youth Camp, but we heard stories about not just dozens, but, like, *hundreds*. Hundreds of couples, giving in to someone not because they'd been brought together by mutual interest or chance encounter, but brought together because they'd been compressed into a relationship by surviving ten days of some well-meaning but misguided twit's idea of a "good time" for kids between the ages of nine and fourteen.

As I've already stated, my father was no help. He used to walk up to the girls I was interested in at our church— the only ones I was *allowed* to be interested in, remember—smile creepily at them and say "So. You wanna marry my son?" Sadly, he was only half kidding.[43]

So I don't know a whole lot about "dating." From the time I decided that girls were maybe not quite as gross as I'd been led to believe, up until I met your mother, I entered every relationship I was in with the specific goal of marrying her and having kids.

Here are a few things I *do* know; lessons I learned the hard way.

1. Good Manners Never Go Out Of Style. Use silverware. Wipe your face with your napkin, not your sleeve. Don't blow snot rockets on her $500 shoes. Don't empty your spit cup on the dining room table. Don't rinse the chaw out of your mouth in the kitchen sink. Say "Please," "Thank You," and "Excuse me," and for Heaven's sake, if you pass gas don't comment on the piquancy of your intestinal bouquet.

---

[43]Totally, totally true. And just as an aside here, son: once you get to the point that you decide I'm embarrassing you, please remember that I could be *sooooo* much worse.

If you take her out to dinner, you don't *have* to pay for her meal, but it would be polite, at least, to offer.[44] Hold the door open for her; look her in the eyes when she talks to you; listen *and* remember the things she says. Treat her like a person, but treat her like a person you want to get to know intimately. Be respectful, patient, gentle, kind and even a little loving. Don't spend the night talking about yourself. Get to know *her*!

A little side note here on manners that many men don't seem to take into consideration. A Real Man doesn't curse in front of a woman. There's a difference between cussing and cursing. Cussing doesn't involve profanity, for one thing, but there's also an element of intent.

I'm of the opinion that expletives are necessary for life. They're like hot sauce on tuna casserole; mustard on french fries; a hundred miles of straight road in a V8 with Tom Petty CDs. You can live without them, but who'd want to? They add flavor and keep you awake. Try it sometime! Drop a plastic bag full of baby food jars on the floor and then deny yourself a single expletive. I'm betting you'll let go after ten seconds.

I tried for a while. I kept my mouth shut and grunted or groaned instead of exploding with my usual crudities. It wasn't the same and I think I may have given myself ulcers.

It's something I've fought with my entire life and I try—genuinely try—not to use words I wouldn't want to hear you using. But they become ingrained in your brain and you end up *needing* them in order to talk.[45]

---

[44] And for crying out loud, be friggin' prepared to pay!

[45] For the record, my all-time, hands-down favorite cuss word is "doggonit." My father's was "gads"; as in "ye gads" or "gadzooks."

Given the modern ideas of equality in the sexes, telling you not to curse in front of a woman is now considered to be deeply old-fashioned thinking. Some of the finest cursing I've ever heard has come from some of the prettiest lips I've ever seen, but it's still true. Don't think you need to talk like you're fresh out of Camp Pendleton to impress her, son. She probably won't think all that much of you if you talk that way in front of her while you're dating, much less during a first date.

2. There's No Such Thing As An Ugly Woman. Okay, strictly speaking, this one isn't true. There are women who are repulsive, physically. I've never met one myself, but I've watched a *lot* of TV and movies, so I know they *do* exist.

The thing is, we guys tend to call a woman ugly when she doesn't measure up to *our* current standard of feminine beauty. (And that's another important point, because our standards are constantly changing. When I was a teenager I thought a woman was only hot if she weighed a hundred pounds, soaking wet, had long, luxuriant hair, silky, perfect skin, and boobs like cannonballs. Now that I'm pushing middle age, I appreciate a woman with real curves. I like stout women; women with meat on their bones. Ribs are only sexy when they're covered in barbecue sauce.

Don't ever dis a woman on a single glance. No, she might not be Marlene Dietrich or Jane Mansfield[46], but she probably has some feature you missed. Taking a second look will reveal aspects about her that you *do* find attractive and before you know it, you might realize that you're into her.

---

[46] Look them up. You'll thank me.

It goes without saying that a woman who finds a man who is into her after everyone else has rejected her is just as grateful to and appreciative of the man as he would be in the same situation.

Don't reject her just because she isn't a Size 4, Victoria Secret Model. The hottest woman I've *ever* known is [47] a size eighteen.

Remember, nobody's a super-model when they sit on the toilet.

3. You Don't Have To Take Her To La Maison Frommage. We guys tend to believe we do so she'll be impressed. It's Modern Man's version of bringing home a haunch of Cave Lion and three bear pelts. Sure, it's always good to demonstrate that you have the means to buy her a five-hundred dollar meal, but one of the best times I had with a girl was walking with her to the local Mall, sitting on the floor and reading comic books. Your mother and I took a long walk through a park on our first date.

Do something that you will both enjoy doing, that doesn't cost her anything other than a couple of hours, and that minimizes the sexual tension. Because-

3. You're *Not* Getting Any On Your First Date. Okay, I know mores are constantly evolving. People accept things today that would have been an abomination a generation ago. But people don't change all that much.

For whatever reason, most of the people I consider friends are women and just speaking empirically, most of them would not put out on a first date. It might be a little chauvinistic to suggest this, but I'm not sure a girl who would put out that early is someone you'd want to know any better. It tells me she either treats sex too casually, or

---

[47] Yo' momma. (Grrrrrrrooooooowwwwwwlllll.)

she has such low self-esteem that she believes the only way you'll *continue* to like her is to put out. Either way, pursuing an intimate relationship with her might cause more harm than good. And yeah, your old man has some old-fashioned ideas about love, sex and relationships, but he's been a life-long student of the human condition, too.

Don't *ask* her for any on the first date, either. She's probably had a couple of guys try to rut with her by now, and she's not looking for more of the same, believe me. Be content with whatever she gives you. If she holds your hand during the date and gives you a peck on the cheek and a hug after, you could probably accept that she thinks you're pretty much a prize-winning stud in her book.

Chapter 9 - Sex:[48]

I tried to write this chapter in a frank and earnest way. Sex is powerful, scary, sometimes a little weird and terrifyingly important to the human species. I didn't see any way to get through this without being blunt and straight-forward. You *have* to know this stuff, I have to be the one to tell you, so arm yourself appropriately for the ordeal ahead. We'll get through this together.

I've set out to try and write a graphic, yet dispassionate description of sex. I'm not sure I managed it, but the following pages are everything I think a young man really needs to know in order to develop into a healthy young man.

For whatever reason, men don't really like to talk about sex in a serious way. That seems like a contradiction, but hear me out. Men like to *brag* about sexual conquests, they like to *discuss* sexual perversions and weird sex acts; they enjoy *talking* about sexy women, women they'd like to have sex with, women they *claim* to have had sex with; the pros and cons of the physical attributes of women of their mutual acquaintance and most anything else to do with the actual *experience* of sex, but men don't like talking about sex in a clinical, dispassionate way.

---

[48] I realized something pretty quickly as I was writing this chapter. There is an unavoidable component of comedy in human sexuality. And while it's certainly true I didn't make a really big effort to avoid it, I *did* try. I'm sorry, son. I'm only human.

My theory about this is that we're all aware, deep down, how inadequate we are, but we continue to lie to ourselves because our male egos are so incredibly fragile.

Learn it now, son: you're not a sex-god, you're not an all-weekend-long stud and women will not be screaming your name at the top of their lungs every time you take your underwear off.

Bascially, if you can make love to a woman without any complaints, you're doing fine.

For men, sex is primarily a visual experience. If we see something we like we want to have sex with it. The evidence of large-breasted, large-hipped cave paintings from nearly a million years ago suggests that this has always been the case. We see it, we like it, we want it.

Sex is the most powerful motivating force of human existence. The lies we tell ourselves to justify the actions we take in order to rut are stupefying. Given the right set of circumstances a man will throw over everything he loves, everything he honors and everything he holds dear in order to have sex with a total stranger. Somebody once said that "An erect penis has no conscience."

People claim that the accumulation of vast riches or power motivates them, but peel away the veneer of sophistication and it's all just sex.

People have died because of sex; killed their families because of sex; started wars that killed tens-of-thousands of people and lived their entire lives in a paroxysm of lies and fear, all because of sex. If you're a student of history and human behavior you realize that sex has changed the face of human existence—and altered the course of its history—more times than can be conveniently counted.

It is terrifying and holy; comedic, banal and inexplicable.

As men, we are wired, by biology, to spend our entire lives trying to have sex with as many people as we possibly, possibly can and there's not a whole lot we can do about it.

God invented sex. It's one of those logical puzzles. If you believe, as I do, that God created the universe and everything in it, then it follows that God invented biology, along with all of its wiring and drives and pushes. Further reasoning would tell you that God invented sex. Ergo, sex is normal, good and, yes, holy. The problem with sex is that like everything else in life, people get all twisted around the axle with excesses and perversion, but I'm getting ahead of myself.

Chapter 10 - Pornography:

If I had my druthers, you'd never be exposed to pornography. You'd live your entire life without pornography becoming part of it and forever be innocent of the crimes we men inflict on women and women inflict on themselves. But I can't protect you forever. This will be something you'll have to deal with on your own terms. The best I can do is educate you.

There is empiric evidence that suggests that many rapists and serial killers got the foundations of their behavior from pornography. I don't know how accurate this is but I have to believe there is some truth to it.

There is further evidence that demonstrates that pornography mimics the actions of narcotic addiction in the brain. A person who uses a lot of pornography has a brain that looks and acts like a person who is addicted to an opiate. When he gets his fix his brain responds in the same way. Common sense will tell you that isn't normal or cool.

Our society is soaked in sex. From birth to death we are surrounded by a never-ending litany of sexual dialogue, imagery and input. As I've already discussed, everything in our society is geared toward making sex happen. Given this set of parameters, it's no wonder that modern, American men treat sex as casual entertainment, with no repercussions. Sex *is* normal, healthy and good for you. You should have as much of it as a loving, consensual partner will agree to give you, but you should never treat it casually.

We don't respect sex anymore. Pornography feeds into this because it creates a further set of parameters where it's possible to instantly have any kind of sex you'd like to have without any of the messy business of relationship building.

My father claims there is a Jewish belief that declares you are married to everyone you've ever had sex with. If you tie that into the teaching of Christ that states "If you look at a woman with lust in your heart you have committed adultery," then you begin to appreciate how serious sex can be. If you're married to every woman you've ever *watched* having sex, things get heavy.

It is my hope that you will eventually meet a woman you love, marry her and have kids. Should this be the case, she is entitled to *all* of you. Even if she doesn't want all of your sex, it is hers to want or not. All of your seed, if you will, belongs to her. Since that is the case, it is disrespectful—and an argument could be made that it's even adultery—to your future wife to be jerking off to some other woman in a pornographic setting. Yes, this is a sophisticated argument, but think about it for a minute. Would you want *her* watching porn and later comparing your body to some of her favorite actors?

Another good point is that your wife/girlfriend doesn't deserve to spend even a second wondering if she isn't good enough to give you what you need. Don't let her think that way by consuming pornography. Give her *all* your love, your energy and your sex.

Pornography is *powerful* stuff. We men love it because it depicts hot, naked women doing things we think we'd like our wives and girlfriends to do to us. It's purely visual sex, and it wires directly into our brains and flips all the triggers that make us hum.

The argument for porn is that we can have unlimited sex with unlimited women we don't need to know and there are no repercussions. At worst our wives and girlfriends might catch us viewing the stuff and yell at us; a small price to pay to get your rocks off that hard, right?

I've heard this argument and any number of others about pornography; that it's safe sex, harmless and an acceptable outlet for men to have sex without cheating on their wives.

For me, at least, the problem is that none of it is true.

It's been my experience that most women don't like their bodies too much. This is society's fault for telling them they're too fat, too short, their boobs are too big and their butt is too flat. Modern American women aren't allowed to age. Once they get a wrinkle or start to show some sagging they're encouraged to get Botox and plastic surgery. And then we come along and compound the problem by watching eighteen-year-old-hardbodies having sex and fantasizing about how nice it would be to have sex with them.

Do I need to point out how much of an issue this is for someone who's feeling insecure *anyway*? Leave aside the issue as to whether watching pornography is adultery or not. Making your wife or girlfriend feel bad about her body is a crime, a sin and something you deserve to be punished for.

Anything that takes up space in your head is something you're allowing into your life. These days most pornography is about out-perverting the other guys. The watchwords in pornographic production are abuse and maltreatment.

As nowhere else in our society, pornography treats women like objects, at best, and sexed-out animals at worst.

They are slapped, yelled at, ejaculated on—among a wide variety of body-fluid choices—and treated like something to be punished. They are called "bitch," "cunt," "whore," "cum-dumpster," and other names even worse. The actresses are encouraged to refer to themselves as "sluts."

While it's *believed* these women have *chosen* to be treated in this way, given the renewed trend for slavery in modern life, it has to be suggested that some of these women are sex slaves.

Further, do you honestly think someone is on the sets of these movies and photo shoots, checking birth certificates? How do you *know* the woman you're looking at is eighteen? Because the website says so?

Is there a medical professional on hand, monitoring health and wellness? Who's preventing the spread of Sexually Transmitted Disease on these movie sets? Is the couple being provided with medical care of any kind?

If you consider those features you can hardly think of pornography as "safe" or "harmless." *Someone* is being hurt and mistreated. It just might not be you.

Those women are *not* sluts, son. They're not vessels of lust, designed for a man's pleasure. They are someone's daughter, someone's mother, someone's sister. They get cold and scared, hungry and lonely. They hurt. They have dreams and hopes and desires; a favorite color; days they wish would never end and days they want to see the back of as soon as possible. They are *people*. They deserve to be treated with the same dignity and respect as everyone else.

Whatever her reasons, being in a pornographic movie doesn't make a woman an object or an animal and watching her degrade herself shouldn't be treated casually.

Having said all that, let me say this: wanting to view pornography, or even giving in and viewing it doesn't make you a sexed-out monster who deserves to go to hell. Looking at naked people doesn't make you a bad person. It's normal, every guy does it and it's something you will probably end up doing more than once during the course of your life. I will not freak out and become Dad-Monster when I find your porno stash. We're men, this is something we like to do and you shouldn't feel like you're going to die and go to hell for using pornography. You just can't use it without being *aware*. It's like junk food: if you use too much of it something will go wrong inside you.

Pornography is a problem for me, but I think it becomes a problem for *everyone* when we start thinking that it has anything at all to do with real sex.

Pornography is an edited fantasy of what we men *think* sex should be like. It's well-lit, fake, there are no broken hearts, pregnancy or STDs. Subservient, hot women are happily doing everything they can to please the man. Part of us—no matter how much we might deny it—wants that. Do I need to point out that this has nothing whatsoever to do with the reality of sex?

There is no *effort* to pornography. There are no long nights in ERs because she had a stomach cramp; no spending thousands of dollars on the back end of her car; no holding her while she cries because a beloved pet died. It is just sex; the visual equivalent of ten-million empty calories. It has no substance, no value, it destroys your appetite for healthy sex and it isn't good for you.

Your wife/girlfriend *isn't* a porn star. Don't treat her like one. She doesn't want to have to learn a safe word. She doesn't want you to slap her and to be told to "Eat it, you crack-whore." *No one* wants to be treated like an object.

And I can keep right on going, but nothing I say will be nearly as important as what I do.

As your *father*, let me say this: don't let this stuff get its hooks in you. It's bad for your soul, it fills your head with garbage and it creates an unrealistic ideal in your head as to what sex is and what it should be like. When you look at a woman and see "nice tits, good ass and great legs" instead of "A beautiful woman with wants, dreams, hopes and desires," you're part of the problem. When you reduce her to her component parts, and value her for the way she can shake her butt instead of for her soul, you're debasing her.

Even if you never meet her, even if you don't know her name or anything about her, when you view a man mistreating a woman, however obliquely, you are complicit in that mistreatment.

As a fellow *Man*, let me say this: you get to choose what you put in your head. You get to choose what gets you off. If, despite everything, you choose to use pornography, try to make sure it doesn't hurt anyone, including yourself. Be aware of what it is and be aware of what it does to you. Don't rely on it, don't expect sex to be like porn and don't treat it casually.

Chapter 11 - Rape:

You can't talk about sex without talking about rape. Rape is "forcing someone to undergo a sexual act." *Any* kind of sexual act. Whether she has her clothes on or not, whether you think she wants it or not, whether she's even *asking* for it or not, if you have to force her to do it, it's rape. It's not about sex, it's about power and it's a vile, despicable act comparable to murder.

Rape is one of the worst things you can do to a person. Any person who has been raped is a brutalized victim with scars that go all the way down to their soul.

Anytime she says "No," regardless of how far along you are, proceeding one micro-second past that point is rape. This is important to remember, son. She might've expressed interest and desire through the entire process. She might have given you every indication of strenuous enjoyment. She might've been screaming your name at the top of her lungs and scratching your back, but she can change her mind *at any point* in the proceedings and if you don't stop, you're raping her.

Things get even more complicated when you add things like alcohol, age and informed consent. If she's incapacitated enough not to be able to resist you; too drunk to stand ; too high to stop you or too young to know better, you're raping her.

If you're older than eighteen and she's not at *least* eighteen, whether she's sexually developed, a virgin, or the best lay in the neighborhood, you're raping her.

The bottom line is, you shouldn't ever "encourage" a woman to have sex with you. Don't dose her with drugs or alcohol until her inhibitions drop. Don't push yourself on her "just to get her started." Don't ever have sex with anyone under the age of thirty. Don't have sex with strangers.

A good rule of thumb when thinking about sex in general: consensual, pain-free sex between husband and wife is ideal. Anything else is iffy. At a minimum, make damn sure you're going into it with someone who is awake, aware, legally able to make an informed decision about sex, and that she wants to have sex with *you*. Anything else is asking for trouble.

Chapter 12 - Pregnancy:

Men believe a lot of myths about pregnancy. These myths are perpetuated by our gender because it allows us to continue to have guilt-free sex. Here's the truth of the matter: assuming there's nothing biologically wrong with you, if you have enough sex, you *will* knock a woman up.

Babies come from sex and there is no position, no time of the month, no ointment, cream or other magic potion that can prevent pregnancy. There is no 100% effective method of birth-control.

That's a terrifying thing to consider, son. Once you're created a life with someone, you are tied to both of them for the rest of your life. Even if she never speaks to you again, even if she has five kids with another man, even if she has an abortion and it never goes further than one night of sex, you are forever tied to her as "The man who got me pregnant."

If she decides to keep the baby, then you are "Her Baby's Daddy." Every decision the two of you makes from that point forward affects a third person and you are *fully responsible* for those decisions. Everything you wanted from your life takes a back seat to the needs of your child.

Not many men understand that and it deserves underscoring: Your. Baby. Comes. ***FIRST***. For. The. Rest. Of. Your. Life. There is no job, no college education, no woman, no goal, no career, no dream, aspiration, hope, fantasy, vacation, appliance, car, truck, dream-girlfriend or *anything* else in life that should come as a higher priority than your baby.

Any man who puts anything before his children is committing an unforgivable crime and deserves to slapped about the head, face and neck. (Yes, God should be first in our lives, but an argument can be successfully made, I think, that putting your baby first is doing exactly that.)

Pregnancy is one of the primary reasons it's such a good idea to wait until you're happily married before you start having sex. Baby-making should be done in love, reverence and fear, not over a sixer of Schlitz and lowered judgment.

Chapter 13 - Homosexuality:

I went back and forth on an essay on homosexuality for a long time. I thought of all the people I know and love who went through the agonizing process of admitting to themselves that they were gay. There were no parades for them, no celebrity shout-outs. They were brave, lonely people who decided they were done lying to themselves.

I wrote this essay for them.

I don't understand homosexuality at all. People have tried to explain the spectrum of human sexuality to me, and I've listened with what I believed was an open mind and a willing heart, but like much of human existence, homosexuality is a closed book to me.

I'm okay with that. I've come to a place in my life where I've decided that some people are different from me. I might not understand it, but I don't need to understand a person's sexuality to love and value them as a person. I understand *my* sexuality, and the only person I have sex with is your mother. Why is it any of my business what other people do?

When I was growing up in my church there was a doctrine called "The Age of Accountability." The doctrine—for which I have found no Biblical evidence— stated that a person was not accountable before God for their actions (sins) until they had reached an age where they could determine right from wrong. See, the way it worked was the congregant asked the preacher "My baby died. He had not received the gift of the Holy Ghost with the evidence of speaking in tongues and he was not baptized in the name of Jesus, as outlined in Acts 2:38. We all know that's the only way to be saved. He was only four years old. Will he go to hell?"

The preacher would reply that the worried parent shouldn't worry about that since the child was doubtless below the threshold of The Age of Accountability. It allowed us to think warm and fuzzy thoughts about innocent children when we believed that God would send people to hell forever for the foul sin of cutting their hair the wrong way.

My Father believed that The Age of Accountability was right around thirteen; when "real" Jews had bar and bat mitzvahs.[49]

I have since amended the doctrine for my own use. To my thinking children really *are* innocent. Once they hit a threshold where they can determine their own moral code, they have reached The Age of Accountability.

I bring all this up because it will determine my response to you if you come to me at some point and say, "Dad, I think I might be gay."

I will discuss it with you in a rational, intelligent manner. I will listen to what you have to say and I will love you, accept your decisions and be proud of you.

But my question will be "Have you decided this after thoughtful consideration of yourself as a person who is no longer a child but a Man, able to make these decisions about himself? Was there deep soul-searching involved? Have you talked to God about it?"

You will always be my beloved son, and nothing you do, say or decide about yourself will ever change that. No

---

[49] Something we never got since Dad couldn't read Hebrew.

one you bring home will ever change that. I will always love and accept you for you, but grow up first, okay? I only say that because it's my job, as your father, to protect you from yourself until you are old enough and mature enough to make your own decisions.

I will try to *let* you be a child for as long as possible. It's okay to grow some facial hair, let your voice even out and allow your testicles to finish descending before you decide who you are and what you're about.

As you grow older and make decisions about yourself, here's something to remember: people are *people*.

When Jesus Christ—the person I believe is God Almighty in the flesh—fed the 5,000, there were people in that crowd who were gay. And Jesus didn't require them to give anything of themselves up. He didn't make them sign a piece of paper that said they'd stop being gay. He didn't try to convince them that they were something other than what they believed themselves to be.

There were murderers, thieves, rapists and pedophiles in that crowd. There were people who murdered people for money. They were prostitutes, drug-dealers and pimps. And Jesus fed them *all*.

In fact, he broke the bread with his own hands and had his disciples—people we Christians have come to believe were perfect saints—*serve* the food to everyone.

Jesus made no distinctions. Any sins they had committed were none of his business as he fed them. Anything they hid from themselves was not something he dragged screaming into the light. 5,000 people were hungry, so he fed them. No one had better meals than anyone else. There was no VIP section, no special seating for fervent believers. Jesus treated everyone in that crowd *exactly* the same.

Black, white, brown; gay, straight; slave, free; Roman, Jew, Gentile, he fed Every. Last. One. Of. Them. The miracle—and the love that accompanied it—was for everyone who came. He handed out bread and fish to everyone who asked him for food. His love was there for everyone to take.

If we call ourselves Christians, how can we do any less?

People are people, son. Jesus said it with his words and with his actions. Jesus loved everyone and he made it clear that some things are just none of our business.

We all want love, respect, kindness and gentleness. What people do in the privacy of their own home is none of your business. Who people choose to love, marry and have sex with is none of your business.

Individuals are special, unique, terrible, wonderful, ugly and pretty and should be valued or dismissed on their own merits, not on who they like to get naked with. Don't buy into the rhetoric or the hate. Don't be a homophobe. Treat everyone with love, kindness and respect and you'll be well on your way to true manhood.

Chapter 14 - Marriage:

I'm not going to talk about marriage too much since I think I'm beginning to repeat myself.

There are only two kinds of marriages: successful ones and failed ones. A failed marriage is any marriage that ends in divorce. A marriage can be thought of as successful when the two of you are lying next to each other in the dirt. Everything between those two states should be thought of as a work in progress.

So you manage to overcome all the odds and find someone to love. She loves you back and the two of you decide to tie your hearts into a knot. Guess what? That's only the beginning of the struggle.

Marriage is *hard*. And it shouldn't be entered into lightly. You should accept that there are awesome and powerful responsibilities associated with it. You belong to another person, now. You are one half of a whole. Everything you are and everything you will ever be has stopped as *"me"* and become part of *"we."* You have told that person "I will love you, honor you, work to your good, respect you and stay with you until death separates us." And if you violate that oath, what kind of a man are you?

People these days don't think about it. They treat marriage as a convenience that can be ended at the drop of a pin. And it shouldn't be. It should only be entered when you're absolutely sure that you want to spend the rest of your life putting another person's happiness and well-being above your own. If people did that there wouldn't be nearly as many failed marriages.

It's hard to do that. It's hard to look at another person and say "What she wants and needs is my job to provide for her." You never get to quit working at it, you never get to take a break and you never get to give up.

I'm of the firm belief that the only acceptable reason to end a marriage is adultery. An argument can certainly be made for abuse and neglect, and I would never suggest that anyone should be forced to stay in a loveless, joyless, painful marriage. But the decision to end one should *never* be made lightly.

You have to accept the good with the bad. You can't bask in the successes and good times of a marriage without weathering the bad times. You're going to fight. You're going to argue. You're going to not want to touch each other, you're going to go broke and you're going to go out of your mind with frustration and anger toward each other, and despite all that you *still* can't quit.

Most marriages end badly. Most couples can't get over the hurdles in their way and they get tired or give up or just quit trying. It's hard, son. Most people never get it right. They treat it as a license to have sex or as a means to an end. They marry people who are horribly unsuitable for them and they end up in either a joyless, loveless marriage, or in a messy, expensive divorce.

It's not enough to talk to each other. It's not enough to have great sex or be rich or beautiful. It's not even enough to love each other. In order to have a working marriage you have to be willing to work at it, every day. You have to communicate with each other. Love comes into it, but sometimes *liking* each other is more important.

Man Quotes:

"What is hurtful to you, do not do to your neighbor. That is the whole of the Torah. All the rest is just commentary. Now go and study it." ~ Rebbe Hillel

<u>Part IV - Homeland, Spirituality, Politics & Philosophy:</u>

<u>Chapter 15 – Celebrating Where You're From:</u>

It's important for a Real Man to know—and celebrate—what he believes in, what he stands for and where he's from.

It defines you as a person; tells the world who you are and what you're about.

What follows is an exploration of my beliefs. This is me, son. You'll have to find your own history, religion, politics and philosophy, but I thought that maybe you'd enjoy finding out about mine while you did it.

Being from somewhere is much more than "I was *born* here, so this is where I'm from." It's about the place you call *home*.

I'm from down south; Kentucky, specifically. I grew up there, found love there and buried people I care about there. If anyplace can be called The Home of Nescher Pyscher, then Kentucky is that place.

I moved up north into the forbidding, frozen wilderness of northern Ohio to marry your mother.

I remind her, every chance I get, that I am not a Buckeye. I am, at best, a reluctant immigrant.

In turn, she reminds me every chance *she* gets that while I posture and preen about being a Kentuckian, I was actually born in Michigan.

My response is "While that's true, I escaped to Kentucky as soon as I had the chance."

I wanted you to be born in Kentucky. Your mother made jokes about wanting running water and electricity during your birth, so you're a Buckeye. That's fine. Nobody's perfect.

I lived there for the best part of twenty years. I loved the climate, the people, and the way life moved. I loved the smell of honeysuckle on the night air. I loved sweet tea and bourbon.

Moving up north to marry your mother was a traumatic event for me.[50]

Here's a random Kentucky story to give you some idea. It's totally true.

---

[50] Just the moving, "ripping-my-roots-out-of-my-native-well-loved-earth" and the "relocating-away-from-everyone-and-everything-I-knew-and- loved," part. Everything else about the experience was AWESOME.

Chapter 16 - Kentucky Song:

I was dreaming about the wyrm. It writhed and fed on the child in full Technicolor surround, and I, the hapless observer, was trapped in the flaming snow globe of my own imagining. And then radical, incipient insomnia—my default state—did its thing and my eyes snapped open.

I went from dreaming to awareness slowly, like a bug swimming through engine oil. And like the bug, I felt as if I was drowning.

This is my usual routine. I sleep. I cease to sleep, but continue to dream. It's like flicking a switch on the world's biggest mercury light.

My eyes focused on the wall across from my bed. I watched a dream spider, made of stars, climb it and disappear.

Groaning, I rolled over. The digital readout on the clock flashed "19:45" in bleary, incandescently red numbers, four inches high. I groaned again. I was due three more hours of sleep, but now they were gone because my brain doesn't know when to quit.

Throwing off the covers, I padded out to the bathroom clad only in my boxer-briefs.

Leaving. Relocating. Abandoning the only home I've ever really known.

I was moving six hours north because of love. This half-submerged, half-forgotten thought hit me in the face when I saw the crates and boxes lying around the living room like the laziest obstacle course ever.

I negotiated my way through the cardboard labyrinth. Deli, the brain-damaged, brindle-haired, devil-cat I rescued from the delicatessen down the street, danced in between my ankles, hoping for a treat. I muttered something reassuring, flicked the bathroom light on and shut the door.

Washing my hands on automatic, I looked at myself in the mirror.

I worry about mirrors. They scare me. I feel like hungry things with scales and tentacles move just outside the edge, mere slivers away from where my eyes can see. I think it was Andy Warhol who said "Don't look in mirrors. You might not see yourself."

"Yep. Still here," I mumbled.

I walked out into the kitchen and scooped some cocoa into one of my spaghetti-jar-drinking -glasses. I added hot water, some instant coffee, and stirred. I sipped coffee and thought about nothing much until the sun went down. Deli hopped onto the loveseat and burrowed her way into her normal spot formed by the angles of my legs. I patted her.

For a moment peace reigned. The classical music station I left on whenever I was home, the cool of the evening, the languid, contented purrs from my cat: it all combined to make a restful scene.

I finished my coffee, lay my head back on the arm of the love seat and found the faces my imagination had carved into the ceiling over two years of staring at the same coat of paint.

Evening had fully fallen and with it a homesick restlessness. I fidgeted, trying to find a comfortable place on the seat and in my head. Deli, irritated, bit me on the calf, hissed and ran off to sulk in the hidden corners cats find everywhere.

Ten minutes passed and I couldn't regain my equilibrium.

"To hell with this," I said, and stood. I padded my way into the bedroom, threw on jeans and a t-shirt. I rooted my sneakers out from their usual hiding place. Wallet, knife—because you just never know—and keys were placed in their appropriate pockets.[51]

"Bye, Deli. I'll see you later," I said. She ignored me. I'd left a nice, warm, funky-smelling spot behind me on the loveseat, and she was making the most of it, rolling and rooting with feline abandon.

I closed the door and set out into the night. A rare and lovely evening. The sky was bright with stars; the kind of well-lit night you could only get in Kentucky. I've quietly pursued these warm, slow, spring nights since I was a child, sneaking out to bask in the cool dark. Mild weather, with a hint of cold, a breeze that felt good against my skin, gently lifting my hair from my forehead and kissing my ears and the back of my neck like a playful lover nuzzling, nibbling and necking. The moon shone and that playful wind carried a variety of perfumes. I licked my lips and lifted my face into it: cut grass, wood smoke, honeysuckle, the pines along the road. Tree frogs buzzed and croaked their loves songs into the night.

Radcliff, my less-than-metropolitan hometown, rolls up its sidewalks early. The streets lay empty and deserted.

I had no destination in mind.

Hands in my pockets, I rambled loosely, looking up at the sky. The moon was particularly bright, surrounded by a

---

[51] This is a weirdo aside, but every Real Man should always carry a pocketknife; nothing Rambo-esque or anything, just a folding, sharpened piece of metal. It's a part of a man's basic tool-kit.

glittering, tiara-like fairy ring. Each of the stars around her had the thinnest possible halo of ice or diamond.

I saluted her and her court and walked on.

My universe is full of personal ritual and superstition, so when I passed by the graveyard just down the street from my house, I was careful to keep the boundary of the road in between me and it. Ghosts can't cross boundaries of any kind, even ones you define yourself.

Most of the people I know don't believe in ghosts. I always say "You don't believe in ghosts until you've had one lick the back of your neck."

I rubbed a nervous hand across my face and shot glances toward the darkened gates of the cemetery. Yep. Things were moving in there. Light shadows and dark ones, dancing over and in between the stones. I shivered, doing my best not to be noticed by the playful dead. I didn't feel any particular malevolence coming from those restless spirits, but I didn't want them whispering my name and telling me secrets, either. I held my breath until I'd walked beyond the psychic stain.

The high school, an edifice of light, and the farm undergoing re-zoning were next. I tried not to think about leaving, and told myself that Radcliff was changing anyway. Cold and thin consolation, to be sure.

"This'll all be strip malls in two years," I said, eyeing one of my old apartments. "In five it'll be an urban wasteland." I didn't believe myself, but I felt a little better thinking that home would be different if I left.

My steps took me to the field without my conscious awareness. Radcliff is surrounded by farms, woods and open fields of grass. The field I made for bordered a wood and sat under an inky patch of sky, perfect for star-gazing.

I walked into the middle of the field and I lay down on my back, my head pillowed on my crossed arms. The grass crushed beneath me and the smell filled my nostrils. The cool damp under me felt like heaven. I lay there for a long time, watching the sky, trying not to think about leaving.

The wind picked up and I smelled her long before I saw her: cut grass, wood smoke, sunshine beneath the trees in hollows damp with rain. Something danced in my hair, and I reached a careful hand. A viceroy butterfly, radiant under the moon, touched my fingers and then fluttered away.

I could smell earth and cold, clear, mineral-rich water that coursed deep beneath limestone caverns a thousand miles long; blooming goldenrods and tulip poplars.

I could hear the wind blowing in ten-thousand acres of woods, over rolling hills, and across the tops of small, ancient, rounded mountains. Somewhere close by, a cardinal called, followed by the sweet, sweet sounds of the Appalachian dulcimer, the dobro, the mandolin, the banjo.

A high, clear tenor voice began to sing words I couldn't understand. It was joined by a chorus of voices singing and dancing. A clear alto rose above them, singing a tune I recognized as something older than humanity. It was the song of a place singing about itself to itself.

It was the song of liquid rock in a volcano; the song of water dripping in deep caves; the song of wind in the trees no man has ever seen.

Kentucky was singing to me.

I closed my eyes and sighed. Living in my world of haunted mirrors, playful winds and neck-licking ghosts, this kind of thing happens to me more often than I'd like to admit.

Standing, eyes still closed, I dusted myself off while combing nervous fingers through my hair and smoothing a hand down my shirt, wishing I'd worn something a little less trailer-trash. I turned around, opened my eyes, and there she stood: big as life and twice as beautiful. Tears rushed to my eyes and a honey-like pain crashed against my heart with the force of a sledgehammer. Sobs wanted to rush from me in a torrent and my soul felt as though it had just been given a goodbye kiss.

Kudzu fell from the top of her head in green, undulating waves. The blooms of ten million different flowers, each entwined with the other, made up her body. The miniscule, perfect petals, each a different color, blended so the overall whole was a multi-hued shade of blue, like a certain kind of famous grass under the warm, ever-changing light of the sun. Pure agate eyes shone above lips the color of crushed blackberries.

Kentucky stood in front of me, waving gently with the breeze, as indescribably beautiful as it's possible to be, and a part of my heart shouted with wordless joy while my eyes streamed tears.

God, how I love her. She lives in my dreams, in my heart, in my soul. Kentucky, bluegrass maiden, mother, lover, friend, home.

It took an effort to keep from crushing her in a sobbing hug. I swallowed, tasting the perfumes that wafted from her, and gained some measure of control over myself. I bowed, as I'd been taught, one hand going into my pants to touch the steel of my pocketknife. Not a threatening gesture, merely letting her know it was there. It was manners, like having a gun but keeping your hands in plain sight.

There were no words. Sometimes there are, sometimes not. She chose to speak in impressions, smells, taste, and touch. The lightest possible brush of a warm breeze touched the skin of my cheeks and drew a caress down my face: her greeting.

"A good evening to you, milady," I said.

I'm not a "milady" kind of guy, but the powers that be get touchy about manners. I met the Ohio River once and he was a grumpy old cuss. I suspected it was a trait the powers shared.

Her lips spread into a smile and I was again washed with touch, smell and sensation. A voice that was not a voice sang in my head with the trill of birdsong.

So polite, my son?

"It would not do for one like me to be rude to one like you," I said, my lips crushing the stilted, formal words as they emerged from my uncultured mouth like gasoline pouring from a broken pipe.

She made a sound like water pushing its way, finally, through the last impeding millimeter of porous limestone. I realized after a moment it was her laughter. She showered me with flower petals.

Polite is well and good, but that need not be the case between a mother and her son, surely?

I grinned sheepishly, accepting the loving comment. "No. It shouldn't be that way."

She smiled, the light of the moon dancing in her eyes.

And yet, you are leaving me?

I sighed. "I don't want to. I really don't. But I've met someone . . ." I trailed off as I realized the futility of trying to explain this to her. "I don't have a choice," I finished lamely. It was true. I didn't. Not really.

A whisper-light touch danced on the surface of my mind, and unbidden, *her* face, the face of the woman who now formed the nexus of my life; the woman who'd promised to take me away from all this, to sweep me off my feet and whisk me away to a wonderland of marvel and delight–framed by her glasses and her incredible eyes— opened like a flower. In my mind's eye, my love smiled, and the light in her heart glowed like a constellation. She swore to me, did my love, with her green, green eyes, to keep every promise and love me as hard as she could.

Ah, Kentucky said, looking with sad eyes at the picture of my beloved smiling at me, *I understand.*

She lifted a flowered hand and brushed it against my face.

I was here long before you loved me, my son. My heart will continue to beat. I was here before I was named, here before I was forced into a form by the imagination of man. You did not create me, and your leaving will not destroy me. I will be here long after you are gone.

Her voice was mournful, but resolute, like the flooding of the river once or twice a year.

My response was husky and full of tears. I couldn't help it. I wasn't just moving north, something vital was being stripped from my soul.

"I carry you with me," I said, touching my heart. "Right here. You're as close to me as my own flesh and blood, and I couldn't love you any more if I tried."

She smiled in her impossible-to-describe way, leaned forward and kissed me gently on the lips. Her kiss was warm and tasted of September-ripe blackberries.

Insomnia did its thing, and my eyes snapped open. I licked my lips, tasting the sweet tang of fruit not yet in season.

"I'll be back," I whispered. I closed my eyes, wrapped in the loving arms of Mother. Somewhere nearby, impossible to reach but close enough to touch, a low, contented sigh filled the air with the smell of honeysuckle and bluegrass; a mother watched her son peacefully sleep.

Man Quotes:

"Nil
Desperandum"~Anonymous

Chapter 17 - Spirituality:

My relationship with God is a very complicated thing. It has grown and changed and become something very different from what it started out as. I love God, and I'd like to think I have a vibrant, living relationship with Him, but because I am who I am, I tend to balk and kick up a fuss and be all hard-headed about stupid stuff.

I have a problem with authority, and unfortunately, that includes God sometimes. It doesn't make sense, but not much about my life does.

When I was a kid, God was this faceless, loveless, merciless being that held a sharpened sword over me, just waiting for me to eat a chocolate Easter Bunny so He could send my scrawny, screaming soul straight to the burning hell I so richly deserved.

I grew up in a Southern, fundamentalist, Apostolic cult. Thinking for yourself was often a reason for expulsion from the church, and a ticket to hell.

We were discouraged from asking questions about the nature of life, like 'Why Did God Allow This To Happen?' We were told to accept things as they came, trusting in the might of God and the words of the preacher.

I tried to be a good Christian as defined by my church's parameters, but far too often I fell short. I found myself at the altar confessing and begging God—at the tender age of fifteen—to spare me from eternal damnation.

We went to church twice on Sunday and once on Wednesday. The services were three to four hours long and every night we heard the same thing from across the pulpit: God's Gonna Getcha.

At some point I grew so despondent that I decided life didn't matter anymore. God, the person I'd tried to get to know, was on the other side of a sky made of brass. I quit trying. I participated in life as little as possible and counted down the days, waiting for death.

I believed this until I was in my mid-twenties. Can you imagine? Serving God not through love or a desire to make Him happy, but through a simple, profound fear that if I screwed up, I was gonna wake up in hell. I preached this, lived it and suffered by it. Jesus didn't love me, He just wanted my servile obedience. I really felt this way!

Then I started actually *reading* the Bible, specifically the stuff that Jesus said. It had been beaten into my brain that all truth was contained in its covers. I started reading it and looking at the things Jesus Christ said and did.

Everything I'd been taught about God being a merciless smiter of sinners was balanced by the infinite love and mercy of the same God for everyone, regardless of race, creed, religion, sexual orientation or political affiliation.

I kept reading, and I saw the same examples of tender love and incomparable mercy. I read the entire Bible, cover to cover, and then I read it again. It became a tradition. I'd read the Bible once a year and absorb a new truth.

It sounds cliché, but my life changed. I started modeling my behavior after Jesus'. Instead of a *religion*, I formed a *relationship* with my God, and I found a new capacity for joy, love and hope.

It blew my wires.

I read about this Jesus-dude. And the more I read, the more I realized that pretty much everything I thought God wanted was wrong.

This Jesus guy, this hippie from some two-bit place in the armpit of the Roman Empire was saying things I wanted to believe my whole life.

I read how Jesus hung out with hookers and pimps and homeless people. He went to dinner with junkies.

He probably didn't smell very good—"Foxes have holes, and birds have their nests, but the Son of Man has no place to lay His head." He most definitely didn't stop to make sure everybody He was hanging with felt the same way about life that He did. He just said really crazy stuff like, "Come. Taste and see. Take my burden upon you. For my yoke is easy." and "I am the way, the truth and the life. No man cometh to the Father but by me." and "Fear thou not, for I have overcome the world."

I read about how the established religious leaders of the day kept trying to make him conform to their doctrines and Jesus kept going, "Look. It's simple. The greatest commandment is 'Love the Lord your God with all your heart, all your soul and all your mind. And the second greatest is like unto the first. 'Love thy neighbor as thyself.' You obey these two and all the rest fall into line."

Well. That took care of that. According to the doctrines I'd been taught as a child, Jesus Himself didn't qualify to go to Heaven.

But here's the biggie. I was looking through the gospels, and I hit upon this one verse. For my money, the single, most powerful words in the Bible. It's in the gospel of John, and it goes a little something like this: "For God so loved the world that He gave His only begotten son, that whosoever would believe on Him shall be saved."

That's it? That's all it took? Accept the sacrifice and you'll go to heaven?

I took all the stuff I'd learned in church, put it up against the Bible, and discarded everything that didn't fit. It was simple: the Bible was right, the doctrines I'd grown up with, where they contradicted the Bible in any way, were wrong.

Simple.

And that's my "religion," if you will, now. Whatever the Bible says is truth. The rest of it is extrapolation and interpretation. I believe in God and I believe He loves us and wants us to be happy.

I still don't have the answers to life's questions. I think those answers are a matter of belief and faith in something more. I don't know why God allows things to happen.

Do I screw up? Yep. Every freaking day. But the glorious part of being a Christian is that I'm *allowed* to screw up. I get up off my face, ask my God to forgive me for being so stinking hard-headed, and go on with my life. I'll never be perfect, but I'll keep trying.

You have to find this out four yourself, but *I* believe that in order to achieve evolved manhood, a Man has to believe in *something* larger and more important than himself; something intangible that can't be held or controlled; something that can only be believed in. Many men never figure this out. They take drugs, sex, religion; money, political ideals or a flag and try to make that into something they can make into a god. I've never seen that work, but every generation keeps trying.

My intangible is Jesus Christ; God Almighty and the body of teachings that bear His name.

In these post-modern times being a Christian seems to mean that you have a pre-determined set of choices, responses to situations you adhere to, and a militant outlook on life in general. Christianity has become a *religion* as opposed to a way of life. Instead of the emphasis on a "deeply personal relationship with Jesus Christ," Christianity has become a club for people who all want to vote the same way.

I tend to believe that Jesus doesn't recognize much of what is called 'Christianity' these days. As I result, I tend toward ecumenicalism.

Christianity isn't, and never has been, about days and words, rituals and causes. Christianity is about loving "the LORD your God with all your heart, all your mind, and all your strength."

Christianity is about believing. Believing that Jesus loves you, that He died for your sins, and He wants you to be free. It's not about being the best person on the outside where everybody can see. It's about changing your *insides*; that place only you and God know about. Read that sentence again, 'cause it's important. It's about changing *your* insides.

I'm not *good*. I'll *never* be 'good.' But I don't have to be. Jesus is. And He forgave me for my weaknesses. All I have to do is accept the free gift of His sacrifice and *try*. God isn't looking for perfection. That's what Jesus was about. God is looking for a willing heart.

Look, you don't have to believe any of this. In fact, since it's *me* saying this stuff, I encourage you not to. Find your *own* path to your *own* truth. But this is *mine*, and this is how I try to live.

Ask Him what being a Christian really means. There's nothing you need to do, just be willing to talk to Him. He's been around for a while and He's heard it all. You'd be surprised at the answers you'll get from Him, I think.

Chapter 18 - Life As A Proto-Jew:

My siblings and I grew up as "proto-Jews."

My parents were both Christians, but my father believes he was born a Jew. What this means for the uninitiated goy is that my father believed *his* Father was born a Jew, and for reasons of his own, disguised this fact from my grandmother, my father and his siblings.

It would probably be more accurate to say "We are Israeli," but that gets complicated.

My father told dire and awful stories about flaming swastikas in his front yard and being beaten up on a regular basis by people who were racially motivated. The way he put it was "They beat me up because I had curly hair."

His response to all this hate and genetic trickery was to marry a rich Irish broad and have four kids who looked like Danish Vikings. All four of us are broad-shouldered, blonde and blue/green eyed. Telling people "I'm a Messianic Jew," has led to some interesting conversations and even a fight or two.

My father didn't know anything about Judaism. Everything he *believed* he knew was taken directly from the Bible. He went further afield when he got older and learned about Kabbalah before Madonna made it cool. Esoteric Judaism blended with Apostolic Christianity made for some really trippy episodes in the Pyscher household, growing up.

Because of his strange and dark nature, Dad made things that were supposed to be joyous into horrible recitations of atrocity, illness and death. Easter was a celebration to a Roman god, and a horrible, blasphemous display in the sight of God. Christmas was even worse.

Hanukkah was a religious holiday, spent cowering before a menorah, waiting for the Bolsheviks to storm into the house with torches and pitchforks after the last candle went out.

Passover was the killer, however. It typically falls somewhere close to Easter during the year, and we were fasting while other kids gorged themselves silly on chocolate and jelly beans.

We fasted for a month prior to Passover to purify our bodies, minds and souls. During that month we were only allowed to eat kosher foods that were further purified for Passover. Do you have any idea how hard it is for a nine-year-old boy to get kashrut-for-Passover-roasted-lamb during Easter in a lunch room in Kentucky?

Dad didn't understand a shabbat meal. He thought the "bitter herbs" mentioned in the book of Exodus meant we each had to eat a tablespoon full of raw horseradish and a wedge of onion. This ghastly dinner was served with grim and fervent reminders to stay indoors after the sun set.

"The Angel of Death is walking tonight, kids. Eat your horseradish crackers and onion wedges."

And yet, we left the door open for Elijah. I'm not sure if that was a good idea or not, what with the horseradish and the onion breath. Seems to me that kind of thing would have Elijah thinking the Angel of Death had already been by our house.

I grew up believing, really, truly believing that I was going to hell. Twice. Christian God would smite me and then Jewish God would smite me again. Probably with a horseradish-smeared onion wedge.

Dad did teach us to play Dreidel. Sort of. That's what we called it: "Dreidel." One word, capital 'D'. We had no idea what the symbols on the side meant, so we made up our own rules and played with our Hanukkah gelt. We spread it amongst ourselves, spinning the Dreidel until we ran out of money. There was even a little song we sang until the Dreidel fell over.

"It's Dreidel, Dreidel, Dreidel!"

"I made it out of clay!"

"It's Dreidel, Dreidel, Dreidel!"

"Now Dreidel I will play!"

Ours was made out of wood. It was no bigger than a child's thumb, and I could get that thing spinning like a top. I can still sing the song and hear the falling Hanukkah gelt as somebody got robbed blind. My siblings are convinced I've learned a technique to make it fall the way I want it to.

I've grown up and absorbed what I felt I needed to from my father's beliefs. I've come to accept that being a Jew, or at least, believing *he* is a Jew, makes him happy somehow. It doesn't cost me anything and I'm cool with that. I still tell people "I'm a Messianic Jew." and explain it as being a Christian who was born a Jew. A short-stop who can also hit, if you will.

I may or may not be a Jew. I'm probably never going to have a flaming swastika burning on my front lawn, and I won't ever expect you, son, to eat onion wedges on kosher toast with a softball-sized dollop of horseradish.

But I will teach you to play Dreidel.

Chapter 19 - The Quest For Truth:

As I've already mentioned, my father is an unusual person. His life has been spent in what he would call A Quest for Truth.

Sometimes he finds the truth and that makes him enormously happy. He spreads it around, like lard on toast, and feeds it to everyone he knows. And sometimes, I think, for his own amusement, he makes it up.

One such example would be The Nazarite Vow he inflicted on the four of us.

A Nazarite Vow, as defined by the first website that popped up when I typed it into a search engine, "refers to one who took a vow described in Numbers 6:1-21."

"The term 'nazirite' comes from the Hebrew word *nazir* meaning 'consecrated' or 'separated.' This vow required the man or woman to: abstain from wine, wine vinegar, grapes, raisins and, according to some, alcohol and vinegar from alcohol; refrain from cutting the hair on one's head and avoid corpses and graves, even those of family members, and any structure which contains such."

It's been my personal experience that refusing to cut your hair for extended periods, whether for reasons of spiritual purity or not, will set you apart in human society.

My father, devout truth-seeker, saw this idea someplace and latched onto it despite being a self-professed "Jesus-Freak-hippie."

I'm not sure when or why he started combining Judaic Laws and traditions with 1970s Christian philosophy and

Southern Fundamentalism, but what came out was so far-afield, theologically, that it represented a giant leap backwards for all of mankind. We had our very own, very weird little cult going within the walls of our house.

The problem, I think, was that dad had no real guidance. He was using a very basic understanding of complicated theological premises from the perspective of a guy who learned how to read in his mid-twenties.

"You're not allowed to cut your hair until your fifth birthday. And when you have children, they're not allowed to, either."

"Why, dad?"

And dad would hide behind that ago-old aphorism all parents use when they don't know how to answer. "You'll understand when you get older."

Food factored into this whole equation as well.

There were a whole slew of things we weren't allowed to eat. The list is too long to go into here, but one example would be that we weren't to eat anything that went through any kind of a process of fermentation involving vinegar or sugar-based alcohols. I'm pretty sure this was a weakness in my father's understanding of chemistry, but there you are.

I got my first hair-cut when I was five years old. I have a picture from the period, and I look like a very pretty little girl with very long, very blonde hair. So did my brothers. My sister didn't get her hair-cut until she was in her teens. I don't know that having all this hair and being *sans* fermented vinegar or sugar-based alcohols did all that much for us spiritually, but it became a family tradition and something I intended to honor.[52]

---

[52] That's, like, literally the definition of a family tradition: something a father inflicts on his son because *his* father inflicted it on him. In some families it's hopeless sports fandom. In ours it was weird, made-up traditions with little or no basis in reality.

This leads us to the here and now. Your mother, being the kind, patient and gently understanding person she is, has come to realize she's married a man who's a quivering knot of superstitions, traditions and neurosis.

She also understands that I can be gently led, but not pushed. When I have something set in my mind as being important, I don't let go. She does what she can to ease my pain as often as she can, but she let me know, quite firmly, that you weren't going to look like a little girl at five and if you wanted it, you could have all the fermented vinegar and sugar-based alcohols you could stand to eat. Since I didn't know what constituted fermented vinegar or a sugar-based alcohol, I didn't have a lot of wiggle room to argue.

We argued about it, and the compromise was hair cut at three. I *still* haven't found any fermented vinegars or sugar-based alcohols in my local Kroger.

Chapter 20 - Politics:

It's a truism of manhood, son. You're defined by what you believe and what you stand for. My politics are strange, convoluted things and I thought I'd inflict . . . I mean, *share* them with you here.

I've decided it's high time to begin discussion on the single most important issue facing this great nation of ours; the issue that will form the central plank of my campaign for President, and the one I'm going to focus all of my efforts on.

I'm not speaking of healthcare reform, or ending war or fixing the economy. Son, the single greatest threat facing this great nation of ours—the threat that will divide and conquer us more thoroughly than any other is hotdog toppings.

We are Americans. The choice of hotdog building material is endless. You can have a beef hotdog, a chicken hotdog, a processed-meat-parts hotdog or even a tofudog.[53]

Being a hotdog purist of the first water, I prefer Hebrew Nationals. Their hotdogs are kosher, which means A. You're going to pay more for them.[54] And B. They're

---

[53] The question as to whether a hotdog made of anything but pure beef can even be qualified as food will have to be answered by a less passionate hotdog enthusiast than myself.

[54] Nescher Pyscher, perpetuating ignorant stereotypes for almost forty years. But seriously, folks . . .

going to taste better than anything you'll be able to buy elsewhere.[55]

A Hebrew National is made of all beef, with a minimum of the handling, processing and juicing practices common to other hotdogs. Where almost every other hotdog on the market today is a mutt, Hebrew Nationals are pedigreed purebreds. Being a connoisseur, I haven't found one yet that tastes better.

You can have a hotdog as long as your arm or a fingernail-length gobbet pierced by a toothpick and pickled in some kind of Viennese brine. Bun selection is also nearly endless, but hotdog toppings are more of a serious matter.

Up until about age nine you can top your hotdog any way you like. Experimentation is encouraged! Feel free to go for the shredded cheese, the mayonnaise and the peanut butter! Go bonkers on barbecue sauce and horseradish; butter and sour cream. You're a kid and these things are okay.

Once you get to be an adult, however, hotdog topping material is, and should be, a matter of very serious contemplation. Without being dramatic, I liken this choice to a college selection or even a career choice. Don't get it wrong or you'll be unhappy for the rest of your life.

When I am elected President of the United Shires of Awesome, the following changes in hotdog topping choices will be enacted and enforced to the fullest extent of the law: Ketchup will be strictly forbidden as a hotdog topping to anyone over the age of nine. Ketchup—or its evil twin brother, Catsup—is a hamburger/meatloaf/french fry

---

[55] Please disregard any smug, Judaic Pride shining through in that last statement. I am very proud of what our people have managed to accomplish with the humble hotdog and I don't care who knows it.

topping. Putting it on a hotdog will be punishable by firing squad.

Calling a concoction of meat, sauce and beans "Coney Sauce" will be strictly forbidden. Any concoction of meat, sauce and beans on a hotdog is a "chili dog"; an excellent choice for the true hotdog connoisseur, but not—repeat—*not* a Coney dog. A Coney dog is topped with Coney Sauce and whatever else you like. No one knows what Coney Sauce actually is, but it *isn't* a concoction of meat, beans and sauce.

All other toppings are permissible and encouraged.

My government will also be pursuing an aggressive agenda of hotdog bun reinforcement. If there's anything at all worse than a disintegrating hotdog bun, I don't want to know what it is.

Once we enact these changes, everything else will fall neatly into place. A happy nation of hotdog eaters with strong buns will not be able to fail.

Chapter 21 - A Brief Political Bio:

You can't run for President without letting the world know who you are. So here's a short bio. Most of this you already know, son, but read it anyway. It'll make your Dad happy.

NAME – Nescher Edsel Pyscher. Yes, it rhymes. Yes, I respond when people sneeze. Yes, I've heard every possible permutation of it and every bad joke about cars made in the fifties. No, it won't fit neatly on a ballot. Yes, I was born in America. No, my parents aren't space aliens. Don't try; you won't be the first person to say it to me.

AGE – Older than my teeth and of an age with my tongue.[56]

Political Party Affiliation – Unapologetic, Liberal Pinko Commie. . . . I mean, "Independent."

Previous Elected Offices Held – I am the Most Original of my graduating class at Ft. Knox High School, despite the fact that I didn't graduate with them; I won the Ft. Knox Eagles' Swim team Sportsmanship Award, despite being completely unable to swim and I won Fanstory.com's Top Five Authors Awards for the years 2004-2006. All of which qualify me for presidential office. Trust me.

Skills and Abilities You Would Bring To Office – I can throw a punch. That's the only skill I need, baby. I will drop you like a hot brick. In order to successfully pursue

---

[56] None of your fracking beeswax!

my duties as President of this great nation, I would, without hesitation, punch whoever needed it dead in the forehead. Doesn't America deserve a President who won't be afraid to throw down?

Where do you stand on oil/gas drilling within municipality limits? – You mean fracking? I am totally down with any economic development that can be confused with a profanity, within the municipality limits or otherwise.

What can you do to attract more commerce and industry to the community? – Listen, I'm running for President. There's something like, eleventy-billion jobs in Washington D.C. that are being done by random, overpaid, entitled clowns. Vote for me and I'll relocate the fracking center of government to our hometown. We'll show 'em! How's that sound? Vote for me and I'll put a Buick in every pot and a chicken in every garage!

Faced with declining state funding to local government, what actions do you feel need to be taken and what outcomes do you for see for your hometown? – We need a bold, decisive, forehead-punching-leader! And . . . and . . . and our hometown rules! Wooo!

Why are you the best candidate? – I maintain my initial position, son. This great nation of ours can't possibly do any worse than the jokers we've already elected.

According to the people I hang out with on Facebook, American officials in higher elected office—Congress and anybody in The White House—have got it made. They get paid billions of dollars to do fifteen minutes of work a week; get a free office with an awesome staff; free, unlimited health care for all their friends, family and neighbors; free retirement and spend all their time golfing on exotic beaches.

I was a little skeptical at first, but then somebody posted a video of Mitch McConnell drinking something with an umbrella in it on a beach in Maui. Rush Limbaugh was standing next to him, swinging a putter. If it's on the Internet it has to be true, right?

At any rate, all of that sounded pretty good to me, so I went back to Facebook and asked people what the current requirements were for being President. I've already decided to run, and I have a platform and a plan, but you have to infiltrate the system before you can change it.

After weeding out all the lobotomy and physical/mental incapacity jokes and the general rhetoric, both right and left, I got down to the current, core requirements for being the big boss. You have to be a natural born citizen of the United States; you have to be at least thirty-five years old, and you have to have been a permanent resident for at least the last fourteen years. Note that there's nothing in there about being rich, well-educated, or possessing of a full head of hair. Nor is there anything at all about being in any way a success. At anything.

Without belaboring the obvious, and despite my skater-rat, post-punk wardrobe, I'm old enough.

Kentucky, my home for the majority of my life, is still in America.

And while it's technically true I was born within the confines of The United States of America, the community of my birth, Sacred-Water-Moonbow-Dancing-Station did secede from the Union shortly before I was born. We were a sovereign nation, all twelve of us, our herd of goats and our tee-pees, on the fifteen-and-a-half acre plot in Uncle Potatoeater Eyebrow's bean field.

Our Spiritual Leader at the time, Shaman Feather Donut, told us that America feared our growing spiritual awareness and that was why they ignored us and our drum circles. We told America we would secede for the duration of The Age of Aquarius.

I *do* have a birth certificate, but it was made out in crayon on the back of a restaurant placemat. As near as I can tell, it was written in a combination of Sanskrit and Hippie-speak. Where my name should be there's a yellow smiley-face sticker and a couple of gold stars.

But don't worry, I've got this covered. I'm going to hire a campaign manager with a full, lustrous head of hair to control the conversation, raise issues and make enough noise to distract the voting public from my massive incompetence, general inability, and intellectual deficits.

Plus, I'm going to use the words 'great nation' so you know I really love America.

As a public service, I thought I'd share my thoughts on what I believe are some of the pressing topical issues of the day since the networks won't do it. These are problems I have solutions for.

We need to improve our image in the rest of the world. I propose starting by changing the name of our country to "The United Shires Of Awesome."

We need a National Song. My proposal is Queen's "We Will Rock You." It's played more than any other song on the planet, and we need something to express how awesomely awesome our new country of Awesome really is.

How about a new flag? My proposal would be a blue circle—my favorite color and shape—with an eagle holding double "Rock and Roll!" finger-prongs outward to the world.

A good motto unites a people like nothing else. Our new motto will be 'Mellita domi adsum,' which, as anyone can tell you, roughly translates as 'Honey, I'm home.'

Where I come from there's a saying: "Never elect the guy who wants the job." Given the clownish state of our current political system in this great nation of ours, I couldn't agree more.

Luckily, I don't want the job. I just want the perks.

You've elected the rich, the famous and the college educated. I'm the best candidate because I think it's time to give an ill-bred, knuckle-dragging, high-school dropout a chance. You can't do any worse.

Chapter 22 - The Crime Of Being A Liberal:

Politics are difficult, son. And if you've been paying attention you've realized by now that I deal with them by being a snarky clown.

Experience has taught me that I should keep my opinions to myself. I've lost friends, I've been ostracized and small children jeer and throw rocks, but you learn to live with it.

I'm a Liberal Socialist. In fact, I'm a flaming, pinko-commie Liberal Socialist. My politics are so far to the left that I can't see the other side of the political spectrum without a telescope and a map. When I make a right turn, I turn left three times first.

I believe abortion is murder, but I believe it is a woman's right to make that choice.

I believe healthcare should be provided to every American citizen for free, in unlimited amounts. The Cubans can do it. Why can't we?

I feel the same way about our education system. Our kids should get free, unlimited education, to the Ph.D. level, if they want.

The land belongs to the people. Anything that exploits it should be provided—free of charge—to every citizen. No corporation should ever control any resource or even own any land. Why are we paying for water? Why are we paying for gasoline? Why are we paying massive, monstrous corporations trillions of dollars a year to be exploited by them? If I had my druthers, corporate land ownership would be abolished entirely.

I believe every American citizen should have the right to think, feel, believe and say whatever they want, wherever they want and whenever they want to, *regardless of how despicable those opinions might be*. With the *sole* exception of crying "Fire!" in a crowded theatre, metaphorically or otherwise.

I believe everyone in our society should be treated the same. Everyone should have the same rights, opportunities, responsibilities and benefits as everyone else. Changing our Constitution to take rights *away* from people is not just wrong, it's evil

I believe that legislating morality is a fool's game. Human beings *want* to do drugs and alcohol; to pay to have sex with strangers. You might not like it, but making laws against these things create a demand for them. It creates a criminal class that wouldn't exist if the government would just mind its own business. Tax it, legislate it, monitor it and punish people who step outside the reasonable bounds of common sense, but let people do whatever ignorant thing they want to do to *themselves*.

I believe in a strict and firm separation of church and state. I don't want to live in fifteenth century Europe. Further, I don't think the government should be involved in religion in any way, shape or form.

I believe anyone who wants to come to this country should be given the opportunity to do that. Follow a legal process, fulfill the obligations of citizenship and become an American. Hell, throw the borders open.

I believe we need to stop writing laws to make life easier for some people and harder for others. Read the

Constitution and The Bill Of Rights and run our government on those basic principles.

Our current system of government is broken. Special interest groups and corporations have purchased the electoral system. Our government is run to benefit the rich, the corporations and the people who give money to the knobs who're *supposed* to be serving us instead of spending all their time getting re-elected.

The biggest industry going in this country is re-election of favored candidates and the misinformation campaign that takes place every four years or so. We don't talk to each other anymore. We just spout rhetoric and wave placards while shouting slogans. Nothing is getting done in this country and we're dividing ever deeper along socio-economic lines.

None of this is necessary if we, the people, would just decide not to put up with it anymore and elect people who actually wanted to *serve* us.

I believe we need to mind our own business, internationally speaking, fix the problems at home and stop messing around with all the nonsense we distract ourselves with.

I'm vocal about it, too; passionately so. I'll latch on to a topic and soap-box it to death, ranting, raving and generally being as obnoxious as only a thirty-something-Liberal can be. I'll happily argue any political issue with you whether I'm in the right on it or not.[57] 'Cause that's how we do things on the loony left. Loud, proud and uncowed—we are not afraid to be completely and passionately wrong.

---

[57] The truly heartbreaking thing about being a Liberal is that you're never in the right . . . (waaaaaaaaiiiiiiiiiiiit foooooooooor iiiiiiiiiiiiit) . . . you're only in the left.

I can't come to the right on most issues and coming to the middle actually causes me pain and nausea.

And then I had you, son.[58] And I started looking at things through the perspective of 'How will this affect The Pants?' Everything I normally go up in flames about is first put through this prism. How will this issue—whatever it is—affect my son and his well-being, whether now or fifty years from now?

A good example of this is the troublesome issue of Free Speech.

We don't have to like what the other guy is saying. We don't have to agree with him. In fact, under our Constitution we can spit our own rhetoric back just as loudly. But we have to let the other guy say what he has to say, and that right is most fully exercised and demonstrated when bugs crawl out from under their rocks and start vomiting hateful, bilious rhetoric on the social landscape.

I'm happy about that. I don't want you to grow up in a police state. I don't want you to grow up in a place where having an ignorant opinion, however atrocious, about something is illegal. While I hope I am enough of an influence on you to get you thinking for yourself and being a decent human being, if you grow up and believe in . . . saaayyy . . . the divinity of sponges, I want you to have that right. I want you to feel comfortable believing and valuing what *you* find worthy, and I want you to be able to answer the questions of life for yourself.

Anything else would be a crime.

---

[58] Well, your Mom *had* you. But I was *there* . . . crying . . . struggling not to vomit in fear . . .

Man Quotes:

"The difference between a Writer and a Storyteller is that a Storyteller can't help himself."
~ Nescher Fraking Pyscher

A Random Poem:

(bliss)
i can see to the end of forever
by the light of my burning bridges
and the view is
just
fine.

Part V: Art, Magic & Mystery:

Chapter 23 – Arting It Up:

Deep in his heart of hearts, every Real Man is, in some way, an artist.

Your Dad is an author; or, more specifically, a Storyteller with the capital 'S.'

I twist pretty words together in sentences and try to leave them ingrained across the hearts and minds of my readers. I leave little smears of myself bleeding across the page; there for everyone to see and admire or revile.

Writing—the written word in general—is something I take very seriously. It's my art.

I write because it defines me.

It's who I am, who I've always wanted to be; the embodiment of all my aspirations. Being a writer is the only thing in the world I've ever been good at; the only thing that's *mine*; the only thing no one can take from me.

I write because the words are *alive*.

They sit in my head, staring up at me in their serried rows, like blind, voiceless grubs.

Waiting.

Waiting.

I can feel them breathing and shuffling; silent and aware. As the light of my consciousness falls on them they stare up at it in perfect unison. The image haunts me and I write to stop them from driving me mad.

Over and over again the people and ideals that I love have betrayed me and the words never have. The words never give. There is no pity, no love, no mercy from the words. They sit and wait, mute and blind until you give them form and voice.

I write because it's better than sex.

Wrestling a recalcitrant phrase or description into place . . . making those staring maggots in my head dance and submit to my will is better than any drug, better than a weekend of enthusiastic sex, better than winning the lottery. That feeling of "This is *right*. This is *proper*," is like being born all over again.

I write because I live.

I write because in the beginning was the Word.

Beating the ones in my head into shape is as close to touching the creative hand of God as I will ever come.

I write because the world is stranger, deeper and more mysterious than we will ever know. Science has reduced everything in the universe to Xs and Os, dancing in test-tubes and obeying arbitrary laws that we have written and defined. Physics, Mathematics, Biology, Geology: it's all created a logical, ordered existence with no room for fairies, goblins, dragons and magic.

I write because I believe that's nonsense of the first water, a crime against everything humanity has ever aspired to be, and I write to keep the magic bubbling along underneath it all. I write because magic and mystery is much more fun and personally rewarding than knowing how or why. I write because someone, somewhere has to give voice to the things we've killed with science and reason. We don't know everything. We *can't* know everything. And once we begin to believe that we do; once we have the hubris to suggest that all the questions have been answered, then life will be flavorless and dull. We will have lost life's majesty. I'd rather be dead.

I write because it gives me a universe under my complete control.

I spent so much time being powerless and unloved; aching and bruised; suicidal and reeling from a life I couldn't understand. I spent most of my life wallowing in a self-loathing so deep that I couldn't see the top, the bottom *or* the sides.

I started writing. Crappy little poems at first; miserable plaints full of words that should have vomited themselves off the page. They were dreadful. Truly. I wrote poems with titles like "Gaol," and "Crucified." No one will ever read them, thank God, but it gave me a glimpse into a universe that I could control.

I fought myself for the words, for every comma, sentence and period. I wrestled myself out of dreadful poetry and into fiction. My first few offerings were bilge-water. Adjectives and adverbs did the duty of description and character development. I rarely had a plot, my structure sucked and none of it was worth the time and effort I put into it.

I didn't care.

The words glittered and spun across my mind, shooting with all the flare of comets and exploding stars. *I* was in control here. *I* was the master and everything beneath my fingers danced to my will. No one could hurt me here. No one could tell me they hated me or bruise me or make me want to die.

The words were the world and the world was the word and I lived there exclusively. I loved it and as hard as it is for me, I still do.

I was weak, boring, small and broken. After discovering the written word, I was almighty in a tiny universe of one.

I write because drugs don't work.

It's gestalt therapy. Free and effective. Whenever I feel powerless or alone; whenever I need friends, sympathy or understanding that I can't seem to find elsewhere for whatever reason, I pull up a blanket of words and bury myself underneath it until the bubbles of psychic poison that have formed on the skin of my soul pop and evaporate their fumes into nothingness.

And I write because I have to. Sounds cliché, doesn't it? I have to write. It's like a song in my brain that forces its way out through my vocal cords, will I or ne'er so.

Ancient man painted mammoths and crocodiles, saber-toothed cats and antelopes on the walls of their homes to attempt to understand them; to control them. I write for much the same reason. I am splashing words across the walls of time in the hopes that they will never be forgotten. I am telling the universe "I am here. I am alive. This is what I have to say." Whether anyone ever reads it or not isn't as important as the *act* of infinite graffiti. *I* will know the words are there. *I* will know that I stood in the gale-force winds of reality and shouted my little poems and stories into the nothing of forever.

The words have saved my life more than once. I don't treat them with the respect they deserve. I feel it when the words aren't right. They twist under my hands and try to go into different directions until I get the hint and line them up correctly.

As grateful as I am, I also know I am their slave. It's something I'm proud to be, even as I bear the sting of their lash and bleed from the wounds of their cuts.

I write because I am a writer.

Chapter 24 – The Random Story:

There is a story buried in the soft, glistening meat of my head.

It's a thing of straight lines and sparkly lights; alien music played by angelic beings from on high; stern faces staring down at me, gloved, gowned and masked, wondering when I will react to the medication, when I will stop trying to chew the padding off the walls, when I will come back down to me.

It itches. It gnaws deep in the sweet, sensitive flesh of my brain, down where my probing, digging fingers can't reach. I can feel it crawling around in there, nibbling at the thin slices of my sweetmeats, laying eggs, and building starry sandcastles.

Every so often I'll get a small piece of it; a snap shot, if you will.

I have this mental picture of myself when those bright lights cascade across my mind. My face softens and my eyes glaze as they lose focus and gaze inward at what is playing in my head.

I'll be standing in John's driveway, holding the heavy end of a door to a Ford Festiva, while John bolts and fastens and snaps it to the Festiva in question, and I'll get a bright sunflash of story heliographing across my mind . . .

The metal was cold in his pocket: a thin, sharp length he took with him everywhere.

He used to go where the people were. He'd sit, surrounded by people, and he'd fondle the cold length of metal in his pocket, and he'd wonder why he felt so alone.

Some distance from where he sat, a group—a collective, if you like—of old men, had set up a shoe-shine stand. They did a brisk business. Everybody likes a nice pair of shiny shoes.

He watched them, those shoe-shining men. He'd take out the knife, and he'd carve hieroglyphics into the cheap formica-like substance of the table while he watched the old men.

Their actions were oddly erotic, in a business-like way. It disturbed him on many levels.

He watched them, and he thought of prostitutes, on their knees, just trying to get a buck. He watched the way their hands moved with slow, languid grace across the fresh leather of the businessmen's shoes

And it was always businessmen. He never saw a construction worker sit down and ask for a spit shine. Never saw a cabbie, or a waiter.

No. It was always some Brooks-Brothers-clad high priest to the god of commerce, with his business newspaper and his leather briefcase. The high priest would sit, make noises of approbation at his newest slave, and wait while he was serviced.

It made him angry. It made him want to walk up to one of them and ask 'Excuse me. Can I ask you something? Did you tip him the same amount you'd tip a whore?'

But he said nothing. He sat there, watching these slow old men service shoe after shoe after shoe, smiles unflagging, shines unparalleled. And he wrote bad poetry while he watched them. And he wrote marching songs, and he carved them all into the surface of the table, his knife-

hand digging deep grooves; deep, terrible secrets only he could read, into the wood . . .

. . .and John will say 'Move a little to the left, Nescher,' as he does some more of his mechanical alchemy to this heavy Festiva door.

And I'll comply, still holding the door. And I'll try to go back to see what happened, but the thread of story is lost.

But only for the moment.

Maybe I'll be standing in line at Wal-Mart, just minding my own business and waiting for my turn to pay for my week's groceries. Something will catch my eye: a woman holding a bag of potato chips; a goth dressed in a pink t-shirt reading 'Bite me' and that sunflash will blind my mind's eye again . . .

His name is Bob.

Bob Smith.

Bob is not short for anything.

It is just Bob.

No 'Robert'; no 'Roberto'; no 'Bobby'.

Just plain Bob.

His parents were plain, unimaginative people who lived plain, unimaginative lives. They had three children. Their names were Bob, Mary and Susan.

Bob Smith works in an office doing office-related tasks. His job is plain and ordinary, as is eighty-five percent of his life.

The remaining fifteen percent of the time, he is the single-most-important person alive.

Bob opened his eyes to see The Specter of Death, sickle in hand, deep, black, faceless hood in place, looming over him.

Bob saw that the cat—named 'Whiskers,' a plain, unimaginative name—had taken up its usual morning spot on his belly. He closed his eyes.

The cat gave a warning yowl. It was the same yowl it gave every morning, from its same place. It was a yowl designed to indicate its displeasure with the food-bringing one. The yowl indicated that the cat, lord-high-master of all it surveyed, had waited for breakfast long enough, and if the food-bringing one, Bob, did not get out of bed THIS INSTANT, then Bob would regret ever having been born.

The looming Specter of Death was bad to wake up to, but the cat was hungry. And that was worse. Far worse.

"Alright, alright. I'm up," he mumbled.

Bob stumbled out to the kitchen, boxers askew, hair firmly bed-headed, eyes partially glued shut. He didn't notice, or ignored, the enormous, stunningly handsome young man dressed in a full suit of gloriously radiant armor, sitting on his living room sofa, surrounded by the remains of Bob's front door. The young man's black hair was gleaming in the sunlight spilling out of the dirty, mullioned, living room windows. His face looked like something chiseled from granite that was then smoothed with the fur of endangered animals. He smelled wonderful to Bob's half-awake and still dozing nose.

"Sirrah! Thank the Heavens I have found thee!" said the armored young man. The words almost seemed to glisten after contact with his lips.

"Mrgulphmpump," Bob said, moving to the coffee machine and dismissing the young man with a wave. .

Bob made coffee.

He fed the cat.

The cat sniffed disdainfully at the food, in the high-minded manner of all cats, and then deigned to eat.

"I'm glad you like it," Bob said.

The cat said nothing. It never did.

Bob poured two cups of coffee.

He drank one cup of coffee.

The Specter of Death glided[59] *into the room.*

Bob handed it the other cup of coffee. The Specter of Death wordlessly nodded its thanks with a slow forward and back movement of the deep, dark, faceless hood.

"Sugar?" Bob asked.

"Please," said a perfectly cultured, mellifluous voice from the hood. The voice sounded exactly like the reassuring operator's who tells you 'Your call is important to us. Please continue to hold. Your call will be handled by the next available representative.' You get this message every fifteen seconds or so. In between, you get this horrible wordless, muzak translation of The Bee Gee's 'Stayin' Alive,' that makes dying seem like less of a horror.

It's been assumed since the concept of anthropomorphization entered the world of man that the Hideous Specter of Death must be male. Anyone who has ever had his heart broken by a woman as badly as Bob has will have no problem considering the alternative that a female Specter of Death would make infinitely more sense.

Bob handed The Specter of Death the sugar.

The Specter of Death emptied the jar of sugar into her coffee without spilling a single drop. Bob wondered, as he always did, if her coffee moved out of the way to make room for the sugar. He was not a stingy man and he filled the cup every morning. He watched, vaguely interested. She lifted the cup to the deep, dark, faceless hood. There was a brief sipping noise.

---

[59] Glode? Glid?

"Ahhh," she said.

"Rough night?" Bob asked her.

"You have no idea," she replied.

"Yeah. I hear that," Bob said, in the vapid way of someone not really listening.

The cat said nothing. It was too busy eating. If asked, it would have no opinion regarding the coffee-time activities of its food-bringer and his guest. There may be a momentary curiosity about the guest, as all the curiosity about Bob had been resolved long before. This curiosity, like all things cat-like, centered around three main questions: is it edible? Can I have sex with it? Does it make an amusingly frantic squeaking noise if I bite it in the head?

The cat ignored anything that didn't fall into those three categories as utterly irrelevant to its life, as most cats do.

Bob drank his coffee.

The Specter of Death drank, with every evidence of complete enjoyment, what must have been something like a coffee-flavored, half-solid, sugar cake.

The cat continued to eat, making an occasional yowly, gurgly noise as it chewed its way through its breakfast.

"I can't understand how you can drink that stuff like that," The Specter of Death said to him, carefully breaking the fragile, comfortable silence.

"Some people just like it black, I guess," Bob replied, not yet awake enough to be more interesting in conversation. "You're one to talk."

"What? This stuff?" she said, waving her cup at Bob. "What's wrong with it?"

"I figure it has to be something like a trillion calories of teeth-rotting, sugar death."

"Well, that's not much of an issue for some of us, is it?"

Bob sipped his own coffee in response. The Spectre of Death shuddered theatrically. Bob smiled and took a deep gulp, smacking his lips. There were retching noises from under the deep, dark, black hood.

The cat lifted an ear, decided the noises were not edible or sex-related, and went back to eating.

Bob finished his coffee while The Specter of Death investigated the refrigerator for scone and/or donut options. "Welp. I guess I'd better go see what his nibs wants," Bob said.

"I'll be here," The Specter of Death replied, around a mouthful of buttered scone.

Bob put the empty cup in the sink and walked out to the living room. The enormous young man dressed in armor, his black hair gleaming in the et cetera, et cetera, et cetera, was sitting on one of Bob's expensive, Italian leather, deep-pile couches—purchased after many long, hard, boring hours working in the office—and he wasn't paying the least bit of attention to the foot-long scratches, gouges and tears his armor was leaving in the couch's surface. The young man had a stern look of concentration on his face. There was a coloring book, left by one of Bob's nephews, held upside down, in both of the young man's hands.

For the first time Bob looked at his front door. Instead of hanging innocently in its frame and providing security from the elements and any wandering Cossacks, it was spread across his living room in several differently-sized shards.

One of the shards stuck out of the dry wall directly across from where the door used to be. It looked like every urban legend told about tornado-driven straw.

Bob watched for just a moment as the young-man's lips slowly tried to form the words he no doubt thought should be under the crazy, swirling, red and yellow crayon.

Bob wondered if the young man's brain had yet registered the fact that it was looking at a drawing of a puppy—intended to be colored by desperately bored youngsters—wearing a straw hat and bib overalls, playing a banjo.

Bob decided that any banjo-related concept was probably a little much for the young man, never mind puppies.

"Lancelot," Bob said, keeping careful hold of his temper.

He wasn't the sharpest pencil in the box, this armor-clad, gleamy-haired young giant. But a closer look at the four-foot-wide, six-foot-long axe/sword at his side, heavily notched and pitted from the young man's many encounters with a world he didn't understand, gave Bob ample reason to pause and carefully choose his words.

The enormous young man stood up with a violent surging motion. It looked like a small, Pacific atoll, Krakato-ing.

"Oh, sirrah! Glad I am that I have found thee! For, lo! I have searched the world over for thee, and I am in direst straits, sirrah!"

Bob knew, without asking, that this sentence probably wasn't much of an exaggeration. Lancelot would, and had, quite literally, knock on every door he came to until he found Bob's house. Not very big on phone books and addresses, is our Lancelot.

Bob's eyes cut to the remains of his front door.

"Lancelot," he sighed, "what did you do to my front door?"

Lancelot tucked his hands behind him, trying to turn his body away from Bob's gaze in a manner that suggested he was also casually trying to hide the four-foot-wide, six-foot-long axe-sword that hung from his side. He tugged at his sword belt belt with his hands still hidden behind his back. He had the good grace to look guilty.

Lancelot? I'm waiting," Bob said.

"Sirrah! When thou didst not answer the door, I feared for thee! I feared that thou hadst broken up with a woman again-"

"Why does everyone think I can't handle a break-up?" Bob interrupted. "Sure, things were bad for a while after Amanda and I broke up but I-"

"You didn't shower for three months," supplied The Specter of Death from the kitchen, around a mouthful of bagel.

"And thou didst smell funky, sirrah," said Lancelot. "I was concerned that thou hadst fallen once again under the spell of thy beer and cough syrup cordial. So I drew my sword." He fitted word to deed, and drew the sword with a noise like a helicopter taking off. The edge drew a thin, red line across his host's naked belly, chest, and chin before burying itself, by more than two feet, into the ceiling.

There was a snort of bagel-flavored laughter from the kitchen.

Bob looked at The Specter of Death. Bob took slow, even breaths.

She took another bite of bagel.

"Leave me one of those, will ya'?" Bob said, not taking his eyes off her and taking slow, even, measured breaths.

"Freaking things'll kill ya'," she replied.

Bob stared at her for a full second, mentally counting and breathing. With deliberate movements The Specter of Death took a bagel out of the bag and popped it into the toaster.

Only when he thought he was fully in control of himself did Bob turn and look at the sword.

He looked at Lancelot.

He sighed, closed his eyes and felt blood gently seeping from the razory wound. He dabbed at it and looked at Lancelot again.

" . . .sorry . . ." Lancelot mumbled, looking down.

Bob wiped his face with a weary hand. "Look. Tell me what's wrong before you knock my freaking house down."

Bob looked at Lancelot's face, and was surprised to find Lancelot's eyes were filled with tears. Lancelot gestured wordlessly to his highly-polished, burnished, pointed, and sharpened steel shoes. Bob looked at them while wiping absently at the blood on his gut.

He looked up at Lancelot and sighed.

"Lancelot, you've got them on the wrong feet again. . ."

"Okay, that should do it," John says, and just like that, the story evaporates.

But I'll get it. I'll get it eventually.

Man Quotes:

"Duty is ours; consequences is God's." ~ General "Stonewall" Jackson

Part VI - Cars:

Chapter 25 –Dreaming About Four Wheels:

At some point you will meet, fall in love with, and yes, eventually destroy your first car. Every man does. There's something about the internal combustion engine, strapped to four wheels, that reduces every man to a glistening puddle of covetous lust.

There's no avoiding this inevitability, so let me tell you about some of my experiences, and maybe . . . just maybe, you won't buy the 1972 AMC Gremlin with the pink interior.[60]

---

[60] 1978 Mercury Capri – owned it for something like two months. A 1985 Pontiac Bonneville – owned it for a couple of years. A 1984 Buick LeSabre - a couple of years. 1985 Chevy Camaro – owned it for, like, twenty minutes, blew a rod driving it to the gas station after buying it off a buddy of mine. He gave me my money back. 1991 Nissan 200 SX – owned it for two years, maybe. 1985 Saab 900 – owned it for a couple of months.

I am mechanically inept. That's a hard thing for any man to admit to anyone, much less his beloved son—whom he desperately hopes will grow to worship him as a masculine hero—but a Real Man knows his limitations. One of mine is mechanics.

That's a bit understated. If mechanical devices were alive, and had like, Bibles, I'd be the rider on a pale horse in the book of Revelations. If mechanical devices had nemeses, I'd be depicted as a wide-eyed man, holding a blow-torch and a roll of duct-tape, a befuddled look on my face. Generations of mechanical-device-parents would warn their little mechanical-device children about me, The Breaking Devil Man.

I exist in a dark, life-eating cloud of mechanical-device destroying particles. I can blow a light bulb from twenty feet away. If the device is more complicated then say, a zipper, I can, and will, destroy it after a short period of time. At one point my co-workers liked to tell each other that if you need a door opened, regardless of whether it was locked or not, call Pyscher.

I have accepted this facet of my life with what I believe is a certain amount of good grace. What makes it such a problem is that it's totally unwitting on my part. I've destroyed keys simply by using them. Doorknobs crumble under my hands. I've proven that 'unbreakable' and 'flame-retardant' isn't. I considered it my personal duty to ensure

---

1994 Hyundai Sonata – a year, at best. 1985 Chevy Celebrity – a year or two. 2004 Kia Sonata – Uncle Eleazar lent me that one for a year. 1991 Ford Festiva – Uncle Gower lent me that one for a couple of months. 1994 Ford Aspire – a couple of years. 1995 Ford Taurus – a couple of years. 2006 Ford Focus – Six years and counting. I've been driving since I was eighteen. I'm thirty-eight now. You do the math.

that civilization didn't descend to anarchy because of Y2K. I stayed off-line until that period had passed.[61]

You're welcome.

I've given this some thought, and I've concluded that mechanical devices represent an oblique, subconscious desire within me to prove my superiority over them. I do this best by breaking them. I tell you this to give you some background of the story that follows. My father's car needed its alternator replaced. At the time I lived within easy driving distance of him. We were getting along for the most part, and since we were the only ones living near each other, we had an unspoken agreement to rescue each other whenever necessary.

Now, your Grandpa Pyscher knows darn good and well that I'm a mechanical clod. I'm not really sure what he was thinking when he called me, but he did. The disastrous repercussions of that decision should be placed squarely on his shoulders.

At the time, my father owned a truly fly ride. It was a 1984 Oldsmobile Omega. It had all the Old-School power goodies on it, tinted windows, and a V-6 engine that could've easily been really killer if it hadn't been owned by my Dad. It was[62] the original 'Little-old-lady-drives-it-to-Sunday-School' car.

See, my Dad is, if anything, even more mechanically inept than I am. He'd owned the car for something like two years, and he'd already replaced the engine, the radiator,

---

[61] Believe it or not, people genuinely believed that the world would end on the first of January, 2000, because our wired society had not taken the proper number of zeroes into account when we hooked everything up to the internet. People built bunkers, stocked up on antibiotics and huddled down, preparing for the worst. Without saying anything about it, my family gathered together on that New Year's. The collective exhale when the world didn't end at 12:01 actually moved the curtains.
[62] Resounding emphasis here on "was."

five or six alternators and assorted other components on this car. He'd paid more getting it worked on then he did to purchase it initially, and it was in fine shape when he bought it.[63]

My father is also a hoarder. One of the bad kinds. He's got junk mail from 1970 that he steadfastly refuses to part with. Everything he's ever owned is lost somewhere within the confines of either the back seat of his car, his trunk, or the cavernous spaces of his house. He is in serious danger of creating a black-hole, or at least a negative dimension of some kind. At one point he had so much miscellaneous crap stored in the back of his two-door car that he could only go up hill in reverse. Fossilized species of insect that hadn't been seen in this century were found in the floor-boards of my father's car.

He began having more trouble with his car one early Saturday morning. The car was telling him[64] that the alternator was not charging the battery. I'm still not sure what that means, but evidently it's bad. He took it to his usual mechanic, who hemmed and hawed, and undid things and eventually told my father "That'll be $87.50."

Naturally enough, my father wanted to know exactly what he was paying for. The mechanic told him that in order to even *begin* fixing my father's car, he'd need $87.50 to run a diagnostic. My father asked if there was maybe someone else who could tell him what was wrong with his

---

[63] This does not include the assorted dings, bings, and actual cracks in the body of the car itself. Dad falls asleep at the wheel a lot, and tends to wake up shortly after he's wiped out a mailbox or two. He'd gotten better about pulling over after his car went cross-country one night. He likes to think of mailboxes as alarm clocks.

[64] The interpretive devices of assorted gauges may as well be alchemists' alembics for all the sense it makes to either me or my father. We managed to figure it out after eliminating everything else.

car, and the mechanic gave my father the hotline number for The Psychic Network Dionne Warwick used to run.

I showed up at Dad's house the next morning after work in order to help him get the alternator replaced. I was pretty sure the day would be filled with horror, but I was hoping to learn something, too. This is an actual transcript of the events that followed, presented here for your elucidation and delight.

"Mornin', Dad. Let's get crackin' on this. I got to be at work tonight, and I want to get some sleep."

"Okay, Nescher. I got some stuff to take care of real quick. Unhook the battery for me, will ya'?"

I stared at Dad in horror. He looked back at me.

"Which one's the battery, again?" I asked.

"The square one that says 'Everready.' It's got the wires coming off it."

"Oh! You mean the 'jumper-cable-thingy!"[65]

Dad shook his head and left me to fight with the battery. I popped the hood and stared. The first thing I felt I needed to deal with was what looked like a beaver's nest in my father's hood space. A tribe of squirrels had taken up residence above my father's left front tire in a small area just big enough to accommodate them. Dad's car had been idle for a while, and Dad lives in the sticks of Kentucky where this sort of thing is actually quite common. I guess I should be grateful it was only squirrels and not raccoons.

---

[65] I'm going to fast-forward this a bit. It's pretty tedious. I ask my father which tool to use, he tells me. I ask him if that's the 'pointy-thing we use to dig out screws,' or the 'shovel-headed thing we use to pound in nails.' He tells me. Then I ask if I need to avoid the dark liquid coming out of the battery. He tells me. Then I ask if smoke coming off my trousers is normal from the dark liquid coming out of the battery. He impatiently tells me. Finally, I ask if I should rinse the tools off, as they are in danger of liquefying from the dark brown liquid coming from the battery. As a side-note, any dark brown liquid oozing from a battery should be avoided, son.

The squirrels didn't seem to be too bothered by the occasional muted bang of me removing my father's battery, but spraying them, however accidentally, with the hose, got them pretty riled. I was rinsing the thick, black, syrupy material that was congealed on the sides of the battery off as best I could when I managed to hose the nest pretty thoroughly. All seven of the squirrels came boiling out, hell-bent for leather. This resulted in what had to look like a circus waltz of biting, irate squirrels and one maniacally screeching, hose-wielding mad-man spinning and pirouetting less-than-gracefully in my father's front yard.

Ever been bitten by a wet squirrel?

Eventually, the squirrels found a quieter place to observe the proceedings in the tree above my head. I managed to clean out their nest, finish removing my father's battery, and awaited further instruction. I amused myself while I waited by trying to see if I could figure out which one the alternator was. I figured it was either the little square thing connected to the windshield wipers, or the big round thing with the screw piercing it through the center on top of the engine. Dad came back out.

"You done yet?"

"Yep," I responded proudly, "got the battery out and everything. I only burned myself three times, too!"

"Okay. Which one's the alternator?" he asked me.

I stared at the confused jumble of parts confronting us.

"The big round thingy with the screw?"

"I think that's the air-filter."

"That's the fan belt, right?"

"I think that's the windshield-wiper reservoir."

"Reservoir's a funny word, isn't it? Reservoir . . . reservoir . . . reservoir . . ."

"Yeah, okay. So which one is the alternator? Your brother Eleazar replaced the alternator last time, and he told me that this one has a lifetime warranty on it. So if we figure it out, we can take it to the store and get a new one."

"Okay, cool," I said "Why don't we call Eleazar, and ask *him* which one the alternator is?"

"Now you're thinking!"

Your Uncle Eleazar's a mechanical genius. The ineptitude that infects your Grandpa and me seems to have skipped him entirely. We used to make him fix things all the time when we were kids. I firmly believe he joined the Army to get away from the constant demand on his services and abilities.

Twenty minutes later, all three of us were impatiently shouting at each other on the phone. Dad was in his bedroom, I was on the extension in the kitchen, and Eleazar was at his house in Alabama, manfully suppressing his agitation.

"No! The *round* thing *mounted* on the engine block!"

"I friggin' *looked* at the round thing!" I replied. "It's big, black and round, and it's got a screw in it, right?"

Eleazar sighed. "Okay. Look. Undo the screw and tell me what happens."

I put the phone down, did so, and was surprised to find what looked like a round paper filter. When I relayed that to Eleazar he told me, "Congratulations. You've found the air filter. Now remember that. *That* round thing is the air filter. Say it with me, Nescher: AIIRRR FIIILLLLTERRRRRR."

"Okay, okay. No need for sarcasm. I got it. So now what?"

At this point, my Dad chimed in with, "Is it this thing in the book over here that says 'catalytic-"

"No!" Eleazar yelled over him. "Look. Both of you shut up. The alternator in Dad's car is right next to the AIIIIRRR FILLLTERR. Okay? Look for the little round, knobby looking thing connected to a bunch of belts."

"Belts . . .?" I began.

"Belts. You know, they look exactly like what you'd hold your pants up with, but no buckle . Okay?"

Eventually, between the three of us, we were able to finally determine what, and where the alternator was. Next we unhooked it.

Well, unhooking it isn't exactly right. It would be more accurate to call it an extraction. See, Dad's tools consisted of three screwdrivers[66], a hammer, four rolls of duct tape and several wrenches of varying sizes, at least three of which were in the process of liquefying from the dark brown liquid still seeping from the battery.

After several trips to Wal-Mart to buy ratchet sets, soda and beef jerky, we managed, through might, main, and sheer unrestrained masculinity, to pry the offending alternator from its foul embrace with my father's engine. With a minimum of injury, I might add!

The squirrels weren't impressed and threw acorns at us derisively from their new place in the tree.

We then took it to the auto-parts store. We were greeted by "Jeff." [67]

---

[66] Two of which were Phillips heads. The third was an antique, rusted thing with Asian writing of some kind on it. It had two heads, terminating in a squared-off-point like a new pencil. None of us had ever seen it in any store. Tool boxes are like that, son. They accumulate useless tools and breed mutant tools you will never use.

[67] You know "Jeff." "Jeff" is the guy who works at shops like AutoZone and Radio Shack and looks at you like you're an idiot when you ask him things about batteries or phone jacks. "Jeff" doesn't respond well to courtesy. "Jeff" responds best to threats like "If you don't friggin' give me the help I need and stop looking at me like I'm impaired, I'm going to rip your bottom lip off and shove it up your nose." Not that *I* would say anything like that. That was all Dad.

Our "Jeff" looked at us like we were idiots. That is, he did until he noted the matching scowls, the grease on our hands, pants, and shirts, and the thin tendril of smoke rising from my trousers. He then became fairly courteous for a "Jeff."

He skittered behind his little counter, hooked our alternator up to some sort of device, and looked at a needle-gauge.

After exactly ten seconds of electrical/mechanical alchemy, he looked up at us and said the one thing pretty much guaranteed to ensure his grisly death: "There's nothing wrong with this alternator."

It probably isn't fair to say he stepped back like a frightened little girl at the feral growls that erupted from our throats, but it was certainly close.

"What do you mean there's nothing wrong with it? We just spent three friggin' hours disconnecting the friggin' thing!"

"I'm sorry, sir. This alternator is fine. You must have a short somewhere else."

We gave Dad's car a hero's burial, later that evening, 'Taps,' and all.

As we shoveled dirt over it in his back yard, I turned to my father and consolingly said "Well, look at it this way. At least it wasn't the alternator."

Chapter 26 - The World's Ugliest Hatchback:

For a while I owned the World's Ugliest Hatchback. I actually drove it for the better part of two years, including several trips from Kentucky to your Mom's house in Ohio.

The poor thing was a 1994 Ford Aspire hatchback. It had close to 195,000 miles on the odometer. I purchased it for a hundred dollars from your Uncle Jerry. The back, right end was caved in from a hit-and-run accident. The right, rear window was covered in duct-tape, as there was a fist-sized hole in that window. The explanation works like this. It was a good idea at the time: keep a spare set of house keys in the car! That way, when you lock yourself out of the house—because you have, over and over, and we know you will again—all you have to do is unlock the car and you'll be golden. Of course, that only works if the car's unlocked, 'cause otherwise you'll have to break a window, and if the keys are in fact, not still there . . .well, you'll feel like a complete jerk.

When I bought the car I took it to a mechanic, who promptly declared it as totaled and I was able to tell the state of Kentucky that I was driving a road-worthy but uninsurable car.

The fuel gauge didn't work, and I had to use the trip gauge—I filled up every 250 miles—to tell me when to put gas in my car.

Neither one of the back doors opened. The hatch didn't open. The right, rear tail-light was held on with decaying duct-tape, fishing line, green yarn, and my good wishes.The front end was in good shape. There's was one of those terribly stylish, horribly useless, and utterly hip black leather bras on it that was slowly falling apart. It always made me think of an elderly hooker slowly displaying her dubious goods.

The back window had several charitable organization stickers on it—I could only claim a few of them—and the following message, in large block letters, to anyone who might have chosen to read it: 'IT RUNS, IT'S PAID FOR, AND I DON'T CARE.'

I also had 'POET', spelled vertically and horizontally, as a sort of 'lazy-man's' acrostic, done the same way. I have my vanities, same as anybody else.

The car was missing two hubcaps, both on the right side. The muffler scraped horribly. It was no longer connected to the car at its nether end, and the back bumper was slowly disintegrating under its own weight. Whenever I drove it I turned up the radio loud enough to overcome any incidental scraping, farting noises my car's diseased muffler may have made.

The inside should probably be left to the imagination. It was, previously, a girly-girl's car, with all the plush and interior decorating that is implied by girly-girl ownership. Most of the car was actually open to the elements, so you can, no doubt, extrapolate what kind of effect that had on the interior. Just think 'EPA Superfund site,' and you've got the right idea.

"Dad. Seriously?" I hear you asking in amused tones. "Why did you drive such a hideous thing?"

"Well, son, I'll tell you. First, I got close to thirty-eight miles to the gallon. At the time it cost me less than twenty dollars to fill the gas tank. I liked to smirk and laugh at the SUVs who blasted past me in a thick cloud of wasted money. I generally shouted something like, 'You just blew eighty bucks!'

"Second, the car cost me a hundred dollars. Someone once told me that if you bought a car for less than a thousand dollars and drove it for a year, that car had paid for itself. Using that kind of logic, my beast of a hatchback was an investment ten times the value.

"Third, while my car was ugly, smelled funny and made the same sort of noise a congested, diarrhetic Cape Buffalo would, you can't deny it had personality.

"Fourth, I *never* had problems with tail-gaters."

Man Quotes:

"He has told you, O man, what is good; and what does the Lord require of you but to do justice, and to love kindness, and to walk humbly with your God." ~ Micah 6:8

Fish Story:

No work of this kind would be complete without a fish story. Here's mine.

He pulled a glistening, smelly, oddly attractive globule of chicken liver out of its tub and pierced it with his hook. He cast a gimlet eye at the sun, the sky.

"Rain soon," he said to me in a mutter.

I looked up in surprise. The sky was clear, innocent. The sun shone down on a beautiful day. He must've noticed my reaction, for he snorted derisively and spat off the side of the boat.

"Oh. Aye. Rain soon. You'll see," he said, scowling at me in his usual fashion, his tatty pipe clenched between lips barely visible under his beard.

I said nothing.

"Good for fishing, rain is. Chase those old monsters up from the bottom. Get 'im interested in our baits," he said in his muttering growl. With a fluid, continuous motion, he cast his line into the water. It sailed gracefully out from the side of the boat, looking like a blood-drenched fairy, and hit the water with barely a ripple.

A professional couldn't have cast it prettier. He made a non-committal grunt and settled back into his deck chair, his pipe issuing forth the foul smoke he preferred.

I dutifully baited my own hook, taking a guilty pleasure in the visceral sensation of the separating flesh, the cold liver blood running down my wrist.

"Fishin's part of the human soul. It's a common line 'tween us. My Daddy fished, his Daddy fished, and 'fore both of them, their Daddies fished. Man's been fishin' s'long there's been fish, s'long there's been men. Fishin's part of who we are as men, as human bein's." He paused here to take a mighty pull of his pipe. I admired the way he could speak, fish, and smoke, all with an economy of movement that disturbed nothing. His line was rock steady, his pipe did not move, his speech was clear, if a bit clenched. I hoped, that when I became an old, grizzled fisherman, I could do half so well. "But more important than the fishin' is the fishin' story. I tell you, there's as many fish stories as there are fishermen to tell 'em." He looked over at me. "Got a fishin' story?"

I smiled ruefully. "I've never caught more than poison ivy," I said, grinning in the beta-dog way.

He gave me a lopsided smile. "Ah. An honest man! I'd've had to call you out, you told me otherwise. No shame in it, son. You'll catch one eventually. Everyone does."

I felt a nibble on my line and my eyes widened.

"You pull that up now, you won't get nothin' for your trouble but a naked hook. Let 'im peck at it a bit. See if he's really hungry or just noshin'. Meantime, I'll tell you a fish story. It's a good'un'."

Thirteen men got on the boat. Several of them, including two sets of brothers, had been on the water for most every day of their lives. There were no surprises here. They knew every wave, every shingle, every beach. They knew the meanings of the colored tides, of the shifts the wind made during the changes in the seasons. They knew when and where the fishing was good. They knew where the larger monsters went to hide, and they knew the baits that tempted them forth from their cold, dark holes. They knew the songs to sing when casting their nets, and they knew the songs to sing when pulling them forth. There was a feeling, looking at those men, that here was represented more than a thousand generations of men—stretching clear back to when God had pulled the first man up from the mud—who lived their lives on this very same water, fished these very same spots and told their fish stories.

And did He include a fish scale or two in the mud pie that was Adam?

There was a line between them; strong and solid. The water they fish is their water, and none knew it better.

One of them was tired, sore, sleepy.

One was an accountant.

They shoved the boat from the beach into the water, hoisted sail, and they were off.

It was a lovely day. The wind was just right, the fishing was fine, and they were enjoying each other's company. There was good-natured abuse at the fumble-fingered landlovers' attempts at seamanship, and an air of holiday surrounded them. They sailed around the water, enjoying each other's company, the feel of the wind's spray in their faces.

One of them fell asleep.

The day was going fine. They pulled a few in for a later supper, and even the soft-handed ones, with no sun on their faces and no salt in their veins, managed to catch a few. They slit the bellies open, careful to preserve the good meat, and pulled the filets: fresh, hot and fishy, for cooking over the coaled braziers.

There is nothing finer than the taste of a fish you caught yourself, is there? The sweet, tender flesh tastes like nothing else, and the sea-spray in your face makes for an appetite like no other.

There was laughter, there were stories, and there was more good-natured abuse.

One of them slept through it all. Maybe there was a smile on his face. Maybe, through that same human connection we all share, he was sharing their camaraderie in an unconscious way? Who can say?

And then the storm hit.

There was no warning, no lowering of clouds, no dropping of temperature or pressure. One moment the sky was clear, the next they're fighting for their lives. The boat was in danger of sinking, the catch was flopping and flailing underfoot, and the landlovers panicked as landlovers do whenever the wind kicks up a bit.

They strove to get the boat into the wind, to get the oars in the water, to do something that would keep them all from drowning.

One of them, maybe a bit smarter than the others, goes to where the sleeping one was . . .

He paused then. The sun was reflecting off the water now, casting silvered daggers into his eyes. He squinted in a way I could see was carefully practiced. You felt there were indeed no surprises with him and this water. He knew it, and the water knew him.

I envied that connection. "What happened then?" I asked, respectfully. I knew the answer, but I wanted to hear it from him, in his voice, in his words.

He smiled over at me. "Ain't heard this one?"

I smiled back. My turn to say nothing.

"Master! Save us! We're going to drown!" It was a landlover. You know it was a landlover. Man's asleep, and it's always the landlover that comes screaming and yelling about drowning.

He sits up. His eyes are tired. His body is tired. He's cranky, irritable, grumpy.He walks out to the boat's rail. Looks at the roiling sea, the blowing wind, and He's just as cranky as He can be. Who wouldn't be? All nice and cozy in His little nest, and He's got to wake up to settle a temper-tantrum?

He doesn't even lift His voice. "Knock it off!" *He stares at the water, like a Dad making sure the unruly children have gotten the point, and then He goes back to His nest, leaving the wind, the waves and the disciples all still, smooth and silent as clean, new glass.* "Mind you, that's not quite the way Scripture puts it, but a fish story, it changes with every tellin'. I don't think He'd mind, I put my own little interpretation on it. Way I understand it, He was a storyteller His ownself."
I smiled. He reeled his line in, grunted at the empty hook, rebaited it, and cast it back out into the water with that same fluid economy of movement.

"Here it comes," he said, and just as he'd predicated, it started to rain.

It was a quiet, gentle sort of rain, and we enjoyed it, listening to the patter of water hitting water, the gurgle against the boat's side; feeling the ripples and shakes on our lines in the water, and the one between us that stretched to the beginning of time.

Part VII – Work

Chapter 27 – The Nine-To-Five Nightmare:

Let's talk for a minute about the difference between a "job" and a "career." A job is something you do because you have to. You may like your job. If you're really lucky, you might even love your job, but it's something you do because you have to make money *somehow*. You do what someone else tells you to do for a couple of hours a day, you accept the pay they give you and you keep doing it for as long as you have to. Most every job I've ever had sucked to one degree or another. None of them ever told me who I was.

A job doesn't, and shouldn't, define who you are. It's just something you do, for now, to make a little money. It isn't who you are or what you're going to become.

A career, on the other hand, is something you do because you *want* to. You learn it inside and out, let it become part of you and then you go look for someone who is willing to pay you to do this thing you want to do. The only career I've ever had has been as an author. The pay stinks, the hours blow and I have accepted that I may never reach "island-buying" money, but I will keep doing this because I love doing it.

A job doesn't define you. A career, to some extent, does.

I've had every bad job there is by this point, and, as I've already intimated dozens of times in this book, I was a third-shift security guard. That's it. Get it all out of your system. Go ahead and laugh. I've heard it all before.

"What? You failed 'Newspaper Delivery-Boy School?'"

"Pizza delivery wasn't glamorous enough, huh?"

"High school dropouts can't often *find* real jobs. Good for you."

And my all-time favorite: "It's not often you see somebody rise above the esteemed ranks of taxi drivers."

I took a lot of abuse during my time as a security guard. But it's was also the job that seemed to generate the most stories . . ..[68]

---

[68] Probably the worst segue ever written, but okay. I got the job done.

Chapter 28 - Rain, Blood & Steel:

It was *pouring* and I had to do a perimeter tour.

Normally I like doing a perimeter tour in the rain. It's kind of soothing, and it washes all that crud off your face that you get when you sit in a stuffy office-building for hours on end. But this was that 'chunky, fall-down-your-collar, give-you-pneumonia-and-make-you-die' kind of rain.

The buildings downtown make for a natural wind tunnel, so when it rains like that down here you don't want to be out in it. It was the kind of rain that'll have you kiting on the wind and swimming in the Ohio if you're not careful. Naturally, my supervisor wasn't interested. I could almost see the vein in his forehead throb as he bellowed at me in his thick southern accent over the phone.

"Pyscher, I don't care if *Noah* shows up looking for nails! Getcher butt out there and do a perimeter!"

"Can I at least get a parka or something? I mean, it's storming fit to beat the band out here, boss! The thunder's rattling the windows and everything!"

"Have you always been this much of a wuss?"

"No, boss. I'm just not tryin' to die for $9.33 an hour. Okay?"

"Sissy."

And with that, he hung up.

It was even worse than it had initially appeared once I got outside. The rain was falling in what seemed to be horizontal sheets, the wind blew my parka into twisted knots, and I was soaked all the way to the skin within seconds. I pulled my flashlight out, grumbling to myself about 'Even friggin' terrorists wouldn't be out in this kind of crap.' I couldn't *hear* my grumbling, but it felt good to know that the Universe was aware of my objections, anyway.

I turned the corner and I had a brief glimpse of a massive, man-like, steel-gray body hunkered over something bloody; crimson eyes blazing out at me with a sanguineous heat just as my parka whipped around my face.

There was an ear-piercing shriek and something hit me in the chest hard enough to drive the wind from me as it knocked me flat on my can. There was a light, musical 'tinkle' that I felt more than heard as my flashlight broke underneath me.

Through the haze of breathless shock, I could just hear the sound of mighty wings flapping over the storm.

After trying to suck air into my lungs for what seemed like a thousand years, I finally managed a single, gasping breath that was more water than air. Eventually, I recovered enough to get to my knees and wipe the snot off my face. I had the hiccups something fierce, too.

I sat there for a long moment, water running freely over me. I could smell blood, and I was really afraid of what I was going to see when I looked up.

I was right.

My boss wasn't going to believe that the half-eaten corpse of a large dog on our property was the work of some huge, winged beast. Nor was he going to accept any story I told about breaking my flashlight that didn't heavily feature me looking stupid.

I sighed, looking at the eviscerated corpse with an investigatory eye under the feeble light cast by the lightning.

The building is ours. The responsibility to keep it from, like, falling down, is ours. Anytime somebody leaves a dead body on our sidewalk—and it happens, believe me—the initial responsibility of getting it cleaned up belongs to us. You take a close look at all the details in front of you and then you write it down exactly as you saw it. When the real police show up, you give them your report. Simple, easy, and it explains why I was peering at the torn and partially eaten corpse of a dog.

The corpse lay there in an enormous puddle of wet, bloody fur and torn meat. I looked up nervously, half expecting to see something vengeful sweeping out of the sky towards me. Instead, I got a face full of chilly rain.

I'm not inordinately brave or anything. I don't have some kind of death wish, and I probably wouldn't acquit myself with valor on the field of battle. What I am is nosy. It's part of what makes me such a good security guard. I can't leave something like this alone. Most folks'd have an encounter like this and go, "Boy. I'm suuuuuuuuuure glad he wasn't hungry for fat, wet security guy!'" and then run screaming to the nearest church. Me, something in my head goes 'That was a gargoyle. You know that, right? You know it's probably perched on a building nearby, and since the tallest building in the area is the one you work in, you know this thing's probably perched on *your* building, don'tcha?' Then I get to watch in stupefying horror as another part of me answers, 'Ohhhh yeah! Let's go find us a *gargoyle*!'

I really don't have any say in the matter. I don't have an angel and a devil perched on my shoulders, I have two insane idiots, egging each other on.

The observation deck to our building is open to the elements and unlit. It wraps all the way around the building, affording a platform for people who need to work off the side of our sixty-five story palace. This deck is part of the roof, being an eight-foot wide 'perch,' or shelf, that is accessible from a large door on the top floor.

The deck is quite a heady place to be. It's nearly fifteen-hundred feet from the ground. There's a nominal wall around it, but it's really more of an after-thought, being only a foot tall. The thinking at my building seems to be that if you're on the observation deck, you've got good reason to be there and you know not to stand close to the edge. It's not the kind of place to be if you have any kind of aversion to heights.

The storm was still raging around me, whipping my parka into uselessness. I watched, amazed, as a blazing rope of blue-white lightning touched down on the ground about a mile away. I fancied that I could feel the heat of that strike where I stood.

The thunder that followed was deafening.

I had gotten another flashlight and I shined it around nervously, half-hoping I wouldn't see anything, half-hoping I would. I stepped out onto the observation deck proper, my feet slipping and sliding underneath me. It was only as I fell on my butt that I realized how incredibly dumb this was. I stood up, brushed myself off as best I could and looked around for a minute, hoping something would show up.

Twenty minutes later I was soaked to the skin, cold and feeling like a complete idiot. I decided that whatever it was had no doubt winged it to someplace drier and quieter and I turned back to the door with the vague idea of standing there and watching the storm. That was when, in the tradition of every good horror story ever, I heard a feral growl from behind me, loud enough to be heard over the rain, the wind and the thunder.

I turned to the source of the sound, and sure enough, there it stood. All nine hulking, muscular, feet of it; clawed hands opening and closing; teeth working like a bear trap, dripping with the rain and making the deck sway ominously beneath its weight, in-between me and the door. A smell like wet cement mixed with ozone rose off it and overpowered the smell of the rain all around us. I shone my flashlight at it and tried very hard to control those bodily functions in grave danger of failing.

It was a deep gray color all over, like wet steel. Its long, forked tongue was a blazing red against all the gray, as were its eyes. Its teeth were canine-like, with massively prominent incisors. They looked fully capable of biting through anything it pleased to wrap its lips around. It had enormous, bat-like wings that extended out to the sides and over its head. A part of me that wasn't senselessly gibbering in absolute terror distractedly estimated its wing span as thirty feet. This close, it filled the sky with its immensity. Standing there—growling at me over the noise of the storm, its wings spread to its sides and buffeting in the wind—it was the biggest thing I've ever laid eyes on. I could feel a furnace heat baking off of it, coming at me in fierce, angry waves. I'd like to say that there was another dramatic flash of lightning at this point, but to be perfectly honest, a helicopter holding the Norwegian Bikini Team, Metallica, and the Pope could've landed three feet from me and I wouldn't've noticed.

I was wound tighter than a clock, and any real decisive action on my part was probably impossible. I took several panicked steps back and felt my legs bump up against the low wall.

To my credit, I held on to the flashlight as I went over.

You read about people's perceptions as they fall from a killing height. Authors make a real attempt to poetically describe the feelings of 'plummeting weightlessly towards an all too unforgiving ground,' and so on and so forth. What they don't tell you is the way there's a voice in your head going '*Aiiiiiiiiiieeeeeeeeeeeee!*' at the top of its lungs, primal instincts are making you flail your arms and legs in search of a ground that isn't there anymore, and the wind is rushing in your ears in a way that deafens you to all of it. In short, you're not doing anything even remotely poetic.

As if all that wasn't bad enough, add to it the sight of a gargoyle leaping off the deck behind me in furious pursuit. I couldn't scream but I certainly tried to. The air flipped me on to my stomach and some vague part of me tried to fall faster.

I felt a cold metal vise close around my ankle and there was a sudden jerk as I came up brutally short. The wind and the rain nearly froze me solid as my rescuer beat its wings and rose up into the fiercely combative night sky.

Somebody was making a noise that would've been hard-pressed to emerge from the throat of an eleven year old girl and that same, distracted part of me kept wishing they'd quit screeching like that. I don't remember much after that, but my throat hurt for *weeks*.

The next thing I knew I was opening my eyes to see the gargoyle wing its way out into the night. It was making a noise that I've thought about for a really long time.

I looked down to see that I was standing on the roof of the building opposite ours. Everything seemed to be intact, none of my bones seemed to be broken, and I'd managed to keep everything bowel-related inside me. There was a small, warm glow of accomplishment at that. I stood there for a really long time, scared it was going to come back, half-hoping it would. Eventually the wind and rain quit, and I looked around for a way down.

The guys still don't believe me, and I eventually gave up trying to explain how I ended up on the roof of the building opposite ours. 'Specially when *their* guys said their roof door was locked. I showed them the bruise on my ankle, but the guys just didn't buy it. "What? D'you sprain your ankle running from a rat?"

It hasn't been all bad. I had to get a drug test—that I passed, thank you very much—and the job gave me three days off since the boss believed I had some kind of a "nervous episode." Three days off with pay never hurt anybody. Nobody lets me do any perimeter tours anymore, either. They half joke when they say it: "Pyscher might get lost and go secure somebody else's building." But there seems to be an element of genuine worry, too. If nothing else, it's gratifying to know your co-workers care about you.

Late at night, especially when it's storming, I'll look out the windows and think about the gargoyle. I wonder why he saved me, why he didn't eat me and on and on. I wonder if there are more of them, out there in the world somewhere, protecting other clueless security guards.

One really bad nights I'll remember the noise the gargoyle made as it flew away; loud enough to be heard over the storm. I've thought about it at some length and I've   just   about   decided   I'm   right. I think it was laughing fit to bust.

Chapter 29 – Faceful Of Nose:

Find yourself a job that lets you have the flexibility of your own schedule, if you can, my son. Having a job with rigid, inflexible scheduling can be a nightmare. Third-shift security work is like that. It doesn't even matter if you hurt yourself pretty badly, sometimes, as this story I wrote— *chronicling actual experiences*[69]—during that time illustrates . . ..

Monday. It can be in the middle of July, and it is still a dark and dreary day. Even the way it sounds is dreary. Say it with me: "Mooooonnnnnnnddddddddaaaaayyyyy."

I was running late for work. It isn't that I don't have the discipline necessary to get up . . .

Oh, wait. Yes it is. That and the snooze button. Stupid snooze button.

So after throwing something edible down my throat[70], washing it down with some instant coffee, and bathing as quickly as I knew how, I rushed out the door and promptly landed on my face.

The problem begins like this. At the time this story relates, I lived in a cracker box. My 'house' was a one bedroom, 'utility trailer.'[71] My place was small, but it was

---

[69] No, really! Listen . . . would I lie to you?
[70] Generally ends up being the first thing I grab out of the fridge. It's okay when it's like, cold pizza, but when you get a handful of fish or something, well . . .
[71] Have you ever seen those little trailers at construction sites? The ones that are used as offices by the in-charge types? Well, my place could walk up to one of those, neatly fit inside, stretch its feet out, and compliment the owner on the amount of space around it.

also dirt cheap. I paid rent and that was it. My utilities were all paid for. Luckily, I had no compunction about living in a tiny space as it was just where I hung my underwear. Something about that apparently pissed my letter carrier off, because he and I were feuding.

It had started a few weeks previous when he tore my mailbox off the side of my trailer. I don't know how, and I don't know why, but I came home one afternoon, and there it was, sitting like a wounded animal on my front porch with a note that said, "Sorry. USPS."

I am a firm believer in the concept of "You broke it, you bought it."

I left the box lying where it was, along with a note for my letter carrier, stating, in essence, 'No sweat. Feel free to fix it.'

Imagine my outrage when I got one that said, 'Get bent.' This went back and forth for a while, with the notes becoming increasingly aggressive between our two sides.[72]

Eventually, the hostility boiled over into direct action. I placed a line of duct-tape trip wires, attached to the dog's fence next door, right at shoe height. Walking through them shook the fence and woke the dog—something my letter carrier avoided. The dog's name was 'Plague.' No one could quite figure out what breed it was, exactly, but it resembled the result of a drunken night of love between a bear and a gorilla.

My letter carrier nailed my letters to my front door for a week.

I left puddles of asparagus-tainted urine along the walk and porch.

---

[72] My coup was "Oh, yeah? Well, your *Momma* didn't think so!"

My letter carrier left my mail *in* the oh-so-strategically-placed puddles of urine.

I acquiesced. I put the 'box on my porch, with a meek note asking him to resume placing my mail in it. That was yesterday.[73]

On exiting the front door today, I managed to launch myself over the 'box—newly secured to my front porch with what looked like, after later inspection, a railroad spike—and landed on my face.

The fall from my front door to my "driveway"—a patch of gravel big enough to park my car—is a little more than three feet. Running late as I was, I managed to launch myself four or so feet vertically before landing on my face. My first reaction was desperate shock as I tried to remember how to breathe. The wind had been so thoroughly knocked from my lungs that I'm pretty sure an event horizon began to form somewhere near my belly-button.[74]

After several moments of inaudible groaning and panicked gasping, I manage to draw in one, thready breath.

I rolled over onto my back, seeing stars as I went. I could feel blood gushing out of my face from several different areas. There was a shocked and unutterable numbness in my nasal area.

I pulled myself together as best I could, and crawled—weakly and with lots of painful moans and bright, red droplets—back up my porch stairs and into the house. I grabbed a towel from the bathroom and held it to my nose as tightly as I could for a minute or so, until the worst of

---

[73] Look, I'm not at all proud of my behavior. When you're young and dumb you do young and dumb things.
[74] Top that for obliquely nerdy. I dare ya'.

the arterial geysering had stopped. I then balled the towel up and called work.

One of the things about third-shift security work is that calling off is strictly *verboten*. If you aren't there to run your shift, someone has to stay over and/or come in early to cover you. Our contracts with the building stipulated a certain minimum of officers per shift. This would not be regarded with favor by my co-workers.

For the most part, I got along great with them. There was an atmosphere of mutual respect and camaraderie that can only be found in places where lots of Vets work.

Every job has that *one* guy, however. That *one* guy that everybody kinda wishes, on their bad days, would have a horrible accident with the shredder; the kind that you hear Urban Legends about: "They called his wife and told her, 'The only thing keeping him alive is the pressure on his heart. We can't save him.'"

Our guy was named Filson. He worked second shift, and nobody liked him. He was an oily, weasel-y guy in his mid-fifties with truly epic hygiene problems.[75] He was also balding and wore a toupee that looked as though he bought it second hand. None of that made him unbearable. Filson's problem was that he went around the office bad-mouthing *everybody* to everybody else. He'd buddy up to somebody, chat them up, and then go tell somebody else five minutes later what a jerk that guy was. One of the conversations he had with me before I knew what a toxic co-worker he was started with him jerking a thumb over his shoulder at one of my buddies and asking me "Did you know his wife is a whore?"

---

[75] Boy don't bathe none! He stank! Stank like a horse on fire that don't bathe none!

There had been a couple of questionable incidents in the parking lot after his shift.[76] But when he complained to management, nobody ever saw anything and the cameras were mysteriously pointing in different directions at the time. Management wanted to fire him, but thanks to our less-than-reasoned approach to employee development, they were afraid they'd be sued if we tried. So we were stuck with the guy.

I dialed my work-number hoping and praying. . ..

"Good afternoon! This is Security Officer Filson! How can I help you?"

Suppressing a shudder at the oiliness in his voice, I responded as best I could, "Filthon. Thith ith Pychur. I kneed to call ofth. I phell ofth my portch, and I think I brog my noth. I'm goink to tha EeAre."

I can only assume he recognized my voice, as he responded whip quick, "Pyscher. You are supposed to be here in just over an hour. This is an Improper Call Off.[77] You know darn good and well all call offs have to be made at *least* four hours in advance of your shift! And why doesn't it surprise me that you're calling off on a Monday? Hmmm*mmmmmmmm*?"

It still amazes me that a guy who smelled almost exactly like a compost heap on a warm day could be officious and pompous. Gathering my waning strength,[78] I gave him the most sarcastic reply I could think of in the nonce. "Well tha nexth time I brake my noth, I'll be shure to scthaedule it for at leasth four hoursth prior to my shifth."

---

[76] We came from around dark cars and hit him from behind. Kind of like a soap party, but with rolled up security belts instead of socks full of soap.

[77] I could actually hear him making proper nouns of the words. Improper! Call! Off! It was eerie.

[78] I'd been watching it pool on the floor in front of me in large, crimson puddles.

I guess I struck a nerve, because he rapped out an "I'll pass it along," and hung up. I detected a distinct lack of sympathy on Filson's part.

I dialed 9-1-1, and after many fits and starts, and through a voice that was gradually clouding over into what I thought must sound like an incredibly stoned Donald Duck, I finally communicated to the operator that I was bleeding to death due to a slip and fall injury, and could they please send an ambulance with lots of pain medication to my address? Maybe a young, pretty, sympathetic, EMT of the feminine persuasion?

I clambered painfully to my feet and took a quick peek in my bathroom mirror to scope out the damage, dreading what I would see.

Okay, I'm your father. So you know I'm not a pretty man. And it probably wouldn't surprise you to find out that I've *never* been a pretty man. When my hair gets long, I have more than a passing resemblance to Sean Astin's Samwise Gamgee; both in facial appearance and height and weight. So a trip down the stairs, face first, wouldn't do a whole lot of aesthetic damage. But what I saw in the mirror made me yelp and jump back in fright.

I had managed to break my nose, which was merrily soaking my brave towel with blood even now, but I had also busted my lips a good one and my two front teeth felt cracked. I had a large gash above my right eye that was gently pulsing blood, and I could feel both eyes beginning to swell shut.

I decided it might be easier to deal with the fresh tragedy of my face if I was sitting down, and suddenly it became more of an issue of not being able to stand and that's all I remember for a while.

My first thought on waking was, "Why does my face hurt?"

Pulling up the stretch was, "Oh yeah. And by the way, where am I?"

Where ended up being my friendly, local ER. Luckily, I hadn't thought to close the door behind me when I'd engaged in my Mailbox Ballet, and the EMTs had walked in, patched me up, slapped an O_2 mask on my face, started a main line, and dragged me off to the hospital. I found out all this later from the beefy, unsympathetic, good ol' boy doctor who handled my case.[79] He told me I had lost a good two quarts of blood, broken my nose, gashed myself pretty good in a number of places, and had sprained or sprung three or four ribs. They'd given me blood and some fluids, slapped a splint on my nose and put some ice on my eyes—which was probably why I could see at all. He wanted to do X-Rays and CAT Scans, MRIs and EKGs, and he was convinced I needed over-night observation.

I told the doctor I didn't have insurance.

He smiled ruefully, sighed and handed me a prescription. "Yeah. I figured you were going to say that. Take it easy for a week or so. Make an appointment with your doctor to see about that nose." They left me alone for a couple of hours, then a nurse[80] walked in, discontinued my IV, and sent me to the sign-out desk.

They had me sign a bunch of papers. I think we both knew that the bill would be paid in five dollar installments over the next fifteen years, if at all, but they had me sign the papers that said I would pay the bill promptly anyway. I took some solace from the resigned look on the clerk's

---

[79] Like most Real Men, whenever I am sick or hurt, I want to be loved and nurtured back to health. Not told to "Walk it off, you pansy!"

[80] Beefy, ham-handed and unsympathetic.

face. I wasn't the first broken-faced chump they'd been asked to rescue.[81]

I called a cab, went home, kicked my offending mailbox, pulled open my door, sighed at the large puddles of blood, and crawled miserably into my recliner.

My face ached abominably. I looked at the prescription the doctor had written for me. Enough of my days as an Army Medic and Nurse remained for me to cipher out— through a broken noise and steadily blackening eyes—that the doctor had written me a truly stout prescription for Vicodin.

I couldn't afford Vicodin. After paying for the cab ride I couldn't afford *aspirin*. I sighed and my face chose that moment to twinge. The moment stretched across all of space and time and I fought back the urge to sob.

I couldn't afford Vicodin, but I had alternatives. Luckily, I was born poor, so I know how to get money in a pinch. There is an industry that catered to people like me; an industry I hope you have no experience with at any point. I am speaking of Medical Products: sperm, plasma, blood, a woman's eggs, et cetera.[82] It was a fact of life at my economic level at that time: most anything the body produces can be sold.

I'd only sell plasma. I tried selling blood a time or two. It usually paid more, but it also seemed to hurt more. I usually feel really loogy after I *give* blood; much less *sell* it in quantities that would have done me any good. It's probably only in my head, but selling plasma didn't seem

---

[81] At the time, my normal policy regarding bill payment was to pay as much as I could when I could, and to move without leaving a forwarding address when I couldn't. I don't recommend it as a financial foundation.

[82] It was largely relegated to urban legend among us, but supposedly there were places that would even buy your urine. I shudder to imagine to what use human urine is being put, but so long as the money was good . . . right?

to hurt as much, and after they separated the plasma out, they give you your blood back. That was important to me.[83]

I had a great relationship with my local Medical Products franchise. I went in maybe twice a week or so, let a ham-fisted "phlebotomist" shove a spike in my arm, and I watched cable TV for the three or four hours it took to separate out a couple of pints of plasma. My understanding is they take the blood, put it in a centrifuge, separate out the plasma, add a little mint, some cumin, and give it back to me. I got twenty-five bucks, all the free cookies and juice I could eat, and they got some plasma. If it hadn't been for selling plasma, I probably would've starved to death a long time ago.

Three pints of plasma, a bellyful of strawberry juice, half-a-dozen cookies later, and I'm standing on my "doctor's" front porch.[84]

Let's talk about drugs for a minute. My parents tried to tell me they had never used drugs, despite having met in a seventies-era commune. Despite growing up the way I did, most of the people I knew in my twenties were stoners of one level or another. And as much as I hate to admit this, I did say I would be truthful in this book: I enjoy weed. I smoked quite a bit of it in my twenties and I liked getting high. I never got caught with it or anything; never sold it, grew it or distributed it. I just smoked it when it was available, and I enjoyed it enormously.

I don't understand why so many people have such a hard time with weed when alcohol—a far more deadly

---

[83] I'd only recently lost most of it, after all, and I was feeling kind of selfish about what I had left.

[84] I was worried that my peeps at the 'plasma place' (As I like to call it.) would give me grief over my appearance; maybe not even wanna deal with me. They didn't so much as blink. People must come in there all the time who look as though they've been resurfacing a road with their face.

drug—is freely, readily and cheaply available everywhere, but the law is the law. I don't smoke weed anymore and I won't for as long as it's illegal. In fact, unless it's something over-the-counter or prescribed, I don't touch it. I don't even drink as much as I used to. As cheesy as it sounds, I want to set a good example for you.[85] At the time, however, my attitude toward drugs of all kinds was much more relaxed. If I could get high on it, I'd probably at least try it.

I didn't have a typical relationship with a health-care provider at the time. My normal policy regarding sickness or injury at the time was to ignore it if I could, suck it up and drive on if I couldn't. Unless fluid of some kind was actively spraying from a gaping wound, or I had a broken bone pointing in an awkward direction[86], I didn't go to the doctor.

Yes, I went to the ER when traumatic injury occurred, but only when I was in real danger of imminent death.

But even *I* knew that I was going to need to do *something* about my nose. It was swelling and it hurt abominably. I had a sneaky suspicion that the ER doc set it incorrectly.[87] I was going to be looking at a long recovery period. I didn't want to be wearing a splint on my face for the next however-long, and I needed *something* for the pain. While I didn't have a doctor, and I was probably

---

[85] I've told your mother that if the government ever legalizes marijuana, she should take you to your grandparents for a week or so.

[86] I said "awkward." A broken bone wasn't enough. It had to be pointed or jabbing in a non-functional direction.

[87] In my miserable state of pain and self-martydom, I was half-convinced he'd done it on purpose.

going to have to move to avoid the ER bill, I *did* have an Edwin.[88]

It has been my experience that poor people who live in a community together, most especially a Southern community, take care of their own. They have a highly evolved economic system of trade, borrow and barter that works surprisingly well. I lived in a very small trailer park that was populated, for the most part, with retirees, Soldiers, and small families of one or two children whose parents worked in the fast food industry. There were maybe a hundred people living in my park.[89] When somebody *really* needed something, and they couldn't afford it themselves, they'll probably asked a neighbor to help out. Maybe that neighbor had kids, and they probably haven't had any free time in a while, so they'll ask to have their kids baby-sat in return.

"Baby-sit my kids so I can do the nasty with the ol' lady, an' I'll fix that carburetor."

I was occasionally asked to baby-sit. My price was a bag of groceries.[90]

In our trailer-park, the one way to be crowned king or queen was to own your very own washer and dryer.[91] These lucky few found themselves being offered gifts of food, sex, or even small luxuries like perms, mani/pedicures and

---

[88] "Edwin" isn't his real name, of course. People like Edwin would prefer not to have attention drawn to them. I've never known anyone named "Edwin," and the young man in question kind of made me think of one, so we'll call him that.

[89] There were also a hundred generations of unidentifiable creatures roughly corresponding to cats and dogs elsewhere. None of us were sure what they were, exactly. They looked like a rough cross between a small dog, a large cat, and a confused but eager woodchuck. They bred indiscriminately with each other and were as much a part of the landscape as Mrs. Higgins' Ford Endeavour that hadn't moved in twelve years and was collecting a truly awesome collection of pigeon droppings.

[90] My skills left much to be desired. My tactic was to let the kids watch whatever they wanted on my TV—wired as it was with the park-wide cable system—in return for their absolute stillness for the duration.

[91] We called *them* "hoi polloi."

tattoos in return for a few loads being done. I used to fantasize about getting a washer and dryer and quitting my job to enjoy the perks.

It was really quite interesting to watch this phenomenon at work, if nothing else, out of sociological interest.

Edwin was a tall, skinny, white guy in his early thirties that used to be a genuine doctor. He'd worked for some place truly high-end before being popped by the DEA for running a pill-mill ring.

He rolled over on his partners in return for a drastically reduced sentence, spent three years in Eddyville, and got his license yanked. He was released on shock-probation for good behavior, and now he lived with us, *supposedly* getting by as a pizza guy.[92]

He really was a very good doctor. A kid in our neighborhood would come down with a rash or something, and the family would come bang on his door, asking him to take a look and tell them if it was serious or not.[93] He usually charged five or ten bucks. It wasn't enough to make any money, but Edwin implemented this policy to ensure that people genuinely *needed* his help. Otherwise he never got any sleep.[94]

By now it was early afternoon. My night had been spent in the ER and I'd spent the morning in the plasma place. The sun was sparkling off the broken bottles of Ultra Natural Ice House Light next to the dumpster, and the

---

[92] What he *actually* did was doctor. I don't know how he arranged it, but Edwin never paid rent, gas, groceries or utilities.

[93] I hope you never have to do this, son. But at certain economic levels you have to learn to prioritize. You can't afford to take your son to the hospital—no matter how miserable he is—if a four-dollar tube of ointment will accomplish the same thing.

[94] In our neighborhood, 'HMO' stood for "How Much, Edwin?" (I really hope that joke has some relevance by the time you read this, son.)

cat/dogs were furtively prowling, looking for slower rat/weasels.[95]

A furtive "growl-eow" from the dumpster indicated a successful mating/meal. I shook my head at the thought of yet another generation of kitpies.

The head-shaking produced a grinding, grating noise, and a squealing pain[96] in my face.[97] I'm afraid I may have screeched a bit just before I collapsed on Edwin's porch. I was seriously beginning to consider biting my tongue in half and bleeding to death in order to stop the pain, when Edwin, dressed in a tatty robe, a wife-beater t-shirt, boxers, and pink bunny slippers, opened the door to found out what all the high-pitched, glass-breaking-shrieks on his porch were about. "Dude. Is that you makin' all that noise? I'm tryin' to watch Xena in here![98]"

My response was to pant and gasp, spit and hack.

"Dude. Are you okay? You're like, fountaining blood out of your face all over my begonias."

"Grunt, hark, chew, groan, blllllleeeeeeeeeeeeeed . . .."[99]

---

[95] The rat/weasels who were still loogy from the Ultra Natural Ice House Light leftovers seemed to be preferred over the other guys. Something about the taste, I always thought.

[96] I have the perfect illustration for this pain. It was *exactly* like biting on a rotating drill-bit. (See the footnote below.)

[97] Because I'm *much* dumber than you are. That's why. Just because somebody dares you to do it doesn't mean you have to, son. Trust me: somebody has usually *already* done it and can tell you that doing it sucks.

[98] A Shakespearean epic based on the premise that strong, smart lady heroes r 2 hottt . ..

[99] Okay. For the purposes of narrative honesty, I'm gonna have to come clean. This dialogue is totally made up. I was skimming the line between unconscious and mindlessly incoherent from pain when it took place. I don't have a lot of clear memory until Edwin took me inside and made me swallow his burnt-light-bulb-juice. It took a few minutes, but the world gradually became a much nicer place.

My next coherent though was shortly after Edwin poured something that tasted a little like a burnt light bulb down my throat.[100]

I spent a few minutes recovering. By that time, Edwin had moved fully into 'doctor-mode.'

"Okay. Nescher, can you hear me?"

"Yeth."

"How many fingers am I holding up?"

"Ie don't kno. I vergod how to cound."

"Dude. What happened to you?"

"I brog my noth, Etdwhin."

"Yeah, I can see that. But who set it? It looks like they did it in the dark with a pair of pliers."

"Tha EaRe dogter."

"Uh-huh. Did you piss him off somehow? Sleep with his sister? Share some rotten buddha?"

"Yu know, Etdwhin, I'm nod chure. I wath too buthy bleedig to deadh to knodith."

"Alright. Whatever. Look, what do you need? I'm busy here."

I threw my arms up into the air in a moue of exasperation. "I kneed you to fixth my noth!"

Edwin crossed his arms over his chest, looked at my face for a long minute and finally sighed. "Cost you twelve bucks, bro."

"Ogay."

"And it's gonna hurt."

" . . . ogay . . .."

"A lot."

" . . . "

"I mean, a *whole* lot."

---

[100] Again . . . just because somebody dares you to do it doesn't mean it's a good idea.

"Umm . . .."

"I mean, we're talking incandescent galaxies of pain here, Nescher. It'll probably hurt less to-"

I interrupted rather rudely, I'm afraid, by reflexively spitting a large wad of half-digested blood on to Edwin's slippers. My vision was doubling and trebling at this point, so it was kind of hard for me to tell if the look on Edwin's face was disgust or amusement.

"Dude. I just bought those . . .."

I wiped my mouth and looked up at him. "I'm thorry. I kneed thomeding tone abouth thith noth. I kno yu kin fixth id up, and I kno yu got thomeding to mag id hurd leth while yu do."

"Well . . .*yeah*, but . . . but . . .."

"Hack, gasp, spit . . ."

"Okay, *okay*. Let's do it."

He went into his kitchen, and I heard an assortment of clinks and stirring noises while Edwin concocted. I was bravely trying not to think of a deranged alchemist in bunny slippers when he came back into the living room carrying a cracked, chipped, white ceramic pitcher.

"Here. Drink this, but do it *slowly*. When your fingers get numb, let me know."

I reached for the pitcher hesitantly. A viscous, evil-looking, dark green fluid was skulking in the bottom two thirds. It made me think of toad snot. I attempted to smell it, but breathing through my nose hurt, so I mentally shrugged, said a small prayer, and drank.

I couldn't really taste it, but it had the high-octane exhalation of first-rate liquor. Swallowing was becoming an issue, but the drink had the consistency of melted ice-cream, and it numbed and tingled its way down my throat and into my belly. The numbness kept right on going and worked its through my body with a pleasant, spreading ooziness. It was soothing, and I felt my thoughts getting muzzy and fuzzy after the third small drink. In no time I had drained the entire pitcher and was absent-mindedly using my finger to clean off the sides. Edwin, meanwhile, had resumed his seat in front of his TV, and was appreciating the intellectual properties of Xena breaking heads.

After what seemed to me to be a half-hour, but was probably much sooner, he looked over at me rather suddenly.

Seeing him looking at me, I responded with " . . .Whuh . . .?"

He stood up in something close to alarm. "Aww, dude! How much of that did you drink?"

" . . .Huh . . .?"

"Nescher, you weren't supposed to drink all of it! There's enough painkiller in there to drop a regiment!"

" . . .Gwuh . . .?"

It *was* becoming awfully hard to keep my eyes open, so I imagine Edwin may have made this batch of whatever-it-was a little strong. I closed my eyes for a second, and was quite rudely awakened by the feeling of Edwin's strong fingers grabbing the bridge of my detached nose with one hand and sticking two fingers in my badly abused nostrils with the other. It didn't hurt so much as it made me want to curse my parents for ever meeting each other.

Edwin pulled, pushed, twisted and bent, all the time manipulating my nose from both sides. Meanwhile, I've got a noise like an orchestra being eaten by Godzilla going off in my head; tears, blood and snot are running freely down my face, and over it all I can hear Edwin's TV playing the closing credits of "Xena: Warrior Princess."

This went on for a blurry eternity of agonizing torment. It's just when I was at the point of doing something truly horrific to Edwin and all of his relatives that he says, "There. Done," and pulled his fingers out of my nose.

It still hurt, but I could breathe through my nose again. Edwin took the gloves off his hands, washed his hands in his sink and handed me a washcloth to clean my face and some wadded up toilet paper to plug my nose with. "Dude. When you get home, lay down, put some ice on it, and don't leave the house today. Okay? I ain't responsible for anything that happens once you leave here. Don't let them give you a piss test for about three months. You have any problems, try not to involve me. Got it?"

It took me a few minutes to figure out the words assaulting my ears were directed at me, as I was still muzzy from whatever Edwin had fed me[101] and still lightly drifting in a red haze of pain. Edwin patiently repeated his instructions, cleaned me up a bit, and jammed some toilet paper in my nostrils good and tight. He carried me to my house, where he let himself in, plopped me down, and then took his leave. I slept for three days and woke up feeling fine.

Best twelve dollars I ever spent.

---

[101] I asked him about it later. He looked at me for a long moment and then said something no doctor has ever said to me before or since: "You really don't want to know, dude. And I don't want to tell you." Somehow that was more reassuring than the lengthy explanations I've gotten from doctors elsewhere.

Chapter 30 - The Tractor-Trailer Story:

Among my friends, this story has taken on legendary proportions. I will leave the truth here for you before they fill your head with exaggeration.

For five months: March through August, 1998, I was an OTR (Over The Road) tractor-trailer driver. I drove for Hogan Trucking for a month or so, and then followed the money on over to Prime Trucking. I got to see the entire country, a good bit of Canada, and I learned a valuable lesson about sleep deprivation, over-the-counter drugs and height restriction.

People aren't generally aware of tractor-trailers. Sure, we all drive by them ten million times a day, but how often do you notice them? They're like part of the American landscape. Unless they're doing something wrong, like dumping a load, or rolling off an interstate, nobody pays them much attention.

This is very important. A standard tractor-trailer, or semi-truck for the novitiate, is thirteen feet, six inches tall. This has become such an important issue over the years that most bridges and overpasses in this country have the height clearly posted on them, or are well above this height.

At the time I was exiting a truly dreadful rebound relationship, unemployed, burned up and drying out from a bout with a drug-soaked lifestyle. I wasn't any kind of an epic junkie; I did weed, got drunk all the time and experimented with all the freely available, over-the-counter stuff that mimicked speed and weed. I never did coke or heroin or anything else. It wasn't that I had any integrity, I just couldn't afford it.

My experience with drugs was enough to use up my savings. It cost me my job. I let my nursing license lapse through apathy and spent a couple of years partying.

I've had time to think about it, and I believe that breaking up with my girl at the time sent me into a deep spiral of depression. It sounds like an excuse, and maybe it is, but at the time I genuinely believed that if I couldn't be with her, then life had no point and I might as well do what I wanted.

Cleaning up was a real uphill climb, and I was unemployed to boot. My self-esteem crawled into a closet, and I started looking for something, *anything* to turn me back into a human being again. A man needs to work. I firmly believe this, and I didn't want to go back into nursing, or the Army. I didn't think I could cut it anymore in either one.

Your Uncle Ari told me about this commercial he had seen on TV advertising a truck driving school. At this point I was looking at picking tobacco, so I called and signed up.

I arrived in St. Louis, Missouri a few weeks later. I showed up at the Midwest Training Center with hair down to my shoulders, a titanium stud in my upper ear lobe and a slightly dopey expression on my face.

The school was supposed to be two weeks long. I took considerably longer than that to pass, but after two months or so, I finally managed to get a Class-A, Commercial Driver's License from the state of Missouri. I had a guaranteed job once I had my license in hand, and I started driving as a co-driver for Hogan trucking.

I love driving. Even if it's just in a small car. Driving a tractor-trailer is a whole different level of experience.

You're sitting in front of 40,000 pounds of freight that's being pulled by one big ol' mutha of an engine. I loved every second of it. I was a member of a two-person team. Essentially, I drove and he slept; he drove and I slept. The truck kept moving day and night, and we split all profits eighty-twenty. It was his truck, and I was still technically a student driver. But twenty percent of the profits of this truck was still an absolutely phenomenal amount of money. I was staggered. I was being paid to do something I actually enjoyed, and I was being paid a lot. If you're reading this and you're looking for a way to make some money, look into truck driving.

The general rule of thumb whenever you first start to drive is to be put with a more experienced driver as a member of a team. Your co-driver gets paid a whole lot more as a result, and you have a veteran showing you the ropes, including how to drive, how to run your logs, and how to beat the system. My first co-driver looked like an evil Santa, beard and all. He was roughly four-feet-tall and he weighed close to three hundred pounds. His beard encircled his face, was snowy white, and extended to his navel. He was the randiest, dirtiest, sluttiest man I have ever met in my life, bar none. The only thing he ever wanted to talk about was sex. We got along fairly well, and I am considerably grateful that he was a heterosexual.

After driving for Hogan for a month, I started to hear good things about Prime Trucking. They had the best trucks, they paid the most money, and they encouraged truckers to drive their own trucks. In other words, after driving for them a while, you could buy the truck off them and run it as a sub-contractor if you wanted. That meant you could make an obscene amount of money. I jumped ship at my very first chance.

My co-driver with Prime was a clean cut, middle-aged, conservative married man. He was also a staunch, right-wing Republican. When we met, I had a Gen-X Mohawk. Remember those? You shaved the sides of the head up to a certain point or so, and let the remaining hair grow long. I wore mine in a ponytail, and I still had quite a lot of metal in my face.

He was married, had three kids and he enjoyed training. We got along famously because we learned early on that we needed to stay away from politics whenever we talked.

He even introduced me to his family, and tried very hard to turn me into an Amway convert. It was a close thing.

The entire time I drove, I could've passed a urinalysis at any point.At the time, ephedrine was a freely available over-the-counter drug that really never should have been. It was advertised as a weight-loss product, or an alertness aid. Drivers discovered it fairly early, and you can probably still find quite a lot of it at most truck stops. The basic action of this drug is what is known technically as vasodilation. That's a fancy way of saying it makes your arteries and veins open really wide. This causes the blood pressure to plummet, which in turn causes the heart to beat faster. A very neat little drug, really, but very easy to abuse. The recommended dosage is one or two every eight hours. Too many can cause all kinds of interesting cardiac effects, including death.

I was first introduced to it in the Army. I was stationed at Ft. Bragg, North Carolina, home of the 82nd Airborne Division. There aren't many places anywhere in the world where there's a higher concentration of testosterone and machismo. Guys who routinely throw themselves out of planes are constantly looking for ways to prove they are tougher than other guys who throw themselves out of planes. I liked to think of it as "Lawn Dart Mentality."

Evidently, driving yourself for days on end without sleep was considered very manly among Lawn Darts, and one of the ways this was accomplished was through a handful of ephedrine tablets. The brand I liked to use was called *Mini-Thins*. These were so ubiquitous at the time that any ephedrine product was called a Mini-Thin. You can run for three or four days, with no sleep, after taking Mini-Thins by the handful. Plus, it wasn't tested in most drug screens.

I don't recommend it.

After driving for Prime for a few months, my co-driver decided to allow me to run a trip. I would make the route decisions, I would make the switchovers when I thought they should be made, and I would determine when and where we stopped. I was pumped and ready, and I had a brand new bottle of Mini-Thins.

Our trip started in LA. We went from LA to Barstow, California, and picked up a load to go to Miami. We were going from Miami to my home town so I could stop for a day or two. I would be driving from Miami to Ft. Knox, Kentucky as that was home at the time. The distance between the two is roughly a thousand miles, give or take. Assuming a constant speed of sixty miles an hour, that's roughly eighteen hours of driving. An OTR driver can only drive eight hours at any one sitting. You are required to keep logs to prove that you aren't breaking this rule. I started in Miami, and I drove the entire distance after taking a handful of Mini-Thins.

I had a problem and I wasn't aware of it. The pills were freely available everywhere and so far as I was aware they were as safe as coffee. You'd think, given my recent bout with drugs that I'd be more aware, but I just wasn't getting it.

I think I made it in sixteen hours or so, and I was looking forward to spending some time with my family when I pulled into Ft. Knox.

Have I described my tractor yet? It was a beaut! A big, yellow, brand-spanking new F2000. It had a two-sleeper berth, one on top, one on bottom, a desked area, and a whole lot of space with lots of interior goodies. I believe my co-driver told me that it was worth $250,000. It had a lot of extras though, and I may be remembering this wrong. It may have been as high as $400,000.

When we pulled into Ft. Knox, we had a fully loaded trailer. We were carrying concentrated orange juice to Missouri. By the time I pulled into Ft. Knox, I was pretty incoherent. I had been driving forever with one or two short stops. Now, I had lived in Ft. Knox since 1985 at that point. I knew it from front to back, inside and out. You could drop me off from a helicopter with a blindfold on anywhere within a hundred miles of Ft. Knox, and I'd know within twenty minutes where I was. This makes what happened so damned inexplicable.

When it happened, it happened on a street I had driven down ten-thousand times. I had never noticed something very important about it. The road passed under a railroad trestle.

Driving along, mumbling to myself, and seeing bright, sharp little flashes at the periphery of my vision, I drove under the railroad trestle, at thirty miles an hour when I heard a horrific crunching noise, and the tractor came to a dead stop, flinging my co-driver violently out of his berth almost into the driver's area. It slowly crawled across my sluggish consciousness that something was badly amiss. I looked up and saw that the top of my tractor had been crunched beyond recognition. I put the tractor in reverse, but all it did was wind the engine up real good and shake the tractor violently.

Not only was the railroad trestle about three feet too low, but it was a good foot too narrow, too. I had been going just fast enough to wedge the tractor so tightly in that it wasn't going anywhere. We wriggled out somehow, and surveyed the damage. The tractor was demolished from a point approximately a half foot above where the windshield ended. If I were a little taller, or had the seat adjusted a bit higher, I could have been killed. There was sadly destroyed tractor bits falling now and then with muted clunking noises. Walking around, we saw that I had also driven the trailer in by about three feet, effectively destroying it as well.

The end result was I got fired for destroying not only a tractor-trailer, but the cargo as well. Ask me how much 40,000 pounds of frozen concentrated orange juice is worth. Ask me how much it's worth after it's been sitting in the Kentucky August sun for a day or three.

If you are in Ft. Knox, drive to the Knox Boulevard/Bullion Boulevard intersection, and look up at the bottom of the railroad trestle facing Bullion Boulevard. I'm betting, given governmental repair contracts, that you can still see the scars. You'd think, given this experience, I'd give up drugs forever. But I was still doing drugs until I got married the first time. Sometimes it takes more than one bad experience for you to learn, I guess.

Man Quotes:

"Everything has cracks. That's how the light gets in." ~ Leonard Cohen

Part VIII - Family:

Chapter 31 –The Birthright:

Family is a lot like your eye color, son. You're born with it, you can't really do anything about it if you don't like it, and changing it might make you go blind.

You have this consolation, at least. As bad as you think your family is now—and I'm sure you hate us on some level. Every son does—mine was galaxies worse.

I am the eldest of four. In our family that means I have the obligation of "The Birthright." In Biblical times, the possessor of The Birthright was entitled to a double share of his Father's possessions and the obligation of becoming the Patriarch of his family after his father died. In our family it means that I have the obligation—placed on me by my father when I was five years old—of taking care of my family.

My siblings have all grown up and gone on to success in their chosen fields, so me taking care of them isn't so much an issue anymore, but I do *worry* about them constantly. My mother died and now the only person I have The Birthright obligation of caring for is my father.

I love my brothers and my sister. We used to be much closer, but something about our family needs distance. There's too much pain shared between us, I think, for us to be truly close. Eleazar and Ari have both had spectacular success in the Army. I'm enormously proud of them, but their shared experiences have taken them away from me. My own stint in the Army was a year-and-a-half on Active Duty and some time as a Reservist. I never went anywhere or did anything. My brothers have been deployed multiple times. The Army they're in is worlds different from the Army I was in. We have very little in common anymore and that shows when we spend time together.

Naarah and I are probably closer than the rest of us, but she's become a cosmopolite, where I am increasingly provincial. She'll call, and we'll talk, and she'll tell me about her life. Her stories make me tired. I can't imagine trying to live the way she does, twenty-four-seven, with jobs, obligations and friends who call her, need her and show up at her house at all hours of the day and night.

Don't get me wrong: we all love each other, but we've got our own lives. When we think of each other there might be a phone call or two; a fly-by-Facebook-message, or a scatter-shot email exchange, but there is nothing like the close-knit bond we had as children.

I don't like to talk about my childhood.

My mother is dead, and for all her inadequacies as a mother and protector; for the things she could have done and didn't; for all the hurt and rage I feel toward her for abandoning me and trying to kill herself over and over, the strongest emotion I feel towards her *now* is guilt at having failed her so miserably. She died alone, surrounded by strangers, in a nursing home she'd signed herself into after qualifying for Medicare. Your mother asks me what I think I could have done to help her when I wasn't even in a position to take care of myself and I respond with "I don't know. But I should have done it."

When people meet my father now they go on at length about how cool he is, how wonderful his work is and how he seems to be such a nice, all-around wonderful person. And they're right. He is. Now. But back then, before the years of therapy and the admissions of guilt and abuse? Before the apologies? Back then when we were helpless in the face of his ungrounded, relentless, unfocused fury? Back then he wasn't.

My father has tried to apologize for the things he can remember doing to us. He's admitted that he was wrong and he's told me any number of times that he was sorry.

But sometimes you get hurt and you never come back all the way. Even after years of physical therapy, some injuries are too deep to ever properly heal.

Your mother has heard more about this stuff than anyone alive and I can see it causes her real pain. I don't want to tell her this stuff. I don't want to have to tell *you* this stuff. I don't want this to be a part of your history. But I don't think you will get to know who I am as the Man I believe I am and would like you to surpass unless you have some kind of back history.

As near as I have been able to determine from brief conversation with her one surviving sister, my mother came from deeply conservative, Irish-Scottish-German stock. Her parents had money and my mother was a child of privilege.

My mother's mother had taken Thalidomide—a morning sickness drug of some popularity in the 1950s that caused horrific birth defects—causing her to be born missing most of her left arm from the elbow down.

This could have created a cripple, but my mother adapted. I watched her, as a child, bend over at the waist and tie her shoes with her one remaining arm and her *teeth*.

As the years went by she gave up quite a bit of that self-reliance and ability, and by the time I was a man, my mother seemed to be counting down time, waiting for death.

As children we heard half-whispered stories of a late-term abortion my mother endured before she married my father. I have no idea if these stories are true or not, but my mother used to scream for her "baby boy, Barucha." Her keening and wailing would frighten us so badly we'd cry and wet our beds.

It was my father's theory that "Barucha" was actually Ari. My theory is that "Barucha" was the name she gave to the child she'd aborted in the 1970s. Shortly after she started weeping for "Barucha" was when my mother's mental illness begin to be cyclical and debilitating.

I cried at her funeral, but the relief that her pain was finally over deeply overshadowed my grief.

My father's family was blue-collar all the way up and all the way down.

My mother and father met, fell in love and started a family. Depending on who you ask, my parents were either together for a couple of months or got "married" shortly after they met. This marriage was questionable, at best. I wasn't actually present at the ceremony, but I'm sure anyone who was is pretty hazy on the event. I've seen pictures, and everyone was wearing white, flowing gowns.

The "preacher" had beads around his neck and my father looked like he was higher than a kite. Don't misunderstand me: I'm not criticizing, I just wonder how much actual cognizance was present that day.

I was born a little more than a year later. My little brother Eleazar was born eighteen months after that. My father was working as a general laborer, and as near as I can figure, mooching off his in-laws. In 1976, my father joined the Army because, as he puts it, "God told me to go be a light in the midst of darkness."

In 1978 the Army sent him to Germany. My baby sister, Naarah, was born shortly after we joined him over there. We lived less than three hours from The Berlin Wall, during The Cold War.

My mother's life-long mental illness was cyclical, with brief periods of functional lucidity followed by long periods of screaming, self-injuring insanity. It manifested itself in weird behavior mannerisms that made my mother an unfit caregiver. She would take a walk in a snowstorm barefoot. Or sit in one place and keen at the top of her voice. She often spoke with other voices, mumbled incoherencies and scared the ever-loving hell out of us on a daily basis.

It was during this time that we began the long transit through foster homes: mostly members of our church. We were split up and housed with whoever could take us. I'd spend a night with Eleazar in one house, be moved to another house and spend the weekend at a third house with Naarah. Meanwhile, my father was fighting the Commies in America's stalemate with Soviet Russia, my mother was in the care of Army Doctors and in the process of being deported from Germany, and all four of us were growing up apart from each other, missing school and hoping we'd never be sent back to our parents.

We eventually left Germany and came to Ft. Knox, Kentucky. I was nine.

My mother needed full-time, round-the-clock care. She needed to be institutionalized and taken away from us. Instead, my father gave *me* the task of taking care of her. This largely constituted of me feeding her her meds and ensuring she didn't wander off down the street naked—something she seemed determined to do whenever I wasn't looking. He took me out of school to be a full-time mom to my own mother and siblings. I was responsible for my mother's well-being, cooking, clothing, feeding and caring for my siblings and the upkeep of the house.

Again, I was nine.

There was never anything official about it; I just stayed home and did the best I could.

I was horrible at it. The house was an EPA Superfund Site, with cats, cockroaches and filth piled everywhere. My mother was a raging, screaming horror who could not be trusted out of your sight, and would, if given the opportunity, hurt herself or anyone else. She took a double fistful of meds, several times a day, and often snuck them when I wasn't looking, or spat them out after I gave them to her. I could barely read, much less understand the complicated instructions on the regiment of pill bottles.

I didn't know how to take care of *myself*, much less anyone else, and my brothers and sister suffered under my hands as much as I did under my father's. I did everything the way he did it and that meant shouting, name-calling and hitting.

Dad started to seriously crack shortly after we came to Ft. Knox. He became consistently and violently abusive:

physically, mentally and emotionally. I can understand why, now. My real amazement is that he didn't crack sooner.

I can still remember being a child and thinking that my father was the greatest person on earth. I wanted to be just like him. I wanted him to look at me with his ruggedly handsome face, smile and tell me that he loved me, the he was proud of me and that he approved of me.

When I got older I still thought he was awesome, that he was never wrong and if I could just somehow win his approval maybe he'd tell me he'd love me.

When I got to be a teenager I hated him with every fiber of my being and prayed, constantly, that God would take him to Iraq or somewhere else where I wouldn't have to deal with him anymore.

Please understand: my father didn't hate us. In the fractured, toxic atmosphere that was out home, his presence was the only stability we had. As terrible as he could be, my father *did* love us and cared for us as best he could. He kept my mother out of the institutions for as long as he could because he was genuinely convinced, I think, that the Army would take us from him and put us in an orphanage. He actually taught us a script we were to say, asking to be sent to a Christian orphanage[102], should that ever happen. I don't know if they even *have* orphanages anymore.

Now that I am a Man myself, I recognize that my father never had it easy. His life must have been damn near impossible, and as much as I can, I have forgiven him. I love my father. I respect him enormously. I want him to be happy, healthy and well, with a life full of rich reward and

---

[102] "Ask to be sent, as a family, to The Tupelo Children's Mansion."

happiness. But I live several hours away from him and I think that's for the best.

I never ran away. I could have pretty easily. There were concerned families—the observant parents of a girlfriend, maybe some kinder people from our church, John Gower's parents—who would have taken me in. I could have gone to the MPs and shown them the bruises, or I could have simply left.

It would have been pretty easy to leave it all behind me. I wanted to. I thought about it constantly, but I never did. No, I stayed, and I suffered in silence. I often wonder how much of my life would have been different if I'd been just a little braver.

I never said anything. When my mother left us defenseless in the face of my father's rage, I never breathed a word.

I lied to anyone who asked about the bruises, but those questions were rare. My father was very careful not to leave bruises anywhere somebody might see. When I was finally allowed to go back to school, I was the only freshman in my high school that wore long sleeved, button-up shirts and full-length pants to school every day.

During one of her rare periods of prolonged lucidity my mother finally took action and called the police on my father. When they arrived and asked me if my father abused any of us, we lied to them. We lied to the Social Workers, we lied to my church, we lied to anyone who asked.

"Does your Father abuse you? Does he ever hit you? When was the last time your father hit you?"

I took their tests, I submitted to their physicals, and I kept my mouth shut.

My father was a hard man. Obedience was expected and demanded. If I took it in my head to rebel somehow, I would be punished of course, but not until I got to listen to how much of a favor the beating I was enduring was. He was saving my soul. Rebellion is as the sin of witchcraft, and a "son who dishonors his father and mother must be stoned." No kind and loving God in my childhood. No, God stood roughly 5'8" or so, and he had two fists that struck like lightning and felt like thunder.

I like to think that if nothing else, I stood as a buffer between my father and my siblings. If I was too scared to protect them by saying something, at least I could absorb most of his anger.

No, I never said a word. I hated my father for a long time, but more, I hated myself. I let it happen, and I allowed it to go on. There was so much I could've done or said and I didn't do a damn thing. That, more than anything else; my cowering fear, is the source of all my resentment.

My father has spent several years in therapy getting the help he needs. Maybe if I had said something earlier my father would have gotten the help he needed sooner. Maybe if I had just once been able to tell someone that my father was abusive, maybe, just maybe we could have prevented everything that came after. I don't know. I will never know, but I've never forgiven myself.

I began fictionalizing my relationship with my father on the website I met your mother on. I told my father about the stories and he began reading them. They got sillier and sillier, eventually taking the place of a real relationship between us. It was bullshwa of the first degree, but it provided us with a bridge. We don't talk much, my father and I, but when we do I find I am addressing the fictional character I invented much more often then the Man who is my father. I don't know that is healthy, or right or even *sane*, but it also provides us with the ability to communicate with each other without screaming.

He has any number of faults, but he never abandoned us. He never gave up on my mother, never gave her the divorce she asked for, and so far as I know he was faithful to her for the entirety of their marriage. Most important of all, my father loved us and still does. I can't say the same thing for my mother, and I have long suspected that is the genesis of the problems between my father and I.

My father went to college, achieving a Master's Degree in Social Sciences, got a license as a Social Worker, and now does tremendous work for Louisville, Kentucky's homeless population. He helps people on a daily basis. He just can't help *himself*. He doesn't take care of himself. I've tried to help him but he steadfastly refuses to change his lifestyle in any way. I've actually threatened to have him placed, legally, under my care as being unfit to care for himself, but he got all puffy and Social Worker-ese on me. I've resigned myself to sending him money every month and letting him live, and yes, die, any way he wants to.

A few years ago my father came to me and told me he was sorry for everything. In some ways it would be much easier if he'd never done that. It'd be easier to hate him for the rest of my life and blame him for all of the problems in mine. But a Real Man doesn't do things that way. My father has accepted the consequences of his life. He has made amends. He has tried—given the crippling limitations of his stunted abilities—to be a good father and grandfather. For me to hang on to the past and to continue blaming him for the pain of my childhood would be to make those crimes my own.

I've also talked to people who had it much rougher than I did. I've had conversations with people who didn't have a loving—albeit abusive—parent. They were unwanted, unloved and treated like garbage. I've talked to people whose childhood stories have made me feel like a sniveling crybaby.

Given all of their flaws, my father at least loved us and he and my mother never stopped being our parents. They never sold us for drugs or sex, never allowed us to be taken from them on a permanent basis, never let someone else abuse us.

What kind of a man would I be if I held on to hate and pain with those facts staring me in the face?

It hasn't been easy, or even very nice, but my father and I have a relationship that works. We yell at each other more than a healthy family should, but neither one of us is hitting each other or calling each other names. It works and we can actually spend time in each other's presence without wanting to die.

The last time I saw my father he gave me a hug and told me he loved me. I hugged him back and told him I loved him to.

I'm pretty sure we both meant it.

And that's why I don't talk about my childhood much.

Chapter 32 – My Father's 50ᵗʰ Birthday Party:

I was driving through the dark, listening to my CD player and thinking about the past.

The fog, the night, the music; it all matched my mood perfectly. I was in a contemplative frame of mind. I get that way a lot, but today was special; a life mark. My father's fiftieth birthday had me pensive, withdrawn, and thoughtful, all at once. Our far-flung family was all coming together and while I intended to enjoy myself, I couldn't help but think about the things that had brought us to this point.

The idea was we'd have the party at my sister's new house this year. She and her husband live in the sticks, atop a high ridge overlooking the Ohio River. It's the kind of place that causes ominous banjo music to play in the back of your head.

About a quarter of a mile down the road from their house is a graveyard, a final resting place for many of Kentucky's Civil War dead. The cemetery always scares me when I drive by, regardless of the time of day. The dead there are restless and angry, and things move behind the stones, just out of sight.

The nearest lived-in house to my sister's place was seven miles away. There wasn't much between my sister and civilization save that graveyard and a lot of empty, yet eerily watchful, fields of tobacco.

The party was scheduled to start at eight thirty. I'm not sure why my sister decided to start so late, but it was her house so we played by her rules. I had been asked to take care of the cake, and I was running late, but only fashionably so.

A serious river fog had rolled in, bringing with it a miserly rain that cut visibility down to about fifteen feet. My headlights were cutting a swath through the gauzy swirl, and I felt that I could be anywhere, any place, any time. I wouldn't have been at all surprised to turn a bend in the road and see a party of elves drinking and singing the night away, a minotaur fixing a flat tire, or even Phylegyas poling by in a swirl of dank and corruption. I was halfway hoping for it, to be honest. It was that kind of night.

I was enjoying the overall atmosphere of dark, amorphous blue. The music was turned up just loud enough to be audible, making the drive a sad, almost dirge-y experience.

There's something about certain music that is almost holy. It has something to say and it resonates within the human soul. Popular radio stations know they have no business playing important, relevant music and instead offer pre-packaged filler, saccharined and sanitized for mass consumption. You'll never hear Joe Satriani, Leo Kottke, or Paco Fonta on any popular radio station. No, radio stations know they have no right to worship at the altar of higher human endeavor, so they give us Lady Gaga and Ricki Martin instead.

The CD ended and I put in my bootlegged Robert Johnson CD. The sound quality stunk, but I didn't care. The way he seemed to weep when he sang "Cross Road Blues," the song reputed to be written after he sold his soul to the devil, was profound and bewitching.

The music wove its spell, my thoughts wandered, and I began again to think about my father. He's a hard man to define. He's amazingly well-educated, but it's all self-taught. He can quote the Bible and explain Jewish mysticism in ways that would have a Rebbe standing open-mouthed, yet he can't spell. He hasn't a prejudiced bone in his body although he's suffered the sting of anti-Semitism all his life. My father would give the shirt off his back to a stranger, yet his own family has suffered. He's not a drinker now, but had loved Southern Comfort in his younger days. He's a devout Messianic Jew—a group known in the U.S., at least, for a collective conservatism—yet somehow a Socialist.

My father wasn't very good at his job when I was a child. Somewhere along the way he started to hit and that became the primary means of expression between the two of us.

You can give me all the popular psychology you want. You can give me explanations about stress and his childhood and all the other things that go along with the abusive mentality. I get it. But for years and years it was: he hit me. It hurt, and that was life.

But the truest thing you can say about life is that it keeps going and people change. Dad got help. He looked me in the eyes and said, "I'm sorry."

Then it was my turn to learn how to forgive. It was a slow process.

Eventually it was remembering that my father hadn't always expressed himself though anger that made me realize I needed to let go. I remember taking long rides with my father in our van—a monstrous, fifteen-seater Dodge Ram—his lone concession to the desire for a VW bus, I think. We'd all pile in and go looking for hitchhikers to give rides to, seeing the sights and waving at strangers.

We'd stop at a gas station, buy a soda and just talk. Dad took us for long hikes in the woods and taught us each to love every living thing—trees, weeds, bugs—it was all part of God's creation, and should be valued equally. He instilled a tremendous love for God and all of His works in each of us, and I have always cherished those memories.

Perhaps more than anything else, I was able to love my father because of his stories. He had so many and he infected me with a love for stores at a young age.

My favorites are his hitchhiking adventures. He started hitchhiking around the country at the age of thirteen or so, and has a storehouse of tales as a result. He claims he was arrested for hitchhiking to Woodstock when he was nine. A year later, he was back on the road, hitchhiking across the country, sleeping under overpasses and eating out of garbage cans.

I once asked him why he did this, why he put himself through the rigors of homelessness. I had always suspected he was running away from something; an abusive home life, a crime, something dramatic.

He looked at me, surprised and somehow mournful, and said, "I did it for the adventure, son."

I pressed the issue. "Then why run away, Dad? Why leave home?"

"It was for the adventure, Nescher. You ever read the book by that guy, the book about that kid and the black guy on the river?"

"Tom Sawyer?"

"Yeah. Same stinkin' thing."

And that was it. My father put himself through hell when he was more than half my age so he could experience the great American adventure. How do you hate that? How do you smother that kind of spirit in resentment and grudge?

One of my favorite stories of Dad's: he had been hitchhiking and couldn't get a ride, so he found a bridge overpass and sacked out for the night. When he woke up, he was some hundred miles closer to his destination. He always explained it as "angels carrying me in my sleep."

I once badgered him for more details, but he simply repeated the same story. My father is either a master storyteller, or it really did happen. I've never cared. I just cherish the mystery in a way that borders on need. I hope he never changes the stories or provides explanation. A little part of me would die if he did.

I had to forgive him. I had to learn to grow up and let go of my cherished victim-hood. I did after years and years of struggle, but I still fought to understand my father, to understand what made him so angry.

What happened to my father? Where had the anger come from? What had happened to poison his spirit?

I drove on into the dark, letting these and other thoughts wash through me with little effort. The CD ended, and I let the CD player start it again. It was working for me in the mood I was in.

I've often felt that music is magic. It weaves a transcendent harmony between possibility and reality, blurring the line between the two into invisibility. So I don't know if it was the combination of the music and my desire, or if it was simply an answer. I was singing along, moving my head in time with the sorcery pouring from my speakers, when I came around a bend. There in a swirl of fog, I saw the hitchiker.

Standing at the side of the road, thumb lifted, a look of apprehension and surging hope on his face. He was only in my lights for a moment, but the way he stood, forlorn yet defiantly continuing to hope, struck me so powerfully that I immediately pulled over and opened the passenger door.

He was clearly illuminated by my brake lights as he ran to the car, and I got a good look at him in my rearview. My heart started to pound and my hands began to sweat. He stopped next to the door, smiled at me, and glanced quickly inside the car.

He couldn't have been much older than fifteen or sixteen. The rain had plastered his long, brown hair to the sides of his head, and his curls obscured the parts of his face the dirt hadn't covered. He was wearing a sort of caftan, in a dirty ivory color, which looked to be made of linen. He wore a pair of stained and well-worn bell-bottoms, and as near as I could tell, he was barefoot. Hanging on a leather thong around his neck was a wooden crucifix. His face shone with a clear, innocent light, and the smile he gave me was genuine. He didn't have anything with him, though I had expected to see a backpack of some kind.

Scientists tell us that a baby penguin can find its mother in a teeming crowd of millions of other penguins through a combination of smell and involuntary subliminal cues. I don't know how true that is, but I knew who this hitchhiker was. My mind had subliminally recognized him before my consciousness did. It was a combination of the way he moved, the way he smiled, and his overall presence.

It was my father.

Add forty years and seventy pounds, some gray and a semi-permanent scowl, and this smiling and smelly young man was my dad.

I was hit with sudden and perfect understanding. It came upon me in the same way these things do in dreams.

Yes, it was my father, but I knew I couldn't tell him that. My role in this drama was simply to drive him to his next destination. I had that much time, and no more.

Apparently satisfied that I wasn't a serial killer or something worse, he got into the car and closed the door. I composed my features carefully, fearful that the whole experience would pop like a fragile soap-bubble if I made the slightest wrong move.

With muscles tensed, I put the car in gear and pulled onto the road.

"Oh, wow, man! Thanks for the lift, dude! I've been walking forever!" His voice had a strange lilt and fall, along with an accent that took me a minute or two to place. He talked with the same undiluted "Don'tcha-know?" Wisconsin/Michigan twang my grandmother did. His time in the South had diluted it.

There is a very specific etiquette followed by hitchhikers and those who pick them up. The hitchhiker's responsibility is to be gracious and courteous to a fault. He is, after all, mooching a ride. Etiquette dictates that you agree with all of your host's opinions (or at least disagree very respectfully), make conversation as much as possible, and if you have any drugs, offer to share.

I realized my father was following this code and that a response was expected of me.

My voice high and tight, I asked, "So where you headed?"

He laughed in a carefree way that I'd rarely seen in his older self and said, "Wherever you're goin' is fine with me, brother. I'm looking for God, and I hope to find him somewhere soon."

I forced a laugh around the sob locked in my throat and said, "Well, there's a truck stop about thirty miles down the road. I can drop you off there if you like. You can catch a ride to anywhere you want from there."

"Hey man, that'd be great! Thanks a lot!" He stuck his hand out and said, "My name's Dale."

I took his hand, found his grip to be strong and sure, and choking back a small cry of delight, I said, "Nescher."

"Nescher. Wow, man. That's a name, right there! Does it mean anything? Are your parents, like, hippies or something?"

It was hard. I was smiling and trying not to cry, all at the same time.

"Yeah. They're really fun people. It's Hebrew, supposedly, for Eagle."

"Oh wow, man! Like that Bible verse! "They that wait upon the Lord shall renew their strength!" That's really far out, man! Your parents are groovy!"

I laughed, a short snort. "I'll pass that along the next time I see them, Dale."

He nodded his head at me and settled into the seat.

"Oh, wow! I almost forgot!"

Reaching into his shirt, he pulled out a small bottle. He unscrewed the cap and the pungent aroma of Southern Comfort filled the car.

He wiped the mouth off and said, "Want a snort, Nesch?"

My hands trembled on the wheel. My father doesn't drink. I've never shared a beer with him, never passed a bottle of anything back and forth. The first time I got married, where other fathers would have a shot of bourbon or a beer with you, he showed up and slept in the car until it was time for the ceremony to start.

He has his reasons for not drinking, and I respect them, but a beer between father and his eldest son would go a long way toward healing the rifts of experience, I sometimes think.

Normally, I hate being called "Nesch" by anyone, but my father has never called me anything but Nescher, son, or a name of some kind. I bit off a very small snort, knowing my father—or "Dale"—didn't have the money to buy more and fought myself for control of my tears.

Dale took the bottle back and drank a bit himself. He placed the bottle back in his shirt and settled back into the seat.

The radio continued to pour out its enchantment, and I realized there was just enough time left on the CD to see us to the truck stop. Only so many songs and a lifetime of questions to ask.

Dale looked over at me and said, "Oh wow! What radio station is that, man? Robert Johnson! Far out!"

I smiled at his childish enthusiasm and asked, "Are you a fan, Dale?"

"Yeah, man!"

We listened to the music for a bit, Dale and me, losing ourselves in the misty harmonics and the devilish wail of the guitar.

There was so much I wanted to say and ask, and I couldn't!

What would I say? "I'm your eldest son from forty years in the future?"

No, I wanted him relaxed and at ease. There was something here I needed to see, something beyond my own wants.

I took a deep breath, composed myself and said, "Hey Dale, it's a long drive out to this truck stop. Why don't you tell me about yourself? What are you doing out here other than looking for God? Tell me all about Dale."

He smiled in a free and open way and said, "Wow. Okay, well, I just need to find God. You know? I mean, I've been going to church my whole life, right? But I don't know about God, and I want to, 'cause I feel like He's got some kind of purpose for my life, you know? And I've just been going around the country to all these groovy churches, and talking to all these preachers, you know?"

I recognized the start of a fire that still burned within him. If I had any lingering doubts as to his identity before, that last statement, however rambling, singed them all away. This was my father, in his first fumbling steps on his lifelong quest to find God.

We talked then, not as father and son, but man to man. We talked about his girlfriend (not my mother, incidentally):

"She's like this totally groovy, absolutely beautiful blonde, and she's got like, the best-tasting kiss."

About getting drunk versus getting high: "Yeah, I've been stoned on weed, and hash and stuff, but I still prefer my booze."

About his various sexual adventures: "Okay. It was like, me, and these three other chicks."

He told me about his family, how he felt about his parents and his brother and sisters. He told me things I never knew or would even have suspected, like how to stay on the road with no money: "Okay? So the first thing you do is make sure there's no store dick, and then you go looking for stuff you can stick in your pockets."

He told me about eating out of garbage cans and getting sick from it; bathing in creeks; sleeping in fields of wildflowers under summer stars; getting beat up by the police; and meeting people from all walks of life. He told me about his hopes and dreams, and his desires.

I told Dale about my ex-wife and the reasons we really broke up (not the sanitized version I usually shared with family and everyone else). I told him about my hopes and dreams for the future.

When he talked about God, his eyes lit up and his face shone with a pure righteousness. There was no profanity in him. Here he sat, Southern Comfort on his breath, talking to a stranger about God, and it was exactly like being at church.

He told me of his desire to be a perfect servant of God Almighty, and was totally unselfconscious about it, seeing no hypocrisy in liberally toasting this declaration with another snort off his bottle. This wasn't hypocrisy to him. He was still too innocent to know what hypocrisy was.

In short, we had the sort of conversation I have always wanted to have with my father. It was totally open and utterly candid. Dale figured I was a stranger he'd never see again and didn't want anything from me except a ride. He'd leave me with some good conversation and the warm glow of whiskey in my belly.

I had become so engrossed in our talk that I completely forgot we didn't have much time. I saw the sign for the truck stop ahead and I began to panic. He couldn't leave now! There was still so much to say and ask.

He looked over at me and said, "Oh wow. That's the stop, isn't it? Man, time has really flown, hasn't it?"

I wiped a tear away surreptitiously and said, "Yeah, Dale. It sure has. Listen, I could take you a little farther if you want . . . ."

He looked at me seriously and said, "Nescher, that's okay, man. I saw the cake box in the back seat, and I figure you've already taken me out of your way. I didn't want to say anything until we got here, but I can't let you take me farther, man. I don't want to mooch off you any more than this right here."

I shook my head, smiled, and tried not to weep. That was my Dad, alright, polite to his own detriment. Somehow I knew it wouldn't be allowed, that he'd be taken from me if we tried to travel farther together. The magic was all used up. Whatever needed to be said had been said; whatever I needed to know had been revealed.

We pulled into the truck stop and I stopped the car at the curb.

He reached into his shirt and pulled out the bottle. He bit off a quick snort and placed the bottle on the passenger seat.

"There ya' go, man. I ain't got no money, but I can leave you some good booze, anyway." He smiled at me again in that clear, beautiful way and I again fought the urge to weep. I shook his hand a final time, trying to impart through the casual gesture the depth of my emotion, fighting a need to hug him with everything within me. He got out, smiled at me, and walked into the dark, drizzly mist.

"Wait!"

He stopped then, and turned back toward me, a questioning look in his eyes.

I reached into the back seat and grabbed the cake box.

"Here, Dale. You take this."

"Awww, Nesch! I can't do that, man! That's for somebody-"

I set my face into a scowl I had seen far too many times as a child.

"Don't argue with me, boy. I think God wants you to have this. You take it, now, or you're gonna end up pissing us both off."

He smiled and took the cake box from me.

"Thanks, man. God bless!"

The music ended then, and I watched him until he faded from sight and then I drove away.

I realized then who my father is, what he had come from. He isn't a horrible sinner, an abusive ogre, or a loud-mouthed bully. He's just a scared, dirty and innocent kid still trying to make his way through the world as best he can. He's a flawed vessel, just like the rest of us. He'd made some wrong turns and gotten lost a time or two, and he's managed to make a wreck of his life.

But thinking back on my conversation with Dale, I discovered something profound: we were the same. And I have the benefit of knowing his mistakes! Who am I to judge him?

~~~~~~~

I drove on towards my sister's house, pulling off briefly for a good cry. I cried for who my father was, and I cried for who he had become. I cried for all the pain and the wasted years, and for the opportunities I missed because of my own anger and pride.

I wiped my face on my shirt and put the bottle in a crumpled, paper sack I found on the back seat. It took me fifteen more minutes to get to my sister's house, and everyone was worried about me when I got there. Ignoring them all, I went to my father, and surprised him with a hug.

I handed him the paper sack and whispered, "I love you, Dad. And you're pretty groovy. Happy birthday."

Chapter 33—Tattoo You:

When we got the message that your mother was pregnant from the doctor, the very first thing I thought was, "Sweet. I'm gonna get that tat."

I'm a Gen-Xer. We're known best, I think, for our sense of near-sociopathic entitlement and skewed priorities. Somebody once said that "If the world ended, Gen-X wouldn't even notice until Starbucks ran out of coffee." I think that's pretty close.

I'd been thinking about the tats since your mother and I started trying to get pregnant. Instead of focusing in on things like college funds and nursery furniture, I was spending my time doodling and picking baby names at random to see how they'd fit. As long as we went with something that had four letters, I could squeeze anything in. If we went with something a bit larger, I was probably screwed.

Problematically, we hadn't yet agreed on a name for either a boy or a girl, and we'd both decided to keep your gender a secret. It made your mother all giggly and excited, meeting either her baby boy or girl for the first time, but I was worried about getting to the tattoo studio with a design on the day of your birth. Because it had to be, like, just after my wee wiggler popped out. That's how we roll, son.

If you were a girl, I'd just about decided on a silky rose, with teeth for petals. Your name—whatever it ended up being—would be embedded in the folds of the rose, snuggled in like a puppy in a blanket. I thought the side of my neck, just above my collar, would be a good spot for that one.

For a boy, you've gotta go with something a lot more masculine. Wolves, crosses, rifles, they all featured somehow in my baby-boy-tat-fantasies. I'd almost come down on a design featuring crossed revolvers over a cross on my left forearm, slightly above the infinity symbols around your Mom's name. Your name would be the cross bar holding the whole design up.

Meanwhile, tears of joy are standing in your mother's eyes, and she's reaching for me in a slow-motion celebration as we hit repeat on the play button for our answering machine.

Don't get me wrong. I had a lot of conflicting emotions and feelings when I heard that we'd kindled a life together. All the usual stuff percolated away inside me: fear, nausea, joy, fear, excitement, fear...

Part of me was ready for this phase of our life; had been ready for a while. I was Scott Stapp, standing on the edge of the cliff, the wind blowing my hair back as I sang mightily to my unborn child "with arms wide open." I'd made myself cry a time or two in the previous months by playing the fantasy of holding you in my arms and softly singing Lynard Skynard's 'Simple Man.' It was a beautiful picture.

And the rest of me was petrified. I've been assured this is normal for first-time Dads, as I've been repeatedly assured since about a lot of other things:

"No one knows what they're doing as parents, Nescher. You'll figure it out."

"Cheese is good for him. Let him try some!"

"Your mother was a lot better at this than you are. Have I told you that, yet?"[103]

Yes, I had the usual responses, I think, and as I enfolded my happily sobbing wife in my arms, I reacted in much the same way as every first-time Dad has since the beginning of time.

But my very *first* thought was "Sweet. I'm gonna get that tat."

---

[103] Thanks, Dad. Yeah, you have.

Chapter 34 – Forever Wrong:

Your mother, God bless her sweet face, is one of those people who cannot admit they're wrong. Ever. For any circumstances. I don't know anybody who likes being proven wrong, but your mother takes it to a whole new level. Her lips and tongue literally cannot form the words "I was wrong." I've watched her bite her tongue and chew on her lips trying to spit the phrase until I got worried about her safety.

It doesn't happen often. Your mother is much smarter than I am and she's got a head full of facts, figure and trivia. I have this mental image of her as a child, reading encyclopedias and memorizing esoterica.

On those enormously rare occasions when I've squeezed her into a logical corner on something, she almost always manages to weasel her way out. Even when she misunderstands me—which, given my fractured thought process and fractalled syntax, happens a lot—it's never the case that she was wrong and I was right after we clarify things. Instead, "Since you weren't clear, it's your fault." It's an amazing display of mental acuity and verbal agility, and I find myself starting arguments with her just so I can watch.

But I got her this time. I won. We had a bet and I've got her dead to rights, with witnesses, and there's nothing she can do about it. I'm right, she's wrong. I won, she lost, and I'm going to spend the rest of my life gloating about it.

The bet was whether you were going to be left handed or not. I'm a South Paw, your mother's a righty and I'd be lying if I said I didn't want you to join the ranks of the ever-shrinking elite. Your mother was convinced you would be "normal" and grow up able to use tools and open doors without flipping them over.

I might've cheated. I'm the primary caregiver, so when I handed you something, I might've concentrated on your left hand instead of your right, but that just points to me being left-handed. Right?

We'd both been carefully watching you, waiting for you to pick a hand preference. Other family members had gotten involved, falling on both sides of the issue. It had become something of a cause in our extended family, and I won. No ifs, ands or buts. No weaseling, no prevarication, no misunderstanding. She lost, I won.

Because I won, your mother had to design, draw and pick a place for a tattoo on my body. If she had won, I had to do whatever she told me to for an entire weekend in the garden. I hate gardening, she hates tattoos, but a bet is a bet.

She could be a sore loser, do something ridiculous and place it on my face, but she married a shameless person who would get the tat as designed and tell everyone it was his wife's idea. Frankly, I didn't really care what the tattoo was or where she placed it. I just wanted tangible evidence that I was right, however briefly, about something.

She drew up a gear and placed it on my right wrist. It's a sort of a rebus for your name and now I have that proof I've always wanted and an awesome tattoo designed by your mother.

Chapter 35 – Laundry:

Wednesdays are laundry day at the ranch. As it's a domestic, house-related chore, it's my responsibility. The day starts with me grabbing the hamper from our room and your room, trudging down the stairs with them, and stuffing the washer until it bulges. I can hear metal-stress noises when I'm done stuffing, and that's the way I like it.

I add soap until I've got a nice, blue, double line on the top of the clothes, spin the dial and close the lid. I open the dryer, stuff the dried stuff into a laundry basket and put it in its respective dresser.

When the washer quits, I take everything out, stuff it in the dryer, add a sheet-y thingie, close the door and spin the dial.

Everything gets washed this way. Sheets, towels, clothes, bedspreads, curtains: Wednesday's the day it gets stuffed into a washer, washed, stuffed into a dryer, dried and put away.

Everything that goes on a hanger gets hangerized, socks are matched and everything else is put where it's supposed to be. I'm kind of particular about the way my clothes are put away, so even if your mother does laundry day for us, I do that myself. I'm protective of my twenty-five year old t-shirts and my molecularly-thin underwear.

I've been doing my own laundry since I was nine. I'm not a sartorial person. My entire wardrobe is of the wash and wear variety, and always has been. Even when I wore uniforms, they were usually a polyester blend of some kind.

Wash 'em, hang 'em up someplace to dry, and forget about 'em. I've never owned anything that needed to be separated, dry-cleaned, specially handled or otherwise molly-coddled. Your wardrobe is the same way, son. Wash it, dry it, put it away. No ironing, no polybagging, no dry-cleaning.

When your mother and I first got married, I offered to do the laundry. It was something I knew how to do and I wanted to show your mother that marrying her wasn't just romantic gold-digging.

Your mother, in one of her less-than-wise moments, let me go ahead and do that. To her credit, I assured her I knew exactly what I was doing and she had nothing to worry about. She might've investigated a little further, but I can be pretty persuasive.

She married *me*, after all.

I had no business anywhere near your mother's clothes. Her wardrobe was full of frilly, lacy, expensive things that came from different countries with names I can't pronounce. Some of the items in her wardrobe were made by blind monks in monasteries in the Andes. She owned silk underthingies that should never have seen the inside of a laundry room, much less a washer running at the seam-bulging level. Her wardrobe required very special handling skills that I did not—nor do I now—possess. The words 'Unmitigated Disaster' do not even begin to describe the scope of the laundry apocalypse that rained down. I didn't separate. I didn't wash things according to material, color or item. I didn't wash and then allow the item to air-dry.

There was color running, shrinkage and something I think she referred to as 'wilting.' I'm not sure how a piece of clothing 'wilts.' And when she told me what the dress I'd ruined was made of, I didn't know that word, either.

She's never told me how much money I cost her in clothing ruination, but I'm no longer allowed to wash her clothes. I learned a valuable lesson doing that, though, and I share it here: if you really want to lessen the burden of a weekly chore, foul it up big time.

Chapter 36 – Disposable Dilemma:

I have a feeling this will generate some controversy, but I thought I'd go ahead and poke the hornet's nest. If people aren't banging on my door with pitchforks and torches, I don't feel as though I'm doing my job properly. So here goes. Deep, settling breath. Steady, and release: I used disposable diapers. There. Let the hate begin.

Okay, so maybe not, but in my personal credo this is really a sin. I am a liberal, tree-hugging, earth-loving, conservation-monger. I conserve, I recycle, I re-use and I rehabilitate. I try to keep my carbon footprint as small as possible, I pay attention to my daily energy consumption, I compost, I leave the thermostat at just above 'imminent divorce' levels and I look for ways to make the world a greener, less-energy-consumptive place to be.

I'm the kind of tree-hugger who actually feels guilty about not leaving his dryer lint out for the birds as nesting material.

I'm serious about this. It's a lifestyle choice and I am pretty militant about it. I won't actually club you about the head, face and neck if you're not right there with me, but I might chain myself to your SUV and chant inane slogans at you until you change your mind.

"Hey! Hey! Chevrolet! How many miles did you drive today?"

And then I had—well, your mother did—a son and the specter of Disposable Diapers reared its ugly, non-biodegradable little head. See, they're bad because they clog the landfills—yes, the place we send all our trash, anyway—and they don't decompose. The alternatives aren't much greener, but they don't fill landfills.

Nobody asked me, but I've spent a lot of time thinking about this, trying to solve the problem and come up with a way to make baby elimination green. I haven't figured a good one out yet, but once I do I'll let you know.

I've considered buckskin. I've looked into flaxen cloth. I even went so far as to look into woven grasses and rushes. Nothing appealed to me and I haven't made any improvements on convenience. I used to wonder what people did before the invention of the cotton diaper, and I have to believe that there were an awful lot of besmeared, smelly parents with sickly grins on their faces, not to mention rashes, chafing and other general baby-elimination-related unpleasantness that I'm not equipped to deal with.

The obvious choice is reusable nappies. The idea is you put the nappy on your child, the child uses it in the usual way, and you rinse it out in the toilet, wash it, and re-use it. I like the concept, but the idea of having wet, mildewing, smelly nappies waiting for me to wash them gives me the screaming willies. I have to wear a HAZMAT suit when I empty the diaper pail. I go without eating the day before I empty it and I'm still dry-heaving my way to the trash can with the bag held out from me like it's radioactive.

When you wore diapers, you got your diaper changed eleventy-grillion times a day, so if I went the re-usable route, I'd be doing laundry twenty-four seven. I don't know what the trade-off between doing laundry eighteen times a week and a week's worth of disposable diapers is, but I don't want to have to pay that water bill, either. And I don't know about you, but that's not a laundry day I'd care to face.

There are any number of alternatives, but what it basically boils down to is you're either disposing of the diaper in some way or you're washing it. Either option leaves a lot to be desired, but you can't beat the convenience of the ready-to-apply disposable diaper.

I feel really guilty about it, and I suspect they're going to yank my Tree-Hugging Earth Lover card any day now, but until we come up with some kind of an alternative that involves lasers or disintegration or something, in my humble opinion, disposable is the way to go.

From Left to Right: your Aunt Katie, the day after she ran a marathon through downtown Anchorage, AK; your Uncle Tim, your Aunt Lisa, Me and your Momma, atop Mt. Something-Or-Other in Denali National Park in Alaska.

Yes, I'm holding a metal pole that's been driven into the ground with those nice, dark clouds in the background.

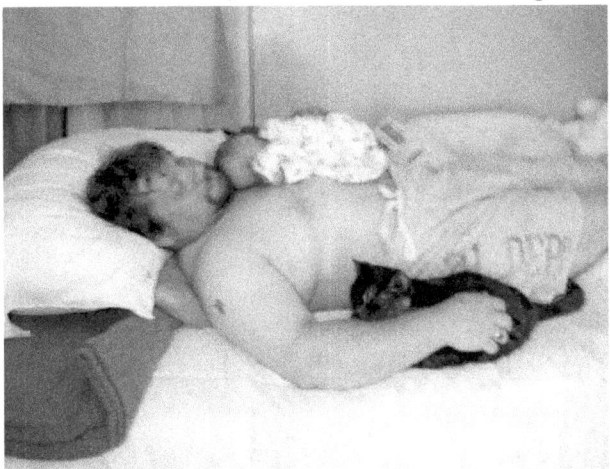

This is me in my "swimsuit modeling phase." That nice pear shape is what you've got to look forward to, son. Me, you and Deli. Deli was psychotic in the extreme and enormously protective of you. Remind me to tell you the story of how she jumped in the back-window with half a coyote in her jaws. (I still own those shorts. I plan to drive you to school in them.)

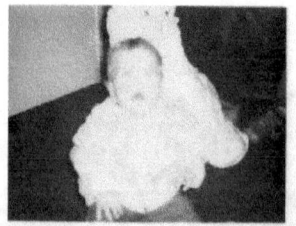

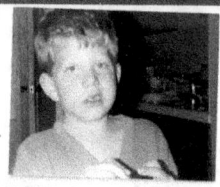

Random pictures of Eleazar. The woman sitting next to him is my mother. I don't know who the people are behind them. The porcelain cat-thing behind Eleazar in the left-hand picture featured prominently in many of my childhood nightmares.

His front tooth was broken off by me bouncing his face off the bumper of a van. I broke his nose with a cardboard tube. He has other scars on his face inflicted by me. Naarah hit him in the back of the head with a three-foot long machete my father stupidly left lying around.

Of the four of us, Eleazar has the most reason to hate our guts. When we hug now there is always a brief moment when I wonder if this is when he is going to finally snap, twist my head off my neck and mount it on his car like a hood ornament.

The last picture is of me and Eleazar and it's my absolute favorite. I've always had a special place in my heart for Eleazar, despite the war wounds I've inflicted on him. When were children, and it was just me and him, I would crawl into bed with him whenever I was scared of the dark. He made little puppets out of his hands and entertained me with stories and songs until I fell asleep. It's not macho to admit that you love your little brother, but I

do. I really do. Eleazar's lovely family: Michelle, Shawn, Sarah and Patrick.

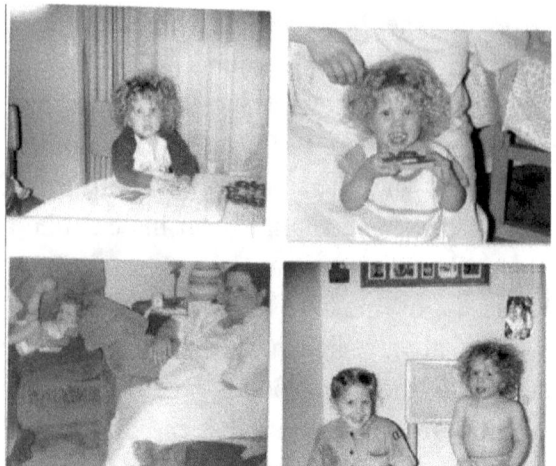

Ari, Ari, Ari and Mom and Naarah and Ari. Ari was born a boy. He's always been a boy. I know this because I changed his diapers. The long-hair-thing was a "tradition" inflicted on us by our dad.

My mother was born missing her left arm. The look on her face tells me she was going through one of her bad phases.

This picture is a perfect illustration of why you want to get a career instead of a job.

I dug graves in north-east Ohio for about three years. When it rained, I got wet. When it snowed, I got cold.

When it was sunny I got burned and when it was just nice I . . . well, it was never nice. Face-down over a grave, helping the back-hoe center a burial container in weather cold enough to kill a boar is no way to make a living.

From left to right: my mother, my sister Naarah, Ari, Eleazar, my grandmother and my father. This is the only picture I have of my grandmother; taken at her trailer. It'd be nice to perpetuate the illusion that I was as tall as my father was when I was eleven or so, but I am standing on my grandmother's fireplace. Eleazar and I were within a few inches of each other.

Random pictures of Naarah. True Story: My father came racing downstairs one morning because my baby sister was shrieking in agony. She might've been seven at the time. When my father reached her, he found her sitting in the middle of the living room floor, sobbing fit to die, Eleazar standing fearful and chagrined over her.

"Daddy!" Naarah said, still hiccupping and sobbing, "Eleazar said that when I turned ten you weren't going to get   me   a   credit   card!" Naarah was the only girl in a houseful of deeply fundamentalist, quasi-Jewish men. Her life was ordered around a strict interpretation of scripture and she was treated like a fragile glass object instead of a little girl. Her mother was a non-entity for most of her childhood, her brothers had no idea how to address issues of feminine hygiene and good mental health. There wasn't a lot of love in our household. What little existed was given to Naarah. We grew up resenting her as a result, and she grew up feeling isolated and alone.

Despite all this, she managed to become a healthy, successful adult who runs marathons for fun and makes celebrities cry over their non-existent physical fitness.

I am enormously proud of her and all of her successes . . . even if she still can't beat me at arm-wrestling.

Your mother, circa 1976. Her smile is one of the things I love most about her and it's always been perfect. Note the cowlick, right in the center of her head. You have your mother to thank for the way your hair is, son.

You hated this costume. We had to wrestle you into it, we had to coerce you to take a picture wearing it and nothing short of God appearing and making it happen would induce you to wear the hood. This is one of those things that parents do because they think it's adorable that makes children need to get therapy later. You scored serious cute loot, though.

I love this picture. It highlights so dramatically everything I've been saying about the Huths being nice, generous, kind and loving people. You've got all these skinny, successful, talented and beautiful folks, smiling happily at the camera and off in one corner is the gargoyle, come to eat them all.

I look at this picture and think, "Those poor people! Taken hostage and forced into a photograph by that evil hobbit!"

Believe it or not, that look on my face isn't dyspeptic gas. I am actually trying to smile.

I love my in-laws. They rock. It gives me hope that you resemble them so strongly. Hopefully you'll be skinny, successful, talented and beautiful and not take after my side of the family where the only gift we have is the ability to bite through bricks.

Your mother is wearing the god-awful helmet-wig we got her for when the chemo caused her hair to fall out. I hated that wig. I hated the way it sat on her head, I hated the color, I hated the way it smelled, I hated everything about that damn wig and everything it represented. The happiest moment for me in her post-treatment period was when she got that filthy thing out of our house. That told me, more than anything else ever could, "This is over. You've survived. Love her a little harder now."

From left to right, bottom row first. Your Aunt Karen and Sid (or possibly Ollie), your Uncle Ian with Ollie (or possibly Sid), Aunt Lisa, Uncle Tim, Ian and Cameron. Me, your Mom—holding you—Grandma Huth, Grandpa Huth, your Aunt Katie and your Uncle John with Aaron on his lap.

 Baby Geir, chillaxin' with Daddy. You were born a month premature. Four pounds, four ounces. I could hold you cupped in the palm of my hands. You were no bigger than a large snowball. I was afraid to touch you with my gargantuan gorilla paws and I was the primary care-giver for three or four months. It was a nerve-wracking time and I spent ninety-percent of my life during those months tip-toeing around, talking quietly and singing nonsense songs to you. You have to be fed every two hours and your diapers were apocalyptic   nightmares.

Never doubt it, son. I love you with every fiber of my being and I am more grateful, proud and delighted that you are my son than you will ever know.

Nescher the band geek. The instrument I'm holding is a Marching Baritone. It's a little bigger than a standard-size trumpet, to give you some scale. I was a dreadful player and I only picked it up because my mother played it all through high school and on into college. She was so good she got a four-year, full-ride scholarship, playing baritone.

I could—and still can—mangle my way through a B Flat Concert scale. One of the advantages of growing up as an Army Brat when I did was that we got free, unlimited health-care. This was good news for me as a teen because I had truly horrific, cystic acne. I was under the care of a dermatologist for most of my teen years. I took an antibiotic and applied three different facial medications, two or three times a day. One of the medications warned you not to spend any time in the sun. So there I was, with zits the size of golf balls bursting out of my skin, band-geeking it up all over the place and not allowed to go outside. I wasn't off to a good start in life.

Rolled pants are cool. Don't let anybody tell you otherwise.

This picture was taken at my mother's funeral. I am so hung over I can barely see. This picture was taken by a cousin I met for the first time this week. The woman standing next to my father is his mother.

Your mother and I have been wondering why no one has approached us yet and asked you to model. It'd be nice to be able to pay for your college before you start exhibiting any of the characteristics of my side of the family. Stay adorable, my son. Stay adorable forever.   Your mother, post-treatment, at my mother's funeral. She hated her hair, I hated her wig and she loved me enough when she had just enough hair to cover her scalp to go out in public without it. I liked to rub her peach fuzz. She was a real hero that week and I will never be able to express to her what having her there meant to me. The tattoo on my right wrist is a gear; a rebus for your name and the proof that I will always have that your mother was wrong about something and I was right.

She drew it up for me in a surprisingly demonstrative gesture of good-natured loser-dom. Whatever. I was right, she was wrong. Suck it, Christine! Suck it, forever!

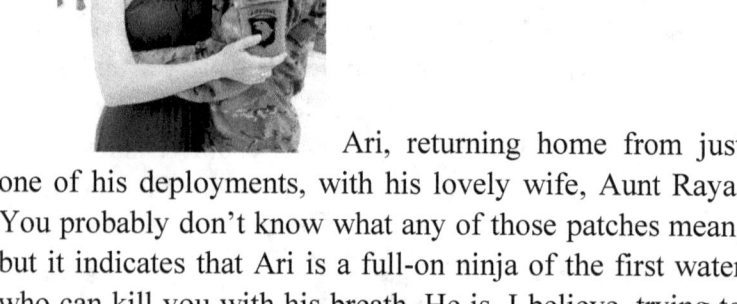

Ari, returning home from just one of his deployments, with his lovely wife, Aunt Raya. You probably don't know what any of those patches mean, but it indicates that Ari is a full-on ninja of the first water who can kill you with his breath. He is, I believe, trying to smile.

Ari lived with me and my first wife for most of his time in high school. I was his primary care-giver during that time and I was pretty miserable at it. He ate whenever he wanted to, did whatever he wanted to with his free time and only had to put up with me being a complete ass. I'd like to think I did more good than harm, but I was so wrapped around the axle with my own life that I probably managed to screw that up, too.

I have a very special bond with Ari as a result of our time as Brother-Father/Brother-Son. We've outgrown the stupid stuff, mostly, and he's gone on to become a real rock star in the Army, outranking me, my Dad, and even Eleazar.

He still can't beat me at arm-wrestling.

A picture of you with my father. Yes, those are two pairs of glasses on his face. I'm pretty sure he wears his hair like that in the hopes that he will be racially profiled and then beaten up by white supremacist cops.

My favorite picture of you and your mother. This photo always makes me smile, and, incidentally, makes me want to help your mother create a sibling for you. (Grrrrrrrroooooooowwwwwwlllllll.)

Your godfather, Dr. Jeremiah McDole, Ph.D—the smartest person I know, a guy I love dearly, an unapologetic smart-ass and someone we miss terribly. His is a good-old-fashioned, southern boy success story and I hope he will tell it to you someday.

He was married to your Aunt Naarah for a while and then life got in the way. It happens but it broke our hearts. This photo neatly sums up pretty much everything you need to know about Jerry. He sucks at arm-wrestling and I'm relatively certain that he will either save the world or help end it before he's fifty.

Eleazar, accepting just one of the many awards and accolades that a lifetime of service in the United States Army has given him. He is the definition of a round peg in a round hole and given world enough and time, I am confident that he will eventually become Sergeant-Major Of The Army. And he can't beat me at arm-wrestling, either.

An incredibly rare picture of the five of us, taken at Ari's graduation from OCS. From left to right: Eleazar, my father, Ari, Naarah and me.

Chapter 37 – Dealing, As A Dad:

I once read somewhere that men are ill-suited, by biology, for child-rearing. Apparently our bodies are designed to make us able to hunt, stalk, kill; *make* babies, but not rear them.

If the research was correct, an infant's cries actually inspire a very different set of responses in us.

I don't know how much credence I give this theory, but I'd like to add some observations of my own to the mix. Men are problem solvers. Even when there isn't a problem that really needs to be fixed, we look for ways to solve it.

Full diapers are a problem.

If your dog gets into a fight with a skunk, you can make the situation a *little* nicer by putting him outside and hosing him down until the worst of the smell lessens enough for you to get up close and personal with the tomato sauce. Neither one of you will enjoy the process and you're probably going to get bit, but you can at least minimize the mess.

It's a Man-Solution: take the mess elsewhere. The same concept doesn't apply to infants, and I've had to learn this the hard way.

Your mother and I are richly blessed to be your parents. You were never too picky as an infant and would at least *try* most anything we gave you to eat. You were, in fact, so eager to expand your dietary horizons, you often expressed an urgent desire to eat things that weren't food, and we stayed on top of that as best we could.

If you go to any supermarket, you'll find the baby-food aisle. They have organically-balanced, nutritionally-superior, space-shuttle-packaged foods on display for twelve dollars a pop; guaranteed to provide your child with the ability to speak Chinese and balance your checkbook by the time he's five.

I tried the infant superfood. I prepared it, and put it on the ergonomically designed dish, specially fashioned to appeal to your newly awakening senses of smell, taste and touch. I'd been assured by the books I read that this was the way to go about it. This was the way to get little Mozart's motor running in the right way.

Then *I'd* throw some baloney on white bread, smear mayonnaise on it, and we'd have lunch.

You took one look at the twelve dollar entrée I was trying to feed you, howled, knocked it off on the circling cat, and reached for my baloney sandwich.

So you ate what I fed you and I fed you what you liked to eat. Yogurt, pickles, beef jerky, hot sauce, carrots, animal crackers, well-mushed chicken nuggets and even steak with mustard on it have gone down that incredibly efficient maw. You chewed it, swallowed it and asked for more. As long as it wasn't going to choke you or bring on hives, I was probably going to feed it to you at least once.

The problem was that I couldn't take the later mess anywhere else. Wiping it off just spreads it around. Moist toilettes didn't enter into it. I used bath-towels while muttering lines from *The Exorcist*.

You can't hose an infant down. Even if he smells like the end of the world and you can see his last meal creeping up his back, you can't throw a bucket of hot, soapy water at him and scrub him until the worst of the grease goes down the drain. There just isn't a masculine, problem-solving approach to a dirty diaper. You take it off and you clean it up as best you can while he's beating on you with his toy hammer and howling at octaves that would kill a dog. You thought it was hilarious. The noises I made as I struggled not to vomit made you giggle uproariously.

I tried, but I never could convince you that you really wanted the baby cereal with little red lumps mimicking strawberries instead of my ham and beans.

Chapter 38 – Me, The Muppets & Maury:

Daytime TV is dreadful.

I grew up without a TV. My parents were cultists who were waiting for the end of the world. It was either going to be Cossacks coming across the Canadian border, *vis-à-vis*, Red Dawn, or Leviathan rising from the deep and eating, like, Florida. Either way, TV would weigh you down.

They vacillated on it. We'd own a TV for a year and get rid of it for three. I have vague memories of enjoying Sesame Street, but TV wasn't a part of my childhood.

I owned one off and on as an adult. Mostly off as they represented a cash commodity. I tended to watch whatever was on when I was eating my ramen with cheese sauce.

I wasn't really enjoying the shows; I was using them to fill the silence in my one-bedroom trailer. Even Scooby-Doo's voice was better than the howling shrieks of my crippling loneliness. Money got tighter, and I finally gave it up completely when I was twenty-nine. As I recall, I bought a month's worth of ramen and several dozen cans of cheese sauce.

I went for several years not owning a TV, and I didn't notice the difference. Pop culture is one of those things you don't really miss when you're not immersed in it, and one good way to unplug is to lose your TV.

When your mother and I got married, I hit her with all the facts I made up about it being better for your brain not to have a TV: that it stunted emotional development between married couples and children with TVs in their homes were more likely to grow up with eye warts.

She said something I can't repeat here, and then hit me with the stunner: "Whether you believe it or not, we'll need one after we have kids."

I argued about it, trying to get her to accept a less media-centric approach to life, but no dice.

So you have access to one, and I reiterate: daytime TV is dreadful. All of a sudden you notice how often people are fighting each other, how many f-bombs are dropped—bleeped or otherwise—and how often MacGyver makes an alien's head explode on *SG-1*. Nothing's safe to watch.

We tend to watch a lot of the nerdy stations. *Discovery, The History Channel, The Military Channel and PBS, PBS, PBS.* And yes, I occasionally have to flip away from even those. I justify the violence on *The Military Channel* as being something my son should be aware of.

"Son, this is in your blood. I was in the Army, your Uncles are in the Army, your Grandfather was in the Army, and your Great-Grandfather was in the Army. So far as I'm aware, Pyschers have *always* been in the Army. I'm not saying you *have* to join, but you should be aware of your familial expectations. Now watch Patton run the Germans over.   It's   awesome."
We watch an awful lot of *PBS*. When you were younger I'd plunk you into your play-pen, turn on *Sesame Street*, and sneak off to get a shower while your brain was bombarded by Elmo's manic teaching technique. When I come back, your eyes were glazed, your body was relaxed, and I could tell Elmo had beaten another few facts into your little brain.

I got to watch whatever I wanted when you went down for your nap. The pickings were slim, but I was so grateful for the chance to listen to adults talk that I didn't care. And nobody was singing about letters, numbers and shapes. When I get ahold of the TV, There. Were. No. Muppets.

I know, I know. TV isn't good for your brain. You don't need to be watching *any* of it, much less what little I let you watch when you were a wee lad. But if it weren't for TV, dreadful as it is, I would have had mushrooms growing in my armpits, bugs dancing in my skull, and my eyes would have been as wide as dinner-plates. As much as I hate to admit it, your mother was right: we needed our TV.

Chapter 39 – Ball, Ball!:

I have reached a level of gooeyness that is embarrassing. I have what looks like an exotic cheese hanging off my chest, my arms are mozzarella, and I get winded opening a bag of potato chips. The other day I bent over to tie my shoes. It took me twenty minutes to get my breath back and I was sweating like a boar-hog the whole time.

All the usual jokes apply. My belt size has three digits. I butter my cereal, I bacon my celery.

I'm fat. I'm as fat as butter, soft as runny cheese. I sweat mayonnaise, I can't walk by a chocolate chip cookie and the things I do to food should be illegal.

I'm an author, and that doesn't lend itself to a lot of sweaty, physical exercise. You sit down, you write until your butt falls asleep, you drink coffee, beer, soda or whatever, and you eat stuff you can hold in one hand, as long as it isn't sticky, greasy or crumbly. I can actually type *faster* while eating a ham and cheese sandwich.

My weight has been increasing for years, but it's only gotten worse since becoming a stay-at-home Dad. I've always been husky. I'm 5'2" in my boots, and I haven't weighed less than a hundred fifty pounds since fifth grade. I look like a cinder block. These are assets when you're digging graves or delivering furniture. You're like a tire-jack and your stoutness is appreciated.

But it hasn't been until very recently that I've actually been *fat*. Since entering my thirties, my weight has been climbing, but it's been a slow, gradual process, and I haven't really noticed.

Your mother has tried gentle remonstrance. That never works. I'm really a "Slap him in the head until he gets it," kind of guy.

It took you, my son, to pry me out of the comfortable, fried cheese-smelling acceptance of my physical decline. When you were a toddler you had a large, red kickball. It was the exact consistency of the one we used to play Dodge Ball with when we were kids. It was one of your favorite toys and you liked to grab it with your little hands, smile and say, "Ball-Ball!"

I came down the stairs without a shirt on. It was a Saturday and your mother was letting me sleep in. I got my coffee, climbed into the sofa, grunted and rooted my way into a comfortable position and waited for the caffeine to kick in.

Meanwhile, you were grinning at me in a way I had come to recognize was trouble. You toddled over to me, climbed into the chair, gave me a hug, and then stuck your finger into my belly-button. I couldn't see your third knuckle and I could feel your fingernail coming off.

You can probably see where this is going.

You smiled at me, slapped me in the belly and said, "Ball-Ball!"

I have no one to blame but myself, but my excuses are pretty good. My body has gelatinized and I encourage the process by seeing if the refrigerator is still working every fifteen minutes.

Your mother encourages me to get up and get moving, but it was really just so easy to stay in the house, behind the baby gates, watching you play. Yes, you needed to be outside, getting bit by bugs, developing frostbite, and collecting the scars every man brags about later in life, but I rationalized it by saying "He's still so little! Let him get better control of his feet first. Then we'll go outside."

I've gotten better. I joined a local dojo, started eating less junk and more vegetables, and I tried to play with you for an hour every day. It was hard. But I don't want to be the Dad whose son associates his gut with a large, round, red rubber ball, and I never want to experience anyone losing a fingernail in my belly-button ever again.

Chapter 40 - Christmas At The Greasy Spoon:

We didn't do Christmas when I was a kid. Your Grandpa Pyscher spent too much time in tee-pees in the seventies, got religion, joined the Army, got more religion, and ended up in a deeply fundamentalist cult that mashed all his home-grown beliefs together and added a couple drops of its own brand of crazy.

My father was convinced that Christmas was some kind of a Roman holiday; an orgiastic devotion to a false god, incorporating all kinds of fertility myths, and incidentally, a cover up by the Roman Catholic Church.

"It's a stinkin' sacrifice to a sex god! Every year, at Christmas time, they'd dress up a tree, offering it sacrifices of gifts, and then they'd wait for their god to fall out of the sky in a special chariot, to deliver sexual favors to his highly esteemed! It's an abomination!"

He'd spleen on in that vein, for hours, ranting on about 'concessions by the Catholic Church' and 'conspiracies by Principalities and Powers' and 'Santa Claus?' No. 'Satan's Claws!'

And almost every Christmas was the same.

"'What are you getting for Christmas?"

"'Nothing."

"Why?"

"'We don't celebrate Christmas. It's an evil holiday."

Mom and Dad grew up with Christmas and I think that somewhere in their hearts, they knew that denying it to us was wrong. Dad wanted to spout on about being nonmaterialistic, but how do you explain that to a seven-year-old who just wants to unwrap presents on Christmas Day? Is the innocent joy shining in a child's eyes any counter against the steel-lined logic of legalistic religion?

So he'd shout at us, angry at himself for not being the shining scion of faith he was meant to represent, and angry at us for 'tempting' him.

We'd wander around on Christmas Morning, like some Dickensian orphans, picking through the neighbors' garbage, looking at the packages and wrapping paper and feeling miserable. Sometimes you got lucky. A toy would break, and some 'materialistic' parent, better equipped to provide on Christmas Morning, would toss the broken toy out for us to find and play with for a few hours. Those were good times, fighting over one-armed G.I. Joes.

Every once in a while, maybe every five years or so, they'd cave and give us a Christmas. A tree, decorations, presents, a dinner, it was all there, but there was a thick, syrupy covering of frustrated guilt from my parents that soured the whole deal.

We got older, and Christmas stopped. And we went along with it. What choice did we have? He was Dad and he was in charge. Mom was a hollow, voiceless reed that let things happen and pretended her victimization was so much worse than ours.

"I tried. I couldn't do anything." And she'd fade off into some drug-induced bliss, leaving us to fend for ourselves.

And boo-hoo-hoo. Sounds like some awful After-School-Special-Pity-Whore-Extravaganza, doesn't it? We do things differently now. We're bigger than Dad now. Outweigh him, outnumber him, and we're masters of manipulation.

"Dad. Get in the car. We're taking you to Christmas dinner."

"We can't! It's an abomination!"

"Yeah, Dad, it might be, but if you don't get up and walk out to the car, I'm gonna sling you over my shoulder like a sack of potatoes and carry you out. It's up to you."

My sister can be tough when she puts her mind to it.

One year it was just me, my sister and my Dad. She'd driven two hours to be with us on Christmas, her sweet heart blowing holes out all over the place in a swelling gush of pity for the 'poor bachelors who don't have anyone to spend Christmas with.' Evil manipulators we, we milked it for all it was worth.

"Don't know what I'll do on Christmas, sis. Probably sit at home, listening to the radio. Maybe they'll play some Christmas music."

And sniff, sniff, boo-hoo-hoo. We compared notes later and my sister confirmed that bad as my manipulation in getting her home to Kentucky was, Dad was infinitely worse.

"'Sure wish your mother could be here. Your brother'll probably be at his place, sitting in the dark, feeling sorry for himself and listening to his radio."

It wasn't fair of us to tag-team her like that, but she's smarter than we are, so we need whatever advantages we can get.

"That's fine. I'll drive down there. His Nibs"[104] is off performing experiments with guinea pigs in Hong Kong. Something about cancer. I forget."

---

[104] I don't know why, but every opportunity I get I make gentle fun of your Uncle Jerry. Probably because he's infinitely smarter than me, infinitely more successful than I am, and much, much smaller than I am. (Note: I said "smaller" not "shorter.") He's got just enough of that "Okay, I'm gonna hurt you now," lurking in the back of his eyes to keep

Christmas! With the family!

We didn't exchange gifts. Hers was the two hour drive. Dad and I mumbled something about being broke. It wasn't true, but she didn't care. She smiled at us, each in turn, her beatific grin lighting up her face.

"That's okay. It's not about presents anyway. I'm here. Let's go out to dinner!"

It's a known fact. The only restaurants open on Christmas Day are Chinese Diners and the greasy-spoon-truck-stops. Since we lived in what basically amounts to the rural south, we were stuck with trucks stops. Fine eating, if you're not all that particular about your food.

We drove around for a while, chatting, trying to find one. They hide, those greasy-spoon-truck-stops. They hide, knowing you're fuelled by desperation for something to eat. Your gratitude, when you do find one, allows you to overlook the fact that you're paying four dollars for a boiled, overly-greasy, toad-meat-burger.

When we did find one—a Waffle House some thirty-five minutes' drive away—it was packed. Every lonely soul, every forlorn face, every Christmas ghost in three counties had picked this Waffle House to eat their Christmas grits in.

We sighed, squared our shoulders and walked in.

She couldn't have been more than fifteen. Her hair was that blonde color you only get from irrepressible youth, and her eyes were a bright green, swimming with tears. She floated in her waitress outfit; two, maybe even three sizes too large for her. She walked up to our booth, freshly vacated by an unsmiling elderly couple, and tried to ask us what we wanted.

---

me from, like, trying to wrassle with him or something, but I never miss an opportunity to mock him either. It's love, son. Manlove at its most basic.

I heard myself say "What's wrong?"

She swallowed and tried a teary smile on us. It didn't work. All three of us turned the Compassion-O-Meter on her.

"Oh, now! Don't cry! You'll make me cry! You ever seen a fat man cry? It isn't pretty, I warn you!"

"Do you want a hug?" My sister. Her hugs have been known to cause spontaneous healings.

Even Dad contributed in his small way. "You're doing an outstanding job!"

She smiled at us wanly, and then fled. Another waitress came to try to take our order. We asked. She spilled.

"This couple came in here, on Christmas Morning, no less, and they just yelled at her! They treated her like a dog, and she's just here, helping out, trying to make a little extra money!"

There was silence around our table. The three of us looked at each other and the thought raced through our heads at the same time.

No.

No, there was no way this would stand. We exchanged a look and the two of them let me do it. "You go get her."

"What?"

"You heard me," I said. "You go get her. You bring her back out here, and you make her wait on us."

She left, fuming. The trembling, doe-eyed thing came back to our table. She apologized, and in a tremulous voice asked us what we wanted.

We ordered. She brought us our food, hands shaking. She spilled my soda, overfilled Dad's coffee and managed to tip my sister's fries onto the floor. We smiled at her, reassuringly. She brought us fresh plates, "Free of charge," she mumbled. We thanked her. Smiles plastered on our faces.

We ate our meal, talking about this and that, while a psychic wave danced through all three of our skulls.

I looked at Dad.

Dad looked at me.

I looked at my sister.

My sister looked at me.

"I'll do it," I said, grinning at the two of them. They'd already known that, but it was nice of them to allow me to believe the decision was mine.

The shaking young thing came back with the check. For three meals, the total was less than twenty dollars. You could see in her eyes that she'd appreciated our patience and she was a little hopeful we were going to leave an okay tip. A couple of dollars, after spilling food everywhere, probably would've made her entire day. Dad got up to pay the check and my sister and I remained at the table.

Not our style, I'm afraid. With as straight a face as I could manage, I said, "Go get your manager." She stood there, and you could see her trying to understand. Were we going to lash out at her, too?

"What?"

"'You heard me. Go get your manager." Gently, but firmly, I insisted with my gaze and my voice.

She nodded, looked down at the table, swallowed and fled once again.

The three of us grinned at each other conspiratorially. We loved doing this!

The manager came to our table, braced for trouble. "How can I help ya'll?" Her voice was sugary, ready for whatever we were going to complain about.

"You can't," I began, in a voice that carried through the entire restaurant. I can really bellow when I try, and I was trying hard. "Whatever you're paying that girl," a head nod to the poor thing behind her, swallowing and trying not to sob. Then a weighty pause, because even when I'm doing something nice for someone, deep down inside, I'm really just a bastard, "it's not enough. We've never had a more perfectly cooked, perfectly delivered meal. She was nice to us, she was efficient, and she was clean. Her hair smells nice, and she's got a nice smile. She walks on water, and you need to promote her."

This rhino-skinned, greasy-spoon, battle-axe grinned down at me like her head was going to unscrew. I can't swear to it, but I'm pretty sure I saw the barest hint of a tear glinting in one gimlet eye. Her young ward, nearly hiding behind her skirt, sobbed once.

But we weren't done. Dad's turn, and he's even louder than I am, as fifty generations of privates on the drilling ground can nervously attest.

"I have no idea why anyone would need another waitress working here. You should fire your entire staff and pay her their wages. She's strong, she's tough and she can take it."

By now we had an audience. The entire serving staff, the entire cooking staff, everyone shoveling food down their throats; the whole place had stopped to listen and watch.

My sister's was the *coup de tat*. In a voice known and recognized by high school math nerds everywhere, she looked the trembly young thing in the eye and said, "I don't know how you do it. Your job is so hard and you do it better than anyone I've ever seen. I know if it were me I'd probably quit after the first ten minutes."

The battle-axe grinned enough to show us her gold teeth, and there was no doubt about it now. A tear was trembling in her eye, and you could tell she didn't give a damn.

My sister kept right on going, holding this poor, trembling thing with her eyes and with the kindness of her voice. "I want to shake your hand, sweetheart. You've demonstrated that a woman can be tough and smart and beautiful, without compromising those ideals that make us all women."

And she stood up and shook her hand like an equal.

I won't lie. I sobbed just a little at that.

Yes. It was all nonsense. But it was *Christmas* Nonsense. It was the same kind of nonsense that says it's perfectly okay to believe in a fat man flying all over the world, delivering presents just because he's . . . he's kind. And he's good. And noble. And there's nothing even remotely evil about goodwill and kindness among men. It was nonsense the poor thing needed to hear. She needed to be told by random strangers, on this Christmas Morning, that not everyone in your life is going to piss down your neck.

The poor young thing was sobbing by now, grinning at us, and wiping her eyes with her apron.

We three stood up, turned toward her and applauded, grinning like loons from beyond the asylum's walls, and crying like we'd been tear gassed.

The rest of the restaurant cheered.

The young thing blushed and tried to go into the kitchen to hide and recover. We still weren't done.

"Hang on. You forgot your tip."

I have no idea how much it was. I reached in my wallet and pulled out whatever I had. My sister was counting tens from hers. Dad just reached in his shirt, without looking, and pulled out the money he kept there.

When we handed the wad to her she had to use both hands. Tears were running down her face and she couldn't talk. We wished her a "Merry Christmas!" and we walked out.

Best. Christmas. Ever.

Chapter 41 – Dinner For A Diva:

I cook dinner, five-six days out of seven, and your mother is a picky eater—the only one in this family.

She can be forgiven for this. I say it from the perspective of a man whose bachelor grocery list for two weeks represented a starvation diet for much of America.

I've since been introduced to the much wider world of culinary possibilities and your mother has made it perfectly clear that my dietary habits would need to change.

I'm not much of a cook. Part of the reason for that is I'm not much of a gourmand. I don't have a sophisticated sense of taste, and fillage is much more of a priority to me than delicate tastes and subtle textures.

I am perfectly content to eat whatever's in front of me, so long as it's properly subdued and I don't have to cook it. When I *do* cook, I can follow directions and put simple dishes—like peanut butter and jelly—together, but anything requiring more than the boiling of water is completely outside my realm of experience.

So we buy a lot of convenience food. Which is fine for an uncultured palate like mine, but Mrs. Picky likes variety.

"Use your imagination! Expand your horizons a little bit! Try doing something with a meat or a vegetable you've never used before. I'll eat it, I promise."

I *did* try. I bought some chicken and an exotic vegetable well outside of my comfort zone: radishes. I had this vague idea of baking the chicken in Worcestershire Sauce and garnishing them with radish florets. I went so far as to make Flapjacks and even got some wine that didn't feature a cartoon character on the label.

I got flowers and candles and everything.

What emerged from the oven haunts our dreams and stained the walls with its evil. I cut three of my fingers badly enough to require stitches and bent our best cleaver trying to make the florets. The flapjacks caught fire and we nearly blew up when I used the wine to try and extinguish them.

We almost died of exhaustion trying to chew through the chicken. We agreed to never speak of it again. I bring it up here only as a demonstration of my willingness to try.

Mrs. Picky doesn't ask me to expand my horizons anymore and she doesn't look forward to dinner. But she doesn't fear it, either.

Chapter 42 – Shining A Light Into The Grave:

The cops came by today, and there she stood; fearful, hesitant—as if I were going to shout, or turn her away. Her hair blew across her flushed, sickly face.

"Again," I thought.

How many times have we played this scene? Like actors in a Kabuki, we can't move from our appointed roles: her, the helpless damsel, unwilling, unable to cope with the world; me her sole protector, the "Returning One."

She wore no shoes, and I couldn't help but see that she looked tired. Old love; forgotten love; *primal* love swallowed my anger, and I accepted the script once again. The officer escorting her stepped back from my visible frustration, flaring like a collapsing star.

I was there the first time: a handful of pills, a trip to the ER. It was her bland-faced admission: "I tried to kill myself." that I remember. I realized it then, I think, that here was a damaged mind, and I put on my costume, stepped to the lights, and played my bit.

The years have not been kind, but how much of that is her fault? Could she have stopped the fall sooner by speaking up? Did she *need* to fall down the rabbit hole, or could I have done something to prevent it? Could I have spared us years of pain?

I told her this without words, I think, as I drove her home. I spoke of bedside vigils, of being stronger than I am. My rigid posture told of my secret guilt for hoping for an end; an end to her self-inflicted, perpetual martyrdom; an end to this ceaseless struggle.

I sat there hating myself. Hating myself for wanting something beyond this; hating myself for my betrayal, my lack of compassion, my frustration; hating myself for not knowing her anymore, or indeed ever. I was never able to bridge that gap and to touch the woman I had once loved more than life myself.

That very day she'd written me a letter.

I hadn't expected it. She had called and told me it was coming, but I thought I had a day or two in which to prepare—from what, I never know, protecting my feelings, my heart, maybe? I often think that nothing more clearly demonstrates the poignancy or even the outright immediacy of my entire life, than the way I so stridently protect my heart. So when I opened my mailbox, and saw the envelope in her scrawled and shaking hand, it hit me with a bit of a jolt. I read the envelope in the light of my headlights. Her handwriting had deteriorated, but I couldn't exactly attribute that to anything specific. The return address was listed as 'Home for the Aged.' I don't want to dwell on how that made me feel. I put the envelope on the seat next to me, and drove to work. I had actually managed to put it fully from my mind until I was seated at my post at work. It was then that I decided I could put it off no longer, and opened it.

"Dear Nescher,

"Since it is so hard to reach you by phone I thought I would drop you a note. How are you? I am doing fine. I realize that my biggest problem is depression. It's a killer, Nescher - I'm sure you know all about it."

I was struck by that casual statement. It was if she were saying, 'Boy. Your life has sure sucked the past couple of months. Bet you're depressed, huh?' It's funny how we can take the littlest things and attach such importance to them, isn't it? I had made it difficult to reach me by design. My parents had early on seized upon me as a Soldier in their campaigns against each other. I found it necessary to unplug my phone if I wanted to sleep.

"I work on it every day by reading. I read anything! Just so long as I'm reading. Sleep only makes me feel down. It doesn't relieve depression so I push myself to keep moving all day."

My mind cast its way back to my childhood, when she wouldn't move from the couch for anything. Her depression was an acute, living, breathing presence; a hard, brilliantine-like thing that took up all the space in a room and left it dry, sterile and cold. We were too young to understand how afraid we were at the time, and I only reach these understandings now. When balanced against the towering, eternal fury of my father, the two created the two great polar forces of my childish universe: on the one hand, the cold, oppressive, madness-tainted depression of my mother, and on the other, the white, hot, heat flash of my father's anger. Her depression was like a reptile's torpor, driving her to sleep, to become immobile. It drove us to shout, to cry, to laugh; anything to attract her attention, anything to elicit some kind of a response. My father's fury reduced us to tip-toeing and hushed whispers. There was never any warning, never any indication as to what could set the brush fire off. It was like a car accident.

"I'm on the internet now- so if you want my address:"

She had forgotten I no longer had a computer. I noticed these lapses in memory were happening more often, and it hurt me to see. She was only fifty-one! Why she should be having this problem, on top of everything else, and why now? For all her failings as a mother, for all her failings as a person, I loved her as only an eldest son can. I recognized in my hurt as I read this, the lonely cry of a small boy weeping for his Mommy. I missed her.

"I'm learning about the computer at the clubhouse. It's a place where you can do anything. I'm into computers now. I'm happy, Nescher, but I know I must get a place of my own, probably this Fall. Dad is Dad and it doesn't get better. I'm still in love with Dad and that makes it all the harder."

There were small breaks in her handwriting at the end of this. It was nothing overt, or even really noticeable. Just a small squiggly, but it lead me to believe her eyes were filling with tears. I stopped and thought about our relationship then. Our roles were completely reversed. I was the one who lavished praise for every little accomplishment, and I was the one who salved the wounds of heart's pain. It hurt me to see that squiggly. I wanted to hug my mother. I wanted to tell her that I loved her, that I forgave her, and that everything will eventually be okay. I wanted more than I will ever have. I wondered at what point we had effected this alchemy.

"Here are two poems I wrote. I'm excited to share them with you. "I love you, "Mom."

Yes, she had been a poet. She had been a singer, as well as a musician. The great tragedy of my Mother's life was to have the heart and soul of an artist bled out of her by her circumstances. I remembered music from my earliest childhood, how it swelled and swam around and through and over and under. I remembered her singing, high and clear, as though the music dwelt deep within her. Her face was rapturous, and I felt that Heaven was close whenever my Mother sang. And then I thought of her face the last time I saw her, the drugs doing their awful work, leaving her eyes flat, glossy and cold. Thanksgiving Day: we went to visit her in the hospital after her latest gesture. I left well before the visit was over, waiting for my family in the halls outside the ward. There were not tears then, and there are none now. I wish it were different, but no, only a lump, locked deep within my chest, where a sob could be.

I folded her letter up neatly, and placed it back in its envelope. I swallowed the sob, and put it all from me as best as I was able. I loved my mother, and I miss her terribly. I cried when she died. I cried when she was buried and I cried for weeks afterwards.

My guilt was eating me alive.

I always wanted to provide her with more and with better care, but I never had the means. When she signed herself into the nursing home—using her Medicare benefits—I was living in a steel box, making less than ten dollars an hour and living off Hamburger Helper and canned vegetables. I didn't have two spare nickels to rub together, much less the means to help her.

Almost three months after her death I was playing with you in your room. I closed my eyes for a moment and felt myself drift off. The baby gate was closed, I could still hear you and feel you playing around me and the room was warm, snug and secure.

My mother came to see me as I lay there on the floor, aware but not awake. She looked the way she did when I was a child: happy, healthy and smiling. Behind her, just visible, was a little boy I didn't know.

Neither one of them said anything. My mother just stood there, smiling at me. The little boy behind her shyly smiled as well.

After a moment or so, my mother waved at me and I rolled back into consciousness. I hugged you and told you I loved you.

We never could fix the problems between us when she was alive, but I believe her pain is over now.

I haven't cried since.

Chapter 43 – Snapshot Of A Stranger:

The sign on the door says 'Went to Church Dinner. Be back 7:30ish. Make yourself at home.' There's an uncharacteristic little smiley face at the bottom of the page. And even though you don't know it, that's everything you need to know about John. My coffee cup is in its place, the computer has been left on so I can play video games, and there's a self-deprecatory, little smiley face at the bottom of the note taped to his door.

I grin, open the unlocked door, and do so. I play a Hot Wheels car game on his computer until John comes home.

"What's up, dude?"

"Oh, nothing much. You?"

"Same old, same old."

Like a comfortable pair of matching socks, we are. Nothing too surprising, nothing too demanding, just two old friends meeting for Sunday Bible Study. John doesn't know it, but it's the highlight of my week. We talk for a few minutes while John's four-year-old-son bounces around the house, making all the joyful noise a four-year-old, well-loved, little boy can.

The dogs scamper playfully around, hoping for a ball-tossing session, or maybe a treat, or fifteen quality minutes of ear-scratching time. The cats, Pumpernickel and Peach Fox, both make appearances and demand, in feline fashion, their share of attention.

I look around, grinning, basking in the life swirling all around me, and not for the first time, I find myself wondering what John'd say—after he laughed—if I asked him if I could move in.

We inquire about each other's well being. We talk about John's ex. We talk about John's church. We talk about my ex. We talk about my current girlfriend and my prospects for the future. We have coffee and chocolate-chip cookies and we gossip like a pair of garrulous old women.

We have our Bible study. Luke chapter fifteen: "Jesus said this. . .."

"I thought this was cool. Check this out. In verse twenty-one . . .."

"You know, that never really occurred to me like that. Way to bring that up, dude."

"See, this is important 'cause Jesus is talking to the Jews, an' the Jews are like, all fixated on bein' kosher . . .."

John's a Baptist. I'm a very confused Apostolic with Messianic Jew in there somewhere. We don't agree on much, and half the time we're politely demonstrating all the reasons the other guy is wrong, but the insights that do occasionally come as a result of these Bible studies are astounding. For instance: ten years ago, I'd've been convinced John was going to hell, and John would've been ready to break a chair over my head.

"Oh. Hey! Did I tell you I finished my photo albums?" He'd mentioned it. It was to be, in John's inimitably organized fashion, a complete collection of all of his sorted photographs.

He indicates three very serious, very black, three-ring binders on a bookshelf. I waddle over and take a look. He's got ten-thousand pictures of his son, none of his ex-wife, a couple dozen of me, and others scattered throughout. It's indicative of John that each photograph has its own little pocket, fits snugly in relation to all the other photographs around it, and tells a sort of story. He talks about the organization project, while I flip through, looking and remembering. Rowen is off watching a Tom and Jerry video in the other room. Here is a picture of John from his first apartment. There is a picture of Matt—one of our ever-dwindling circle of friends—from years ago. We don't hear from Matt anymore and there is a moment of sadness at the realization of time and lives gone by.

I flip the page, and there he is. For a moment, I don't recognize him. His long, greasy, dirty hair is pulled back from his scalp in a severe pony-tail. He's wearing his usual filthy combination of t-shirt and jeans. There's a dusting of hair on his face, like he's trying, and failing, to grow some sort of a beard. Bits of metal are twinkling around his face, and there are heavy bruises under both of his eyes. He's handsome, in a coke-head sort of way. He's dangerously skinny, and there's an air of poor hygiene around him. I can smell the miasmic funk of old hooch, bad smoke, sweat and crud that he carries around with him. He smells like a roadkill-perfumed-outhouse in the summertime. His mouth is foul; every other word is an obscene one. His eyes objectify every woman he sees. 'Bet she'd like some of this!' he says, with a glottal chuckle, groping himself. He's sitting next to one of my very best friends, petting a dog, ignoring the camera, because he knows it's pointed at him. My friend is being appropriately cheesy in the photo, but the long-hair on the couch is too cool for that. It takes me a few minutes, but I feel the loathing building within me before I realize who he is. I want to crawl into this photograph, jump down his throat, and crawl right out his backside, ripping and tearing at everything I can get my hands on. I want to grab him by the bottom lip and shake until his nose starts to bleed. I want to whip out my knife and carve my name into his face and scream at him, 'Now, remember this! Remember the way it feels! Remember the way you're squalling like an injured, baby pig, your blood running down your face! Remember and maybe you won't screw it all up!'

It won't do any good. I've been listening to him for twenty years, telling me why he can't, why he won't, why he shouldn't; why he's been robbed, denied, looked over, mistreated. He could look into a mirror every day, and see my name in inch-high letters, carved into his face, and think about only how anti-Semitic I must be. There's ten-million excuses and never any reasons. Sometimes there aren't very good words for the description of an individual. Words that I'd usually use don't do the job. 'Jerk' isn't harsh enough. 'Loser' doesn't begin to describe the depths of loserdom this spazz has sunk to. He is an utter shithead. He is a schmuck, a schlimel, a louse, a blood-sucking, parasitic, dumbass.

I'd suggest to you, that for his sins, this creep deserves to be dragged into the street and shot like a mangy, rabid dog, but that'd be wasting a perfectly good bullet and giving mangy, rabid dogs a bad name. I look down at this criminal, this filthy mongrel, and I hate him. I hate him with all my heart and soul; stronger and more pure, in a black, poisoned manner, than anyone else I've ever had any such feeling for. I want him to die a slow, lingering death. And he nods at me, leers at me from his comfortable place in front of the TV, bottle of cheap bourbon in place, and he drinks. Or smokes. Or screws. It doesn't matter. He doesn't need to listen. He's twenty-one and invincible, utterly indestructible and he knows everything he needs to except where the bong and the remote of the moment is, and weren't you just about to take your clothes off, darlin'?

He's a drug addict. He doesn't think he is. He's pretty sure of himself, pretty sure of his ability to 'keep it all together. Won't catch me turnin' inta one a'them druggies.' But there are so many lovely drugs; drugs that he uses on a regular basis. These will get you up and keep you up all day. These will put you down. These will stop the nausea. These will make the world seem like a perfectly groovy place to be. These will stop the diarrhea, the itching, the burning, the muscle spasms. Lovely, lovely cocktails. If one doesn't quite do it, take three. If three don't do it, smoke a joint, do a few shots and then take three more. You'll get it right, eventually, my fair son, and when you do, we'll trip the light fantastic. He sits there, the cockiness of youth on his face, and he laughs at me from beyond his screen of years. Oh. I know he's dead. I've seen his grave. But I'd like to dig him up so I can kick his ass. My teeth clench, inwardly, and I look at his right hand. Sure enough, there it is: a silver ring with a black stone.

"Is that *me*?" I ask, facetiously.

John gets up and walks over to the photo album. I have to show him my ring to prove that it *is* me; a younger me; a selfish, self-centered, egotistical, little bastard, me. A me neither one of us recognize now, thank God.

Sitting there, he doesn't know what the next few years hold for him. Sitting there, all he can think about is crawling into the next bottle of booze, the next convenient, warm bed, the next set of semi-welcoming arms.

He doesn't know about lying awake, listening to the walls closing in after you've been awake for three days, trying to forget your own name. That's two or three years in his future, five or six in my past. He doesn't know about lying on his back, feeling the stretching pain in his chest, wondering whether or not that double handful of ephedrine stressed his heart enough to knock holes in it. He doesn't know about long, sleepless nights, endless days, and the freak-out sessions where he wakes up in the living room, wearing nothing but his boxer-briefs, clutching his blanket and a walking stick, mumbling "In Jesus Name!" over and over and over. He doesn't know about lying in the middle of the street, drunk or stoned or who the hell cares, clutching a family-sized bottle of aspirin and a smoke-shop-katana, screaming to anyone who'll listen, "I'm gonna kill myself!" mHe doesn't know about calling his Mother and reading his suicide note to her over the phone.

He doesn't know about his friends keeping a tight eye on him, asking, "Have you lost weight, Nescher?" with a glint and a worried shine in their eyes. What they're really asking is "Have you started using again, Nescher? Are we gonna need to peel you off the floor again, Nescher? Are you really just that *stupid*, Nescher?"

He doesn't know about any of that. All he knows is, at the moment, he's half-baked and feeling great. He doesn't care. All he knows is that his rent is paid, he's got a warm, dry place to sleep and the woman says she loves him.

"That *is* me!"

No. That *was* me.

I close the photo album and we talk of other things, while a much older, wiser me kicks the ever-living, bloody hell out of a younger, very deserving me. All I can tell you is that the little git deserves it more than you know.

Chapter 44 – Being A Musician:

I used to be a "musician."

I am an old-school headbanger; I am specifically a fan of the genre of music that used to be known as 'Thrash Metal.' According to Wikipedia, the 'big four' bands of the genre are Metallica, Anthrax, Megadeth and Slayer.

For my generation, if you tell someone you grew up listening to Megadeth, Anthrax, Metallica and Slayer, they have a very specific idea of who you are and what you are about: you're deaf. You weren't smart enough to turn your Walkman down on Megadeth's 'Symphony of Destruction' or Slayer's 'Raining Blood' and now you can't have a conversation without a megaphone.

You have very specific opinions as to what 'good' music is. Pop Music makes your teeth hurt; Rap works if it's fast and loud but you can't go anywhere near Soul or R&B without inoculating yourself with some double bass first. You can choke Country down if it's by somebody hard, like Johnny Cash, but anything weaker than The Man in Black triggers your gag reflex. World Music is an urban legend as far as you're concerned and anything else is so far below your radar screen as to be invisible.

You genuinely believe you're good enough to make this music yourself. So you start a band and inflict your creations on the rest of the world.

Our band's name was Cross' Shadow. We were, of all things, a Christian Thrash Metal Band with a Blues-y influence. We were profoundly ecumenical, and as enthusiastic as only teenagers can be for that kind of music. I was responsible for the lyrics and singing. My best friend John—your Uncle Gower—played lead guitar, his brother played drums and his sister played keyboard. Our big hit, 'River of Blood' is still being played in certain parts of Kentucky.

> *"A red river of blood from my precious Savior fell!*
> *Extinguishing the fires of deepest, darkest hell!*
> *Death no longer, no longer flies by night!*
> *For I'm living in the glory of His eternal light!*
> *River! River! River! River of blood!"*

We had three songs: 'River of Blood,' 'Maximum Flash,' and the *de rigueur* power ballad, 'It Was From A Mountain That I Fell (Into The Oceans Of Your Eyes.)' We wrote all our own music and lyrics and we had a great time.

I'm still an enthusiastic singer and I often break into song at the least excuse. I serenade your mother on a regular basis, making up words to popular songs and inserting her name at random. She pretends to enjoy it.

All of this is not to imply in any way that I have musical ability. I can generally be in the same zip code as a note, but any closer is beyond me. My enthusiasm far exceeds my ability, and I've accepted that my comfort zone is the Thrash Metal Guttural Yell.

Your mother, on the other hand, *is* good. She's been cantoring for longer than I've been alive, participated in a number of different competitions, had voice lessons and even been paid a couple of times to sing. She's a professional and I love being able to make her wince in pain with my naked enthusiasm. Every so often she tries to get me to come hang out with her in the 'good voice' area of a song, but I'm having too much fun for that.

Her taste in music is much more eclectic than mine as well. She has twelve billion CDs from people I'd never heard of prior to marrying her. Despite my snobbery and good intentions to be Metal 'Till I Die, I'm getting an education in music that I couldn't pay for. And I'm digging it.

Son, you aligned at a young age with your mother. You liked to sing little ditties and to my tinny, deafened ear, it sounds pretty close to music to me. You've got a natural percussive ability, if the still-healing bruises on my kidneys are any indication—typical to most little boys, I think—and nothing got your attention faster than a song.

I tried to sabotage this unnatural affinity for non-metal music by filling your little world with the stuff I liked. You banged your head, but I was suspicious. When I got the same head banging response from Bon Jovi that I got for Tourniquet, I could tell you were just trying to make me happy. I've still got time to get some Iron Maiden into you, but I've just about accepted that you will probably never experience the sheer joy of torn vocal cords from a particularly aggressive N sharp backed by a thundering double-bass and the wail of broken strings.

Your loss, I guess.

Chapter 45 - A Necessary Lesson:

The dark surrounds me like a warm blanket. I can feel the cat sleeping at the end of the bed. The sound of the radio playing in the other room and the noise of the fan pulls me back into reality. My speeding heart slows.

The dream again. A variation on a tiresome theme, almost life-long. It's like a memory I can't quite coalesce into conscious observation; something I'm repressing. When I was younger the dream featured automobile-related threats. Whether it was a dump truck closing in from a long way away or cowering in a VW Bus while the Frankenstein Monster stomped towards me. That particular variant featured the Muppet Grover. He said not to be scared, but he didn't do anything helpful, either.

There's always a car featured in the dream somewhere, somehow. I've never understood it.

In my adult dreams, I'm almost always driving. Small, fast cars, built low to the ground or hulking tankers with bad brakes. I'm either flying like a UFO or knocking the bricks out of buildings.

Sometimes an impression of space and luxury surrounds me, other times it's little more than a roll cage and a steering wheel--a go-cart arrangement. Small differences exist in every dream, but they always fade in response to the forward impetus of the overall theme: I'm driving and I'm about to have an accident.

One I've had several times features the 'Schwinn Effect'. I'm rolling along. I need to stop suddenly, so I hit the brakes. It's hard enough to lift the back end of the car off the road. I'm rocked forward in my seat as though I'm riding a bicycle headfirst into a wall. The feel of the forward movement makes me sick with fear and phantom pain. Sometimes I get that one over and over and over in the course of one night's dreaming. I wake unrested and cranky, sometimes with sore muscles.

Tonight's dream was only a bit different. I lay on my side, sifting through the fading fragments. I had to think about it for a bit, putting together the thin scenes I could remember.

I often think about the way we receive messages. Whether from God, ourselves, or the universe in general, messages come at us from everywhere. We try to tell ourselves things that are important in dreams. We try to make ourselves heard and all too often we make that impossible.

In this evening's dream, the car I'm driving is starting to spin and I am going fast enough for this to be a problem. The car is spinning like a top. I am missing the other cars on the road by the barest of inches. There's a high-pitched noise generated by my passage. My hands lock on the steering wheel and a traitorous, self-destructive part of me gives in. I watch, removed, as I take no action to save myself. I sit, terrified, my hands on the wheel, and *allow* things to happen. I begin to call on Jesus almost at once, the familiar fear and dread crawling over me.

The fear builds, and I scream to Jesus to save me. Then, like sunlight, awareness breaks. I watch, still removed and outside of myself, as a slowly panning inner camera draws my mind's eye from my terrified face, fixed in a fear-grin-rictus, to my hands, still locked on the wheel and pulling it sharply in the direction of the spin, down to my feet.

My right foot is firmly pressing the gas pedal down.

I stay in bed for a long moment, trying to go back to sleep. I don't sleep well most nights and waking up some three hours before I have to is inconvenient, to say the least. I say a small prayer, in the belief that waking up like this is God's way of telling you someone needs you to intercede for them, and lie still on my mattress, trying to find the inner peace necessary to waft back down the river of sleep.

It's no good.

I'm awake.

I sigh, stumble out of bed and walk into the bathroom, flicking the light on as I pass. I peer at myself in the small mirror over the sink. My reflection stares back, emanating what I categorize as resentment at me. My eyes are dull and tired, and my hair has formed a sleepy crow's nest. Without wanting to I can see the face hiding behind mine in my reflection. His hair's much longer, he's skinnier, and his face, though dirty, doesn't seem to reflect as many years of compromise as mine now seem to. His eyes, below the silent, wordless anger, betrayal and hurt, radiate with the spiritual ambition to change the world and everything in it.

He's not me. I don't think he's ever really been me. Or, no . . . I've got that backwards. *I* was never really intended to be *me*. I was *supposed* to be something leaner and meaner, sharper and harder. I was *supposed* to be an axe; a knife; a sword. Instead, I'm a spoon.

His lips move soundlessly, but I don't need to hear him to know what he's saying.

You've forgotten. You've sold out.

He's so angry, so driven about change and making the world a better place. He's militant and magnificently liberal; furious and impassioned; and he's ready, willing and able to storm the gates whenever the call for revolution comes. I can't remember, now, why he was always so angry, so ready to commit violence in the name of 'the people'.

He never did know who they were, but he was ready to line the 'bourgeois ruling elite' up against the wall in their name.

Sometimes I wonder where he went, and when, exactly, he left. I know he was there in high school, but he disappeared before I hit my twenties. It's easy, when you decide it's time to grow up and put away childish things, to forget who you were and where you came from, isn't it?

Another crime to lay at my feet. A man's got to eat, though, so I don't spend too much time regretting his untimely death.

Deli, the short-haired brindle princess who lives in my house and eats my food, prances around my ankles, grunting and meowing, doing her level best to let me know she wants to be fed, just in case I forgot this is 'treat time'.

I walk into the kitchen, fetch her two treats, and move into the living room, despite her protests.

I sit, picking up the book I left propped on the arm of my chair. I read a few pages, letting the radio behind me tinkle quietly to itself on the bookshelf while I try to relax enough to fall back asleep. The glorified electric typewriter on my desk sits like a gloating toad and I can almost hear it muttering.

Not gonna write anything tonight, huh? Just as well. You suck. Probably shouldn't have quit rolling barrels or delivering furniture. Not much else a dumb gorilla like you would be any good at.

I flip another page, ignoring it. It's right. I *do* need to write. But I don't want to give it the pleasure of knowing that.

The voice on my desk croaks again. *Will you blinkin' credit it? Now he thinks he can ignore me! Well!*

And I'm really not sure why my computer talks with a British accent when it's mocking me. I'm really not, but I continue to do precisely that. Deli, injured and offended, jumps in my lap and purrs like a constipated chainsaw.

A third voice, neither silent ghost or gloating-typewriter-undertoad whispers at me, and it's not going to be ignored. It's like a biting flea in a warm, moist, unreachable crevice of flesh. It flicks around on the surface of my brain, whispering, digging, scratching and calling, and I give in after only a few minutes.

The chair is waiting.

It's not a very nice chair: a thin, reclining thing with a feeble footrest; the kind of piece you'd expect to see in a modern bachelor's home in the 1950's. Covered in a burgundy, shag-like material, it itches something fierce when I sit.

Just a bit used, its condition of the chair isn't all that bad for something rescued from the trash. It's wedged in between my bed and the bedroom wall, with about three feet of space separating them. There are three boards, old shelving material, wedged between the chair and the wall.

I turn off all the lights and move back into the bedroom, where the soft whiff of the fan mingles with the voice of the chair, beckoning me. Some things are just better in the dark. I pull on a pair of socks, and smile, thinking, 'It's *cold* in the void!'

I move the radio from its place on my bookshelf and plug it in the socket closest to my mattress, turning it to face the chair. I pull out the new CD my best friend loaned me—some heavy piece of bluesy-rock—and put it in the radio, turning up the volume to the preset level I've determined is 'just enough'. I don't want to disturb my neighbor any more than necessary, and I have to believe he wonders about the rhythmic knocking noises coming from next door.

I sit in the chair, wedge my legs against the mattress, put my arms on the arm rests and let my fingers find the indentations I've already worn there. I press play, close my eyes and begin to rock.

You've seen it before, I'm sure. It's a forward and back movement, sitting in a stationary chair. It's a telling characteristic of autistic individuals, and people with certain kinds of mental illnesses.

I've been doing it my entire life. At some point in my teens I realized it was a great way to push my consciousness into an inner sanctuary.

My theory is that it originally began as an expression of my enjoyment of music. I'd rock in time with the beat, listening to whatever happened to be playing.

As I got older, I learned it's a fabulous way to meditate. You almost achieve a state of auto-hypnosis. Your immediate awareness fades out. You lose touch with the present and drift through skies of your own making. It's like a drug. You can completely lose yourself in the rhythm, the sweat and the music.

I've done some reading on the matter. Many religions the world over use a very similar technique to achieve an 'ecstatic' state. Voodoo practitioners use drums and dance, as an example. For myself, I've noticed a sensation of 'opening', as though I'm flowing into a larger space than the one behind my eyes. I feel like I'm lightly surfing along the soap-bubble-thin membrane of some enormous sphere.

It's hard to explain without resorting to spiritual, quasi-mystical language, but the basic feeling is I'm a seed opening and rising towards a sunlit sky.

I enjoy rocking. Other than the exercise, it gives me an opportunity to do the 'filing'.

The theory runs a little like this: your head, like anything else dealing with input and output, occasionally fills up. It gets clogged, plugged and stoppered with the constant barrage of crap coming at you on a daily basis. Thoughts, hopes, dreams, ambitions and desires contribute to the general mess, and every so often you need to clean the drains. Take a bit of time, sweat a whole bunch, and move your way through your own head, cleaning house. I don't know if that's really the way things are, but I know I sure feel better afterwards.

The music starts and washes over me. I envisage myself as being a silvery, naked, lance of human-shaped light.

I swim through the dense cobwebs of my head as lightstorms flick on and off behind my eyes. When I was younger, I used to think the display going on behind my closed eyes when I rocked were the skies of another universe, one that existed just beyond the horizon of the seen and known. I'm older now, with some letters in the air above my head, and *intellectually* I know the colors, the bright spirals and the swirling clouds of light I'm watching are probably the result of my brain crashing against the front and back of my skull.

In response to all this learnin', I've taught myself to 'rock' my head instead of 'banging' it. I let my skull 'surf' on my neck with a gentle forward and back movement. It's probably better for me, but I do miss the vibrant 'laser-light' displays.

The music's pretty good. Good hooks, licks and rhythm, but I'm not getting there. I still feel dense, hard, tight, like I'm firmly anchored to myself. The music's okay and I'm working up a sweat, but experience has taught me that there are further depths to plumb if I want to.

I do.

I *always* do.

I stop the CD player, taking the CD out. I put in a CD that always manages to somehow appeal to that part of my brain that responds to rhythms and beats. I like to think of my response to it as being something like a reptile finding a warm place in the sun. The music from this CD goes directly to my hind brain and fires off all the right kinds of responses.

I close my eyes, turn the music up, and rock.

It's like a sonic assault. All at once, the music starts. Primal guitar licks, and a driving, booming, ear-bleeding drum rhythm.

The hairs on my arms and the back of my neck stand up, and a wave of hot adrenaline rushes through me. My knuckles start to itch.

My skin moves against the fabric of the chair. I sweat. My breathing slows to a cadence I've trained myself over the years with, taking on an automatic, almost hibernative nature. My throat closes and becomes dry. My head lowers to my chest and my hair dances around my face.

I rock, finding the beat, and let the music swirl into my needy   places.   It wraps its way around my head, fully cocooning me, and I start to drift. The lights and colors behind my eyes splash and swirl in time to the music. I lance myself upward into them, arms wrapped around me. I'm clothed only with the music, and I move in time with it and the dream of

Tattoos and Baby Food—a Boy's Guide to Life

possibility behind my closed eyes.

The anchors of reality fall away, and I shoot away into innerspace.

I'm rather proud of this sanctum. A scientist would tell you it's all imaginary, existing only within the walls of my skull. I'm not sure I agree, but it isn't all that important.

Description. Yes. You've never been here, so you don't know what it looks like. I'm an arrowed lance of silvery light floating within a nebulous void, swirled with lights, sounds and colors. It's like a nursery for stars. The colors and swirls embrace me. I lose where I end and the music begins. I float on the surface of mind, riding a wave of righteous-music-driven-anger, and drift where the current takes me.

Above, below, and all around are polychromatic, opaque spheres. Some shine like the sun on a perfect spring day. Others are dark, with frightening depths. Still others have a color that makes me think of skin that's been dead for a very long time.

I drift forward, with the music playing all around, and slide effortlessly through the skin of the nearest sphere.

The room is dark and nearly empty. A crib, with a baby perhaps six months old, wrapped in a handmade blanket and sleeping peacefully on its back, next to a cat purring contentedly, takes up the center of the room. A painting hangs on one wall.

The cat, a long-haired black female is named—for reasons only certain drug-addled persons will ever know—'Creamapara'. It and the painting, I recognize. The baby, I don't.

Beautifully regal in the sphinx-like way of all cats, Creamapara sleeps, nose buried, in the warm hollow formed between the baby's head and the head of the crib.

Her contented purring fills the chill, waiting silence of the room. She wakes for just a moment and looks up in the bored, disinterested way of a truly happy, comfortable cat when I glide in. Peering at me for a moment, she seems to shrug. Lowering her head, she goes back to sleep, her purring never missing a beat.

A dirty, badly used, hand-me-down thing of rusty struts and clattering wood, the crib looks like a Victorian torture device. A bare, musty mattress—I remember the smell!—sits within, and if it weren't for the warm, pastel-colored blanket wrapped around the baby, there'd be nothing protecting him from the cold but the cat.

The young stranger who stared back at me from my bathroom mirror walks out of the wall the painting hangs on. He's got his belligerent glare in place before he's even fully through.

I shouldn't be surprised. After all, anywhere I can go, he can go. It's a *shared* universe.

He says nothing. To each other, we are both deaf and mute. I don't know why, but nothing can be said between us across this personal universe, nothing can cleave the distance of time and space separating us. But body language and gesture says more between the two of us than words ever could.

A black t-shirt with an enormous, red anarchy symbol on it hangs from his bony shoulders. It looks like blood. Dirty, torn jeans cover his lanky shanks. 'Poverty-chic,' I think, meanly, on seeing them.

A pair of beaten, beleaguered, outsized, hand-me-down combat boots makes enormous clown's shoes of his feet, and blood drips from his knuckles in a steady stream. It slowly disappears from view before hitting the floor. A neat trick, that.

It's important to remember that none of this is real. It's all an egoist, self-actualized visualization exercise. His knuckles drip blood because he wants people to believe in his anger. The little twat hits walls, making them bleed so his knuckles will drip blood.

Mine ache in a muted sort of empathy. They hurt now, my marble-sized knuckles, and they twinge in the cold. I hate him sometimes for his dramatic tendencies.

Beige calluses, an inch thick, cover his fingertips. He spends far more time in the chair than I do.

Writing covers his arms from wrists to elbows. It is his attempt at tattooing. He uses an ink pen, a marker, lipstick; whatever comes to hand. It's an everyday thing. Songs, poems, lyrics, bits of doggerel; he doesn't care. Whatever occurs to him ends up on his arms.

Today, the left arm has a badly scrawled song by his favorite band. I don't need to see it to read it. The words are a part of my mental landscape, and I mouth the first few words to myself while looking around the room.

"It's never been easy to be who I am, I can only do the very best I can."

He looks at me in disbelief, as if I have no right to remember. He thrusts his right arm at me, and the writing here is clear. Another song. One we wrote together so many years ago. This one I sing in a quiet voice.

"A cold, dark night; a bitter, biting wind, a man walks the streets alone, covered by his sins. Tears many years unshed silently fall, He falls to his knees, broken as he desperately calls . . ."

No, it isn't very good, but it was written with a passion you can only really get to when you still *believe.*

The last three words have been carved into his skin with   the   force   of his feeling. '*NEVER GIVE IN*' has been scrawled, with considerable force, in red ink across his left wrist. I remember that one. He wrote it over and over for a month, re-inking it every day. The skin grew irritated and inflamed. He got an infection that required antibiotics. I remember him hoping it would scar.

This was all long before he started stealing his father's razorblades, before he started reflecting the outward pain of his impossible environment.

I look at him and briefly wonder at the miracle of me. How did I ever survive to be who and what I am? How did I ever manage to live into adulthood? I wonder what he thinks of *my* tattoos. A small part of me hopes he approves.

I nod, teeth and fists clenched. Oh, yes. I remember.

He crosses his arms over his chest, and his dog-chain bracelet twinkles in the uncertain light.

We stand, facing each other, over the Amontilladoian crib and look around the room, curious. There isn't much to see if you're looking the wrong way.

There is no door in the doorway of the room. It looks like the hole left by a missing tooth. Door wood, especially *old* door wood, makes great firewood. Dry and dense, it burns with a smoky, woody odor that mixes well with the musky smell of pot.

I remember that. I remember them being so poor that burning the inside doors in their little pot-bellied stove was just one of the many economies they practiced. Someone would collect old newspapers, cardboard boxes, twigs, even: anything that would burn.

A beaded curtain covers the hole where the door *should* be. Some of the beads look like lovingly polished stones, giving the overall effect a handmade look.

Loud, rough voices, raised in warm, muted

conversation come from beyond the beaded doorway. It sounds as if they are arguing about Exodus.

"Moses, man, Moses was . . . was . . . well, he was, just a *man*, man. Like, ready to be used by God, man."

Rumbles of affable agreement and the voices fade as if conversation has lulled.

A millipede—easily a foot long—crawls along one wall, tracking its way to the ceiling. It looks like something that would've been happy in a swamp with dinosaurs. It finds a crack and disappears inside the wall with a whispery slithering noise that sounds like a snake over sand.

I suppress a shiver.

The painting on the wall behind my companion is also part of my mental landscape. It shows an ephemeral angel, trump raised to the heavens, standing atop a knife-edge mountain peak, while a star supernovas behind it. Sullen colors dominate the scene. Angry purples and blues, they are the colors of a final judgment.

Written at the bottom of the painting are the words 'Many are called, few are chosen' in a contrasting, brilliant white. It is a phenomenal thing. The hand that rendered this painting had a profound understanding of depth, light and shadow. I can almost feel a cold, angry wind blowing out from the wall. When I was a child, I used to stare at it and wonder who took the picture. Where did they stand with the camera so the angel wouldn't see them?

My friend looks over. Then he looks back at me.

The meaning in his eyes is clear. *Many* are *called. Have* you *been chosen?*

I don't need this from him. Not here, not now. I shake my head in annoyance and turn away. I've become what I had to so I could eat. Passion is for young men; practicality is for the adults they grow into.

A pungent odor permeates the thin, dingy peeling walls of this room. I'm not smelling it, of course. I'm *remembering* it. The wood, the air, every surface including the baby's skin and breath is redolent of incense, pot, fried food, cat urine, sex, booze, baby poop, lamp oil, and burning wood.

The baby sleeps through it all. It's a small, sexless, dirty critter; naked, save for the blanket and a cloth diaper that has been washed many, many times. The diaper itself is faded, and while I can't really tell what material it's made of in the dark of the room, I have a sneaking suspicion it is buckskin.

The diaper is held on by one rusty safety pin at the left waist.

It would be quite easy to catalog this household as being monstrously neglectful and abusive. It would be easy to ignore some of the smaller clues, and call these people poor white trash.

They'd say they *are* poor, but only in a material sense. They'd have no response to the 'white', because the issue of race rarely comes up, and as for 'trash', well, opinions varied.

Yes, the baby is a little skinnier than he should be, and dirty, but he also seems to shine with good health. Yes, the mattress is bare, but the blanket is warm and made of all the colors of the rainbow. The making of it required the skills of a weaver: a gift of love.

Poor, yes, but their priorities are exactly where they should be. My companion glances at everything, and then looks at me. He indicates our surroundings with a smug sneer on his face and outspread arms.

For no reason I can adequately explain, I feel hot, guilty tears rise to my eyes. I stare down at the baby to avoid the judgment in my friend's gaze. The baby remains undisturbed by the cat, our visit, or the voices raised in rough laughter from the other side of the doorway.

A quiet moment falls in the other room. I feel a brief tension, like the hardening, all at once, of a vital artery.

The walls of the room, though making no visible movement to my mind's eyes, contract. I feel like a dying moth in the hands of an incautious, over-eager child. My companion watches me, arms still crossed over his chest in a hostile way. Whatever is happening is happening only to me. He remains unaffected. I am being squeezed by the forces around us. My breath comes in hot gasps, and my heart thunders in my chest.

Something is trying very hard to tell me something.

"Alright! I'm listening!" I manage to gasp out The walls around me contract brutally a final time, and then snap back. A voice, like oily smoke, pours out of the other room. And as if I needed this final clue, music I've been listening to for as long as I've been alive follows that voice with a reedy, scratchy, ill-played guitar.

"I'm walking down this beat-up track. I've got dusty tears in my eyes, and I'm trying to read a letter from my lonely home."

The baby opens its eyes. A blue gaze swivels around the room for a moment, taking in the darkness. The cat, sensing the baby has awakened, stretches out her neck and purringly sniffs its nose. The baby screws its face up and gives a quiet sneeze. This bothers the cat not at all, and Creamapara settles down to an extended bathing session, doing what it can to improve the condition of the baby's hygiene.

The baby follows this movement, and reaches out one tiny hand. The cat rubs its jaw along the hand, and the baby giggles.

The music continues to play in the other room. I can hear fingers trying to snap to the rhythm, and whispered comments coming from the listeners.

"Yeah."

"Groovy."

"Sing it, mama."

Creamapara loses interest in the baby's face, having gotten it as clean as possibly with cat spit, and goes to work on the top of the baby's head. The baby stares interestedly at the ceiling. For a long moment, it does nothing. It seems to be listening to the music. Then it rolls over on his stomach. Creamapara meows once, watching. When it becomes apparent the baby isn't returning to its bath, Creamapara begins bathing herself.

Lifting its head, the baby looks toward the source of the music. It listens some more. I watch, grinning, along with my silent companion, as the baby begins to bang its face in time to the music against the mattress of the crib, driving it into the wall.

I can't help myself.

"Alright!" I shout, and bang my head in response. My companion grins too, and starts to mosh with himself.

The baby, lost in its world of metronomic beats, continues to bang its face against the mattress.

A voice asks, "Hey, man. Do you hear that?"

Another voice, torpid and heavy, replies, "It sounds like it's comin' from the kid's room, man."

From the other room there is a sound like a box of wire hangers being dropped, and the guitar stops playing. I hear the sound of strings being scraped roughly across a cement floor.

Bare, running feet slap across the concrete floor. A

young, skinny, long-haired thing walks into the room, an enormous bong with a toad body in its hands, and concern on its face. I know who this is, having seen pictures proudly displayed to my girlfriends over the years, but it still takes me a long moment to decide that 'it' is a man.

He is gloriously dressed in his 'anti-establishment' paraphernalia. A psychedelic, hand-knitted-yarn, knee length serape-thing covers his shoulders. I can see his belly button peeking out underneath it, and the skinny stack of his ribs. His face is dotted with acne, and he can't grow a beard to save his life.

His dirty, ripped jeans probably qualify for EPA Superfund status. They are covered in patches and make up the majority of the material: peace signs, smiling, wise, non-descript, big-eyed creatures, crucifixes, and a large, idealized patch I strongly suspect is supposed to be Gandalf.

He smells an awful lot like the bottom of a well-used hookah. The black curly hair on his head stands out like an enthusiastic tumbleweed.

A rough, hand-carved, wooden cross, a foot long, tied with bootlaces at the intersection, hangs from a leather thong around his neck and swings freely at the level of his navel.

My companion points at the man. I realize my friend is seeing something that maybe *he'd* forgotten and had come to remember. It is a comforting thought.

We all change. We all grow. We all mutate into versions of ourselves that we could never anticipate. Sometimes we change for the better, sometimes, however briefly, we change for the worse.

Bruises cover my friend's arms and shoulders; his thighs and his back. They are up high, under the covering of his tattered t-shirts; always someplace out of sight. I realize why he's here. He's come to see where it all started before it all went wrong.

I can look back and give him *some* perspective. There would be pain, and tears, and blackest recrimination, but eventually, after climbing the mountain until your fingernails bled . . . eventually there would be forgiveness and reconciliation.

He has years yet, and my eyes fill with sympathy for his remembered pain.

The man peers over the edge of the crib, scratching gustily at his scalp as if to dislodge invaders. A moment later he's joined by a short, skinny, brown-haired woman wearing what looks like a beige cape. She's missing most of one arm and smiling vapidly. She smells a bit more bong-like than the male figure. A high, wild light shines in her eyes.

We can see what would later put her in the nursing home dancing around in the back of her eyes; giggling and glinting.

The man puts his arms around the woman and in a heavily slurred voice, asks, "Dana, what is the kid doin', man? Is Nescher alright?"

The woman smiles and pats his cheek condescendingly. Her voice is heavily slurred as well. "I told you, Dale!" she says, grinning widely, "He loves the music!"

"Oh, wow! Far out, man! You guys! Come check this out!"

Other people crowd into the room: long-haired, dirty cast-offs and cast-aways of a society they've rejected or been rejected by. Some look like heavily amphetamined bikers. Others look like vagrants. One fine young specimen wears a clerical collar and smokes a joint five inches long and two thick.

They all share the same look: a light within shines, uninhibited, from their eyes. Stupid, helpless tears pour down my face. They are not my blood, but they *are* my family, the roots I grew from.

My friend throws his head back and laughs. He hasn't learned yet how to cry in joy. He's still a teenager, and I don't learn that for several years yet. Without really thinking about it, I realize it is the first noise he's made that I've heard.

The people crowded around the crib watch the baby, grinning and laughing like stupid, stoned loons. I don't recognize most of them, but there's my godfather, Frank Romano, bearded and in his Road Rat regalia. He smells like his Harley, and the taint of Vietnam still stains his eyes. There's my aunts and uncles, their boyfriends, girlfriends and assorted hangers on which feature in some way in my life. Others, less important and more. My heart hurts with the love I feel for them at this moment.

The baby in the crib, who's belatedly realized he has an audience, stops banging his face against the mattress, and looks at the stoned, smiling faces surrounding him with wide blue eyes.

Creamapara meows inquisitively. She'd been interrupted from a nap *and* a bath! There's a round of spontaneous, bellowing laughter.

"That's my kid, man!" shouts my father, and he picks me up, carelessly dropping the bong. He kisses me on the lips, getting hair, chicken grease, bong water, and his own tears all over me. He carries me in his arms, accompanied by back slaps, and raucous, good-natured laughter, back into the other room. After a moment, the guitar starts playing again. It's a different song, and sung twice as loud, by all.

"Innnnnnnnnnnnnnnn the eeeeeeeeeeeeveniiiiiiiiiiiiiiiiin' . . .."

My father's voice comes from the other room. I can hear the joyous tears in his voice as he shouts, "That's my son! That's my Eagle!"

And that's enough for the two of us. This is where we both began. We can lie to each other, and deny each other as much as we like, but neither one of us can deny the skinny, ratty little thing in the crib, being adored by his stoned mother and father and the rest of their commune.

My younger self looks at me from across our crib, and nods. His face, free as of yet of the beard I will eventually wear, breaks into a smile. His mouth works silently, but I can see what he's saying.

Don't let us forget!

We share a nod of mutual understanding, and he walks out of the memory sphere, back into his life.

I wipe my face and whisper, "I won't, Nescher. I won't." I stand there for a long time, listening, crying and remembering.

After a while, my alarm goes off back in the real world. It's time for me to return, to get up and get ready for work. I sigh and the bubble 'pops'. I resurface, turn the CD player off, and stand.

I wipe the tears from my face and walk back into the bathroom.

I turn the water on in the shower, look into the mirror, and grin. At the edge of hearing, there is a warm gust of all too familiar laughter.

Chapter 46 – Paying For All Of It:

One of the hardest things I've ever had to do was to ask your Grandpa Huth for permission to marry your mother. Don't tell him I said this but your grandpa scares the hell out of me.

There's nothing *overtly* threatening about him. He's a nice man, and like all the Huths he smiles readily and often. His kindness is unimpeachable and he's the kind of old-school Master Pimp-Ninja that can do anything. I have an enormous amount of respect for your grandfather, but he's the standard that I'm measured against, too.

See, when you start the dating thing, initially you'll be dating girls who want to piss off their parents. Dating boys Daddy wouldn't approve of is an accepted and expected form of female rebellion. It's the only reason I got *any* dates in high school.

If their fathers did a good job raising them, they are the masculine standard for the rest of the woman's life. When they grow up a little, they start looking for guys who can measure, favorably, against their fathers.

Needless to say, *everyone* knows I don't measure up to your Grandpa Huth. Your mother's system short-circuited badly somewhere along the way.[105] I live in constant fear that at some point she will realize this and your grandpa

---

[105] Proof positive that your mother loves me is evidenced by the fact the she married me anyway. I'm not sure what undiagnosed brain injury allowed that to happen; I'm just grateful.

will pick me up by the scruff of the neck and toss me into the dark and the cold like a dead raccoon.

We get along quite well, but you can see it in his eyes, too. "Make one wrong step and you're dog food, boy."

And if that weren't bad enough, your mother has a big brother who is vastly successful, charming, witty, urbane and galaxies away from the bib-overall-wearing, chewing-tobacco-eating, knuckle-dragging experiences of my own life.

The two men in her life are, like, Moses and Thomas Edison. I am, at best, Captain Cave-Man or Scrappy Doo.[106]

I respect that. I respect *them*. And I wrote this essay a couple of years ago, detailing the nerve-wracking experience behind meeting your mother's father and big brother *on the same day.*

I didn't throw up. I *wanted* to, but I didn't.

~~~~~~~~

'It's important to her.' I kept telling myself that as I showered and dressed. 'It's important to her. And anyway, the Huths the ones you've met already are nice people! It's not like her father's going to bust a cap in you right there, at the dinner table!'

'Yeah,' sniggered another mean little voice. 'I mean, he'll probably let you finish dinner. The tablecloth might get stained otherwise.'

'Stop it!' said a third voice. 'They're perfectly nice people and they already know you intend to ask. It's about her. Are you willing to make a jerk of yourself for her?'

'Yeah, but, I mean, we're talking about Nescher here,' chimed in a fourth voice. 'He's got the table-manners of a

---

[106] Hopefully your futuristic entertainment device will have some sort of function allowing you to access 1970s cartoons, the absolute apex of animation.

diseased buffalo. He spits when he talks. He tries to be funny and charming by telling knock-knock jokes. He'll probably break a chair when he sits down, knock the table over when he tries to pass the gravy and put his elbow in the butter. This is the same guy who tried to drive a thirteen foot truck under an eight foot-'

"Okay. All of you. Shaddup," I said, to the arguing voices and the falling water.

For a few blissful moments, the only noise was the gurgle of the drain and the patter of the water falling around me. Then I started running through my monologue. "Mr. Huth. I reckon by now you've heard that I asked your daughter to marry me. Wellsir . . . Mr. Huth, sir, this is hard enough without you actually loading the rifle, sir. . ..."

'Yeah. That's good, Nescher,' sniggered the evil little voice. 'Remind him that you're vulnerable, alone, and nobody will miss-'

"Shaddup," I replied. "Okay. What about . . . 'Mr. Huth. I have fallen hopelessly in love with your daughter. I'd like your permission to marry her.' That's good, right? Simple, straightforward, and it demonstrates my level of affection for his baby," I mumbled, spitting soap from my mouth.

'What if he says 'Why should I? You don't deserve my daughter?' The sniggering in the back of my head was getting out of control.

"I'll reply with 'Nosir, I don't deserve your daughter. I don't pretend to. I'm not good enough for her, and I never will be. And despite that, she still loves me. And I just got to ask, Mr. Huth: what's up with that? Does mental illness run in your family?'"

~~~~~~~

"How do I look?" I asked, coming down the stairs, my hands held wide for her inspection.

She smiled up at me, melting my brain. Again. "You look great, honey."

"How'd I do shaving?"

She cupped my face in her hands, a goofy smile eating up the lower half of her skull. She was enjoying this. She was enjoying my miserable state of psychic torment, the incorrigible hussy!

She wiped her hands gently down the sides of my face, smiling like a hyena the whole time. "Smooth as a baby's butt, honey."

I resisted the urge to make the obvious joke and looked myself over in the mirror. Antonio Banderas I'll never be, but I clean up pretty good when I make the effort.

I'm not a snazzy dresser. "Crumpled" seems to be the watchword of my wardrobe. Blue jeans, t-shirts and sneakers are what I wear to church. In the complicated, swirling matrix of hard-core belief and ethnic superstition handed down from ten thousand of my forebears, wearing anything else would almost be sacrilegious.

The first time I got married, I wore jeans. I hope to be buried in them. But Chris had said that her father would appreciate a little bit more of an effort than I normally make. So there I was, staring at myself in your mother's mirror. My hair was very carefully styled, cut short as it was. My jeans were clean and neatly rolled. I wanted to impress, but my wardrobe only goes so far. The *coup de tat*, so far as I was concerned, was the brand, spanking, new, button-down, green pullover, 100% cotton shirt I was sporting. It went nicely with my eyes, even if it wasn't blue. I smiled at my reflection. My reflection smiled back and shot me a wink.

The shirt had been something of an issue. When I drove up, I brought the very best clothes I owned. Your mother looked them over and made a face that looked as though she smelled something awful.

"What the problem is?" I asked.

"Don't you have anything else?"

"Like what?"

"Like a nice shirt."

"These *are* my nice shirts! These are the nicest shirts I own!"

She gave me that look again. "You don't have anything other than t-shirts?"

"I don't own anything *but* t-shirts."

"Huh."

Then she gave me that look that I've learned to interpret as 'There's something I need to say to you and I'm a little worried you might take it the wrong way, and I don't want you to, but I'm going to say it anyway.' "We-e-e-e-l-l-l-l-l, my Dad would appreciate more of an effort . . .."

I spread my hands helplessly.

"I guess we're going to buy a new shirt then, aren't we?" Your mother said, looking at me with a firm smile. "Are you mad?"

"No, I'm mad 'cause I don't have a freaking shirt. Are *you* mad at *me*?"

"Nope."

"You sure? It's not too late to dump me and find yourself a snazzier guy. Maybe a flashy dresser? Somebody who doesn't need his girlfriend to dress him or buy him clothes? I'm sure Colin's still available." I was smiling as I said it, and so was she. I mimicked the picking up of a phone, and held it to my ear.

"Hello? Colin Firth?" In my very best Eric-Cartman-meets-Scooby-Doo voice. "This is Christine. Save me, Colin! Save me from this jeeeeeee-eeeeeerk."

I don't do well with first impressions. Something about my looks, my personality and my overall presence makes people take a while to warm up to me. I find that if I'm meeting people for the first time the very best thing I can do is keep my mouth shut and let them talk to me. Otherwise they might get a glimpse into my psyche and run for the torches and pitchforks.

This wasn't going to be much of an option in asking your grandfather for permission to marry your mother. I was going to have to be engaging, scintillating, witty and urbane; qualities I don't possess and fake badly.

"Dear God, please help me not make a complete jerk of myself," I prayed, while smoothing down the cowlicks on the back of my head.

"You look wonderful, honey," your mother said, smiling at me and giving me a warm hug. I couldn't help but think of a corpse laid out for viewing.

~~~~~~~~

She let me drive: a nice touch on her part. I loved your mother's car. It had this 'Drive me, Nescher. You know you want to,' siren-thing happening. I sat in her driver's seat, and I felt like I was sitting in a cockpit.

"Turn on something that rocks, Chris!"

U2's *Rattle And Hum* started playing from her CD player; she opened the sun roof, rolled the windows down and we took off.

"Okay. Now. You're basically going to be driving down this road for an hour and a half."

There was just the faintest hint of a giggle in the back of my mind at that. The sun was shining, the road was pretty much wide open, and I was sitting in the driver's seat of a car that loved me. It took us about forty-five minutes to make her parents' house, and we stopped for iced tea and aspirin along the way.

~~~~~~~

"Tim and Lisa, Kate and John, Ian and Karen."

"Right."

"Cameron, Ian, aaaaaannnnnd . . ."

"Aaron. Aaron's the youngest." "Dang. Okay. Cameron, Ian and Aaron."

"Right. Just remember 'C.I.A'."

"And Mr. and Mrs. Huth." "Well, yeah, but they probably wouldn't mind it if you addressed them as Martin and Helen," she said, laughing.

"Yeeeeaaaaahhh . . . maybe after we get married."

Kate and John I'd met prior to this. They lived in a home not far from your mother's, in the kind of neighborhood that writers dream about growing up in.

They'd thrown open their home to me, shared expensive food and drink and treated me like some kind of a visiting pasha. I didn't know if this was they way they treated all guests, or if this was some kind of a special effort to impress, but it worked. I wanted to move in with them, do their dishes and wash their cats. I liked them right away and could see myself fitting in with their family.

Your Uncle John is one of those immediately affable people that you like all at once. He has an impressive singing voice that he busts out at the least excuse, tells wonderfully engaging jokes and stories and manages to combine both metropolitan savoir faire with a winsome dorkiness that makes you want to hang out with him all the time. He an interesting conversationalist, he doesn't take himself too seriously, and he isn't stingy with the beer. I like John. When I worked as a gravedigger, I worked in the burial park of the funeral home that he ran. He was my boss, but he was so far removed from where I was that I almost never saw him at work. The guys never let me forget that I was the boss' wife's, brother-in-law, however, and they treated me with the loose contempt that such a thing engenders.

Your Aunt Kate is lovely as all the Huth babes, and has an engaging, outgoing personality. Her laugh was a thing that could infect a room with smiles. Your Aunt Kate is a force of nature. She's awesome with a capital 'A.' She is not only a friendly, warm, personality that knows everyone; makes friends readily and has the kind of personality you'd hate to disappoint in any way, she's also the kind of six-armed, ninjatastic, Mom-Warrior that can do anything needed with energy and ability to do everything else. I told her once, after spending a couple of hours with her family, that she deserved a chest full of medals.

A true story that illustrates Kate's personality better than anything I can make up: Kate ran a marathon for a charity in Anchorage, Alaska.[107] Your mom and I went with her; ostensibly to cheer her on—and we did—but we then spent the next ten days touring Alaska. One of our stops was Denali National Park, in southwest Alaska; a beautiful place, a billion miles from anywhere. We had a cabin in a resort just outside the park, and stopped at the resort's restaurant.

---

[107] Because that's the kind of thing your Aunt Kate does: runs marathons for charities in Alaska. Her kids couldn't come so as the youngest person in our party, I was subject to all of her frustrated Mom-ing. She didn't actually lick her finger to clean dirt off my face; she *wanted* to, but she didn't. She yelled at me a couple of times for packing soda instead of water and had to restrain her head-slapping arm a few times, I think. She *really* missed her boys, that trip.

So there we were, surrounded by miles of nothing but rugged, mountainous beauty. Moose and bears everywhere, with the resort being just one small example of human civilization. Your Aunt Kate walks into the restaurant and five minutes later is engaged in conversation with a guy she's known for something like twenty years.

I'm firmly convinced that if your Aunt Kate was kidnapped by aliens and dropped on the dark side of the moon, she'd find someone she knew within half an hour and have a charity benefit organized a couple of hours after that. Hanging out with Kate makes you want to be a better person and nap more. Their three sons are Cameron, Ian and Aaron. The first time we met they were all younger than thirteen. So there were at the same spiritoemotional level I was.[108] We'd spent an enjoyable afternoon doing lighter tricks, talking about girls in the neighborhood and trying to out-man each other. I adored them right away and was enormously fortunate to have met them when I did; I could still fool them into believing I was cool.

I was hoping to see them at your grandparents' house, as that would provide me with at least one ally in this confrontation.

The first time I met your Aunt Karen was during the visit when I met Kate and John for the first time. Watching her interact with the boys, I was forcibly reminded of a Kindergarten teacher who really liked her job. She bounded on down the hiking trail, laughing as loudly as the boys were, and stopping every few minutes to point out an interesting bug or an engaging flower.

I liked Karen. She was a lot of fun. Karen is the baby of the bunch and the closest to me in age. Because of this, I

---

[108] They were—and are—smarter than me.

think, we spend a lot of time arguing. Not in an animostic fashion; more like an older sister trying to educate a recalcitrant younger brother. We've had an ongoing argument about the nature of morality—and whether God has anything to do with it—for several years now. It's engendered at least one letter-writing campaign and an article from a national news magazine has made a cross-country trip three or four times.

For the record, I'm *totally* winning.

I like arguing with anyone, but Karen's belief system is ninety degrees to mine and that makes things even more fun. Like all these Huths she's stubborn, convinced she's right and willing to take three falls out of four to prove it.

She lives out in Portland with her husband, Ian, and we don't get to spend enough time with them.

I hadn't met Ian at this point, but I'd heard a lot about him.

Ian is a rock star. He's cool, loose and quiet, with the kind of "Hey, man. What's up?" personality I've always tried to affect and could never quite pull off.

Ian is the kind of guy you don't want to play poker with. You're never really sure what he's thinking, and even when you think you've got him figured out, he sneaks around a corner on you and pulls something out that leaves you gasping for breath and giggling. When I thought of being "Cool Dad Husbandman," the image that wouldn't go away was Ian playing Lynard Skynard's "*Simple Man*" on his guitar.

And these are the men your mom's sisters have married. Instead of going for a successful ninja or an icon of cool, your mom wanted to marry a nine-dollar-an-hour slob with self-esteem issues out the wazzoo.

I asked her about it once. "Why . . . why on earth did you *ever* marry *me*?"

She thought about it for a few seconds, smirked at me and said "I was determined to save your cat."

Tim and Lisa I hadn't yet met by this point, but I'd heard so many cool stories about them, I was, unaccountably, looking forward to it. Tim is your mother's eldest and only brother. Where I come from, it's the eldest brother who sticks the shotgun in your mouth when you make his baby sister cry.

I've met Mr. and Mrs. Huth[109] once before and I was impressed. Your grandparents are the American success story written with a mid-west flavor. They've worked hard their entire lives, provided for children who then went on to have successful lives of their own, and are now enjoying what looks like a leisurely and well-earned retirement. Only someone who didn't know them very well would think that for very long, however. Your grandmother has a series of social and church commitments that keeps her hopping seven days a week. Her day begins well before sunrise and ends long after everyone else has gone to bed. She swims, she cantors at our church; there are book clubs and playgroups and dinners to manage; charity benefits to organize and funerals to sing at. She works more hours than I do and she does most all of it for free. I'm not sure where she finds the energy, but the idea of even trying to keep up with your grandmother on her weekly round makes me want to crawl under the bed and hide.

---

[109] I called them that—Mr. and Mrs. Huth—until the day I married your mom. Now I call them "Mom and Dad." Something about your grandparents has scared a level of affectionate respect into me. I'd never even consider addressing them by their first names. Whenever I talk about them to other people it's either "My in laws" or "My mother and father-in-law."

Your grandfather still manages properties in the town next door. He's slowed down a step or two, and he allows me to do the mowing for him, but nothing short of the Rapture will prevent him from doing whatever he thinks needs to be done. I've come over in ninety-five degree heat and found him repairing walls or pulling up carpet in his shirt sleeves. Your grandmother tries to get him to slow down more. Living near them as we do, I'm able to help quite a bit, but when your grandfather decides it's something he needs to do, he gets it done.

He is as tough as teak. It's almost enough to make me bite my knuckles and whimper. Yes, he's slowed down a bit, but the truth of the matter is that he doesn't *need* my help. He's earned the right to step back and supervise, but he doesn't want to. And that's cool too.

Mr. Huth is as lean as a switchblade. He wears a thin beard on sharply prominent features, and his eyes have a friendly directness about them. He looks at you when he talks, and he tends to have a reply ready that knocks the feet out from under smart-assed, Jew-boy, future son-in-laws.

His kids would probably disagree, but as an outside observer, I can make this statement: Mr. Huth is *impossibly* cool. He's the Sammy-Davis-Jr-of-the-mid-west cool. He doesn't talk a whole lot, but when he does he speaks in a soft, gravelly voice that you could picture a poet trying to acquire in front of a mirror. You look at the man, and you can easily picture him with a saxophone slung around his neck, a hand rolled smoke burning on the mic stand.

When he moves, he moves and speaks with a quiet, slow, whispery sort of dignity that I'll never be able to pull off, even if I live to be a thousand years old.

I like Mr. Huth. He's funny and he's kind to helpless creatures (like smart-assed, Jew-boy, future son-in-laws). But more importantly, from my perspective at least, I *respect* Mr. Huth. He's smarter than I am, more capable than I am and a little more aware of where he came from and what he's about. My father has a term that sums it up: Mr. Huth is a self-actualized human being.

The first time we met, he shook my hand, looked me in the eye, and smiled at me in genuine welcome. The whole time I was picturing myself as a knuckle-dragging-bib-overall-wearing-troglodyte, wiping my nose with my forearm, and smiling gap-toothed at this hero. "Wall, howdy! Ah'm Nescher an' I wanna marry yer daughter! You don't mind, do ya'?" Mrs. Huth is a smiler, and after having four children, teaching for twenty years and enjoying retirement for a few more, she's also still a babe.

I don't think I've ever seen her without a smile crinkling at the edges of her face. Even when she's not wearing one on her mouth, her eyes are smiling. There's a lot of Mrs. Huth in your mother's features. The two of them smile the same way, and almost as often.

She taught third grade for twenty years at a small, private school in the town next door. Notice: I didn't say she taught art, or science or history. I said she taught third grade. She taught all the subjects an American third grader is likely to come across. That meant she was as tough as a steel ball bearing, driven, artistic, clever, cunning, a little mean, smarter than you'll ever be and able to spot bullshwa from a mile away.

Luckily, your grandmother is also a wonderfully nice person. I think she met me for the first time and saw something of a three-legged puppy: I was kind of cute, totally helpless and inept in a stupidly adorable sort of way.

If her daughter was determined to marry me she'd just make the best of it, keep a rolled-up newspaper handy and try to keep me away from anything breakable.

If you sawed your grandmother in half you'd find mom all the way down to the molecular level. In a room full of people, half of them complete strangers, your grandmother will adopt them all spiritually and mom it out all over the place. She lovingly corrects me whenever she feels its necessary, intercedes whenever she finds the need to do so, and makes any number of suggestions to make life easier for everyone.

I love her to pieces. She's fifteen flavors of awesome. Our first conversation looked like this: "So, Nescher. What do you do for a living?"

"I'm a nine-dollar-an-hour-security-guard."

Your mom quickly interceded. She could see me turtling and shrinking, I think. "He writes, too, Mom. He's a really good poet. He's been published!"

"Oh! How nice! What kind of poetry do you write?"

"Oh, you know. I mostly write free verse."

Your mom, God bless her sweet face, kept trying. "He writes prose, too, Mom."

"Really? What kind?"

"Well, I write about all kinds of things. I just finished this story about a vampire getting eaten . . .."

Yeah.

The Huths were very kind the first time we met. Of course, I wasn't asking them for their daughter's hand that time, either . . ..

Now I'm telling you all this as a sort of preface for what comes next. Your dad, fearless explorer extraordinaire, had to have dinner with his girl's family; all of them older, wiser, mature-er, and clever-er than he is.

We pulled up in your grandparents' driveway. My hands weren't actually trembling, but I could feel little knots of incontinent butterflies in my stomach and I had to fight the urge to hyperventilate. We walked up the sidewalk, seeing her Dad first. He'd stepped outside for a smoke and smiled warmly as he saw us.

I stuck my hands in my pockets, and slouched down in a nervous way. I do that a lot, especially when I'm scared. "Hello, Mr. Huth," I managed to mumble.

Mr. Huth smiled at us and said, "You have to go inside and eat right now. You're late." '

Awwwwwwwwww, crap,' I thought, wondering how this was going to look.

We walked inside, and there was a chorus of warm greetings from your mom's assembled family. Introductions were made and I did my level best to keep from puking on my shoes.

~~~~~~~~~

This is a wide, sweeping statement, but I'm pretty comfortable making it: The world is designed for right-handed people. You only really notice this if, like us, you're left-handed, but it's true. The world is designed to be used by people who are right-handed. Tools, doors, toilets, ignition switches, mouse pads, stairwells, remote controls, light switches, traffic flow patterns, clothing, almost everything is laid out right-hand specific. If, like us, you're left-handed, you either learn to adapt, or you spend your entire life doing things awkwardly.

I'm one of those adapters. The only thing I do exclusively with my left hand is write. I throw with my right; my right hand is my strong hand, and everything else

I do I can do with either hand. I can bat either left or right; use a tool with either left or right; drive, swing a golf club, chop down a tree, hammer in a stake, peel a potato. You name it; I can probably do it with either hand. I like to call my left my 'smart' hand, and my right my 'dumb' hand. I'm not complaining, I'm prefacing. Lefties are used to this sort of thing by a certain age and we tend to just deal with it. The only time it becomes an issue is when certain delicate procedures are necessary. Like, eyeball surgery, or microscopic diamond handling, or eating a fancy dinner with your future in-laws and having to use silverware. The way I grew up, the common tableware was a fork or a spoon. One or the other. If you didn't have a fork handy, you used a spoon. No spoon? Dig out a fork.

We tended to eat things hunched over our plates and in a hurry. Dinner conversation was limited to threatening grunts if someone reached toward your plate and fearful injunctions to clean up the mess before somebody got killed. We ate fast. You had to eat fast to ensure nobody else got more than you did. There was only so much to go around and getting seconds was purely a matter of getting to the food first. The only etiquette we ever demonstrated was ensuring everybody got at least a *share* of the food and knocking the cats off the table as necessary. We used bath towels as napkin, tablecloth and paper-towel when the inevitable glass of powdered milk we drank with every meal got spilled. The proper use of silverware, napkins, and the directions things were passed around the dinner table was not something that got taught in the Pyscher household. My table manners were more geared toward protecting the space my plate occupied.

I'm kind of a barbarian, and, as a result, I'm a bit crippled when it comes to fancy dinners. I learned how to use a knife and fork in the Army. It was a simple survival instinct. You wanted to be invisible when you were shoveling a meal down your gullet. You didn't want to be eating a meatloaf or whatever, with just a fork. It slowed you down too much. And if you dropped a green bean on the floor 'cause you're trying to eat it with a spoon, you got a hairy, spittle-spraying Drill in your face asking you what your malfunction was. You used the silverware available, and you wiped your mouth as necessary. I still tend to switch hands frequently—knife and fork-wise—and I don't spread a napkin on my lap, if I'm using one. I leave it on the table. A throwback to my bath-towel days, I'm sure.

The Huths had spread a veritable banquet. There were noodles, a baked ham, a sweet-potato casserole, and something called a 'Peace loaf' or a 'Peace bread'. Which, if you stop and think about it, is a pretty ominous foodstuff.

I sat down, and I tried my level best to be comfortable.

Christine immediately deserted me and went into the kitchen, leaving me to fend for myself with her elder brother, her father, and her sister-in-law. I'm still hacked off about that.

There was a long moment of uncomfortable silence that I covered by slowly filling my glass with soda. My hands were shaking so hard, I think my glass rattled. I kept my eye on the glass, and avoided looking at her family.

I wished she'd hurry up from the kitchen! "So. How was the drive up here?" Her brother, thank God, was taking pity on me, and starting the conversation.

"It wasn't bad! I have a really good relationship with Christine's car, so we got here in pretty good time." There were polite laughs, Chris returned from the kitchen, and dinner began.

I think I did okay. I didn't spill anything—something I was terrified I was going to do—and I made polite conversation of the kind I'm no good at. I recognized it, of course. It was the polite, mannerly conversation of people who are trying to get to know the 'potential' without prying his head open and sifting through his brains. An example of the differences between the Huths and the Pyschers: when your godfather, Uncle Jerry asked us—and he had to ask *all* of us, one at a time—for permission to marry my sister, we asked him if he was circumcised. He smiled nervously at us, probably partially horrified, and partially figuring we were having him on somehow. "No, I wasn't born Jewish."

"That's okay," we said. Then we flicked out the pocketknives and looked at him expectantly.

I managed to get through the meal without flinging pieces of ham across the table. And if I sprayed any partially masticated food anywhere due to talking with food in my mouth, your mother's family was entirely too polite to mention it. But I was so nervous, I had to slow down and still my shaking hands every so often. I kept up my side of the conversation, making the occasional stupid Nescherism, and telling stories I thought would be at least partially amusing. I don't remember a lot about that dinner. I think I'm blocking it. I have this sneaky suspicion I said or did something abominable, and my mind is mercifully keeping it from me. I didn't know these people all that well, and I desperately wanted them to like me.

I'm lucky the Huths are such generous, kind people, I think. After a while, the food was eaten, stomachs were pleasantly stuffed, and the conversation had reached that point of 'comfortable lull'. This was my moment. I'd rehearsed what I was going to say a thousand times over in my mind. I took a deep, calming breath. I waited for there to be a still spot in the conversation. I clapped my hands together and said . . . "Okay. I've never done this before, so you'll have to bear with me if I'm doing it wrong. "I've asked Christine to marry me. And for whatever reason, she's said yes.

"I wanted to ask you, her family . . ." I paused here, and looked each of her family members in the eyes. " . . .and you specifically, Mr. Huth, sir. . .." And I leaned forward and looked Mr. Huth in the eyes. He was grinning at me in a way that suggested sharks and schools of fat, slow-moving, retarded tuna. I soldiered bravely on.

" . . .for your permission and blessing. "If you're going to say no, I just ask for a two-minute head start." Time stood perfectly still. Mr. Huth's eyes filled my vision until they were as wide—ironically—as the barrel of a shotgun. . .

~~~~~~~~~

Einstein once said that time is relative to the observer. In my own experience, I've found this to be true. For instance, a weekend when you've got no money, no food in the fridge, and no place in particular to be, can last for three weeks. Likewise, a night where you've got insomnia, and you have been twisting and turning all night long, trying to find that one magical position that'll get you into slumber land can last for a year. . . unless you've got to get up early, and then the amount of time you have to *get* some sleep is flashing by like a cave full of hairspray-incinerated bats, while the time it takes you to *fall* asleep is dragging.

I find it kind of hard to believe it took an Einstein to put the scientific screws to that observation. If you stop and think about it, it's perfectly obvious that time is subject to the whims and fancies of the person floundering around in it. I've seen months fly by with nary a backward glance, and I've suffered through an eight hour shift that could've doubled as a geological epoch. If you've ever worked third shift, or done any kind of factory job, you know what I'm talking about. You've watched fossils form.

Another near Einsteinian truth is that time slows—and sometimes almost seems to fracture—when catastrophe is imminent. Just as a convenient example, pretend you're a doughy, smart-alecky, security-guard, Samwise Gamgee look-a-like who's just asked an artistic ninja for permission to marry his sweet, smiling, radiant baby girl.

Time doesn't just slow, it stops. It gets up out of the driver's seat, and wanders into the kitchen, looking for salty snacks. It curls up on the sofa and settles down to watch some C-SPAN. It has itself a long, leisurely conversation about knitting techniques with the cat.

Time slowed like an insect stuck in amber. The world shrunk to Mr. Huth's face. His eyes were glinting at me, weighing me and sifting my potential, I could feel time shift and slide and bleed across various interfaces.

All I could hear was the thrumming rush of blood in my ears and a double-handful of butterflies puking their cute little guts out somewhere in my lower digestive tract. All I could see was white, toothy smiles.

It kinda makes me think Einstein once asked somebody's dad for permission too.

See, the concept had been a good one. 'Ask the whole family for permission.' My reasoning was as sound as any of my reasoning usually is. I knew that if I got Mr. Huth off by himself and asked, as was usual; traditional and all that other good kind of crap, I'd just bollix the whole thing up somehow. I'd say something, or do something, or imply something absolutely horrible that'd have him reaching for the tar, the feathers and the staple gun. I wouldn't mean to, it'd just happen.

Besides, I wanted witnesses. Your grandfather scares me. He always has. I have a healthy respect for the man and I'd like to not wake up in a sack. What I hadn't really taken into account was that by asking the whole family, I was, in effect, asking the whole family. I was a sweet, bumbling, fluffy, innocent kitten who'd wandered into a kennel full of toothy, hungry Rottweilers.

I could hear them breathing at me and they were all grinning, with the exception of your mother. She was grinning and giggling like the little kid who'd covered the aforementioned kitten in gravy. There was this sort of breathless waiting silence around the table. Mr. Huth's eyes took on a warm, elastic quality, and they stretched this moment into a timeless eternity of personal anxiety. The Universe, suspecting something of import was afoot, held its breath . . . . . .Time had another handful of chips and flipped stations to The Weather Channel . . . . . .the butterflies in my stomach quit messing around with puking and started a messy riot . . . . . .and the smile on Mr. Huth's face; mischievous twinkle that I swear had the lightest glint of temptation, spread to cover the whole world . . . and he nodded.

Nuclear technicians watching those spinning needles falling inexplicably back into the 'safe' zone would know a little something about the relief I felt at that moment. "Mr. Pyscher, as your Doctor, I'm happy to inform you that it's not a tumor. The biopsy has come back and revealed it to be an undigested wad of hamburger and processed cheese." Hosannas and Hallelujahs were ringing and singing in my head. The relief I felt took on dimensionality and texture. The butterflies wandered off to sulk. We settled down to a friendly, laid-back kind of conversation. They asked us about our plans and I—being the wise, experienced young man I am—deferred to my lovely. Marriages aren't about grooms, after all. We just need to show up, on time, in a clean outfit, mostly sober. Marriages are about brides.

Your mother insisted I contribute to our plans. I made all kinds of demurrments, and then planned most of it. I just wanted to marry her.

~~~~~~~

Like-minded geeks can often recognize each other. Your mother had told me about her big brother at some length, and I gotta say, I was really worried about making a good impression on him.

"What's he do for fun?"

"He races Formula One cars. Last year he took a balloon trip across Asia. His wife—have I told you about his wife? She's a model with a Ph.D. in nuclear physics—went with him. They visited a tribe in Mongolia and cured them of a skin disease they'd been suffering from for the last few hundred generations.

"Oh. So a lazy under-achiever, huh?"

Okay, so not quite, but your Uncle Tim is still pretty fraking awesome, and much more successful than I am. In Gen-X parlance, your Uncle Tim is an Uber-geek. He is a ninja-tastic, pimp geek. Tim owns his own software company in partnership with some other guys. These guys like, invent the stuff that goes into our computers. He's very, Very, *VERY* good at what he does, and he's enormously successful.

I asked your mother once, out of curiosity, "Is he a millionaire?"

Your mother hemmed and hawed for a while, and never did answer my question.

I, on the other hand, was a nine-dollar-an-hour security guy who thought making jokes on internet writing sites was the be-all and end-all of existence. Yes. I was a bit worried about making a good impression on him. Uncle Tim is married to Aunt Lisa. Aunt Lisa is a fun character. She is a lovely woman, with an interesting mix of ingredients to her personal stew. She intimidates me.

Like all the women in this family—and yes, the men, too—I adore Lisa. She's got a number of advanced degrees in fields I don't understand and know nothing about; she does serious and important work for international governments, and she's founded at least one software concern. She is an intellectual match for your Uncle Tim in every way, and a total babe.

She's also the *teeeeeeniest* bit of a princess and that reminds me of your Aunt Naarah. As a result, I treat your Aunt Lisa the same way I treat your Aunt Naarah: I make every effort to get up her nose whenever we all hang out. There's just something about getting your Aunt Lisa all riled up that entertains me to no end. By now I'm sure you've realized that the Huths are as kind, nice and generous a bunch as has ever walked the face of our fair planet, and I wasted a lot of time and effort worrying about them roasting me over slow coals. They were—to a person—as nice as they could possibly be.But your Uncle Tim is a freaking hero, and a geek to be admired by all geeks everywhere. Uncle Tim got into Dungeons and Dragons waaaaaay back in the day when it was brand-spanking new. He broke out some of his books, and it pre-dated the first edition stuff I cut my teeth on.

I nearly started to hyperventilate when I held some of his stuff in my hands. I looked at him, happy tears of joy standing in my eyes, and thought, 'Here is a geek above all others. Here is a geek to be admired.' I almost hugged him. I'm pretty sure I bowed. We talked about a lot of different things that day, enjoying each other's company. No, Uncle Tim doesn't race Formula One cars. He may have taken a balloon trip across Asia. And while Aunt Lisa is beautiful, talented and incredibly smart in her own right, I don't think she's ever been, like, paid to model. It wasn't easy asking them to accept me. But I did it and I'd do it again. I will never be able to fully express the love, respect and gratitude I feel toward your aunts and uncles. I hope you grow up knowing them, respecting them, emulating them and loving them. For my part, I say this without shame or hesitation: I love being a part of this family!

Man Quotes:

INVICTUS -

Out of the night that covers me,
Black as the Pit from pole to pole,
I thank whatever gods may be
For my unconquerable soul.

In the fell clutch of circumstance
I have not winced nor cried aloud.
Under the bludgeoning of chance
My head is bloody, but unbowed.

Beyond this place of wrath and tears
Looms but the Horror of the shade,
And yet the menace of the years
Finds, and shall find, me unafraid.

It matters not how strait the gate,
How charged with punishments the scroll,
I am the master of my fate:
I am the captain of my soul.

William Ernest Henley (1849-1903)

Acknowledgements, Blame and General Abuse:

The very idea of a non-fiction book makes me wonder who I'm trying to fool. It's hard to do, I'm afraid it's coming out as belabored nonsense, and I'm just insecure enough to believe that no one will ever want to read it and I'll die alone behind a Dairy Queen dumpster, covered in gravy-eating rats.[110]

I got an idea from a friend of mine—Jen Horton—that sounded like she was smoking crack. I was whining to her about not being special, recognized and celebrated as an artist. It was some first-rate whining, too. I was really hitting some high notes and soaking her ear with spit. She sighed patiently, wiped the side of her face and hit me with a suggestion that saved my life. "Send your local newspaper an email. Tell them you'd be willing to write a humor column for free."

I thought she was out of her farking mind. I made any number of excuses while in the back of my mind I kept praying that she would just shut up. If the universe wasn't

---

[110] Because that's what happens to unloved writers: they die and get eaten by rats.

going to give me a J.K. Rowling book contract for the kinds of books I *wanted* to write, then as far as I was concerned, the universe could stick its head up its own butt and suffocate on its farts.

I was *done* with writing, mo'freaka.

I told her what I thought she could do with *that* idea and tried to change the subject. To her credit she didn't give up. It makes me wonder what I've ever done in my life that would allow me to deserve the kinds of friends I have.

She did the one thing she could do that would make me try. She dared me to.

It's a truism of manhood: I won't want to do it if you present it to me as a good idea, but if you dare me, or tell me I can't, I'll kill myself proving you wrong.

I gave her an "I'll show you, buttface,"[111] wrote a couple of sample columns, sent the email off and waited.

Two days later I got a response that made Jen bust her pants laughing.

Tattoos And Baby Food was born.

It was a simple column about my daily struggles as a stay-at-home Dad. The people in town loved it. I had a lot of fun, and for a time I enjoyed a certain amount of local celebrity.

It was a game-changer for me and made me realize that while maybe I wasn't going to be getting car loads of awards for dense literary fiction, I possibly had a gift for humorous non-fiction. Maybe . . . just maybe, I could give the heavy, cow-killing writing a break and write something a little less chewy.

I sent Jen an early draft of this book, and she came back at me with a stick. With a nail in it.

---

[111] I sincerely hope, son, that you eventually have a friend for whom "Buttface" is an acceptable form of address.

"Where's the section about your struggles with Christine's breast cancer? Where's the stuff about the two of you struggling to conceive? Why is this so vain and self-aggrandizing? It's over-written and full of contrived angst! Get back to your *real* voice, Nescher. Why are you pushing this fake crap? Why are you such a *putz*?"

I took her notes in stride, wiped the tears away and realized she was right. And while I love her dearly, I also have elaborate fantasies about her slow, lingering death.[112]

Having said all that, I have to confess that this book got away from me.

There are a couple of different reasons for that, but here's the explanation I'm going with: *I am a storyteller.*

I get it from my Dad, I think. My parents weren't very good at their job. And as tempting as it is to leave that hanging out there . . . a sort of karmic payback, forever in print, condemning my parents for a truly miserable childhood, I'm gonna clarify a little further: my parents were not *qualified* for the job. So while I live in constant dread that I will fail you, son, I also *know* what a bad childhood looks like. Remember that when you're ready to begin fostering your *own* resentment.

Having a son taught me that *no one* is qualified to be a parent and the only difference between a good parent and a bad parent is the level of effort.

Mom? Dad? I get it now

---

[112] Usually something fake, contrived and full of angst. With ants. And barbecue sauce. You've got to understand about Jen, son. She's that rare friend who pushes you without turning into a monster. She slapped me in the head when I was being stupid about moving in with your Mom, so she's earned the right to give me advice. I listen when she talks. She gets on my nerves, but she has bigger balls than I do. I admire the hell out of her husband. He's either the manliest man who has ever lived or he thrives on challenge. Either way he's an infinitely bigger man than I am and I wonder what keeps him from, like, feeding her to a wildebeest.

As much as I hated my parents growing up; as miserable as I was as a teenager; as painful as my entire formative years were, I can still sit, enthralled, listening to my father tell a story about the time he and Davy Crockett defended The Alamo against t

he Cossacks with a can opener and a Bowie Knife.

I swore to myself if I ever had a kid, I would tell the same kinds of rambling, pointless, utterly enthralling stories, like an over-stuffed word sausage.

And that's what happened with this book. I set out to write a simple collection of essays, stories and columns I'd printed about being a stay-at-home Dad. Somewhere along the way I realized I was writing new material: some of it was auto-biographical, some of it was complete fiction, and some of it was a Man's Guide To Manhood. And then I started writing random stories, telling bad jokes, and generally being a complete dork. In short, I was being a Dad.

It just kind of happened. I wrote the jokes, stories, columns and essays that comprise this book on a spurt of head-slapping motivation, proofed it and found, to my surprise, that it was, in every possible way, a book by a father for his son; a letter, a long night around a bonfire, sharing stories, bragging, telling jokes and drinking beer.

I set out to write something meaningful for my son, something real and honest. I don't understand why, but fathers and sons can't communicate with each other. There's too much between them for words to be able to carry meaning. Fathers are worried about being their sons' hero and sons are worried about getting their fathers' approval.

I decided, while writing this book, to simply tell my son the *truth*. "*This* is who I am, *that* is who I was, and I hope you do better than I did, son. I believe you can."

If it paints me in a bad light, well, maybe it'll help him in his own journey.

It's a Man's book. It's a book *about* Men, *by* a Man and it is my fondest hope one little boy in particular will read it and transition over just a little easier into the fraternal brotherhood. Because nobody tells you how to be a Man. No one gives you a manual and a head-start. Your parents meet, have sex, and you get launched into the universe with a rudimentary understanding of things.

That kind of negligence could get a guy killed.

No, it doesn't tell you how to get rock-hard abs or how to chug a beer while groping a pop star and juggling chainsaws . . . although, that might be my *next* book.

It tells the world I love my son.

This book is dedicated with love, affection, and unending respect to everyone who loved me when I most needed to be loved: The King of Kings; God Almighty, Jesus Christ. Master of All Things, Lord of All and My God.

Johnathan "Uncle Gower" Gower, Christopher "Uncle Christopher" Modderman, the Modderman clan, Mark Kelly, the Kelly clan and the rest of the GCM;

To Jennifer "Sheena, Queen Of Goblins" Horton, for the being the kind of friend you love *and* have elaborate murder fantasies about;

To the Huths, for accepting me so readily—and to all appearances, anyway—without regret;

To every woman who has ever loved me, however briefly or badly. Thank you for helping to mold me into the man I am now.

To Christine Gale Huth-Pyscher, for rocking my world on a daily, for debts that can never be repaid: the perfect wife, mother, and soul-mate; classy dame and all-around swell broad. You are the coolest chick it's ever been my pleasure to know. You're the best, Mud Duck, and I freaking love, Love, *LOVE*! you.

And finally, this book is for my son, Geir Edstel-Joseph "Pants" Pyscher. Son, it is my genuine hope that you grow up to be better than I am in every possible way. I love you.

One final note: Everything you've just read is one-hundred percent true.

Except for the parts that aren't.

Also by
Nescher Pyscher

Tales of the Fallen

Tales of the Fallen opens in a sewer at the end of the world. Mankind has poisoned itself with the toxic excesses of an ultra-modern society. The earth has been pillaged, and mankind is partying its way to the Apocalypse with blind eyes and deafened ears.

One man, Solly Mont, knows what is coming. He knows how to rebuild from the ashes, and he can see where mankind needs to be led to prevent this from happening again.

He's done it before, after all.

His wife, Titiana—the abdicated Queen of Faery, and now the keeper of The Beller Inn, the finest bar and restaurant in all of the Outrealms--fetches him home to celebrate their anniversary. His gift to her is the unabridged story of his life, aided by his unparalleled skill in the power of Storyweaving—mankind's mightiest magic.

Solly's story is an exploration of the experiences common to humanity through the eyes of one immortal man.

Solly's master, the anthropomorphization of the virtue Wisdom, gave him the power of a god. Nothing humanity could achieve was beyond him, and even the spirits of earth and air bowed to his will. Being only human, Solly allowed the might and majesty of his gift to overwhelm his commonsense, and in the end, he spurned his humanity. At the very end of his life, when everything he had accomplished was burning into dust and ash, Wisdom came to him offering her slavery as a path to redemption. Solly agreed and Wisdom stripped him of his name, his power and his very sense of self; a gift and a curse that allows him to relearn his manhood after losing the powers of a god. He took the name Solly Mont, and he agreed to do her bidding without question.

He was now a Soldier in the fight of order against chaos. Solly's teacher Taliesin Sungmeister, introduces him to the mysteries of magic, teaching him how to travel through space and time, and showing him his enemies. Theirs is a friendship beyond measure and far surpassing that of teacher and student.

Jack O'Green, a lying Green Man—or a leprechaun, or a vampire, or a fairy, depending on what he feels like telling you—joins him in his fight. His story is part of the whole. He has lived among humans for tens-of-thousands of years, and his insights are invaluable. He is bitter, cynical, mean, petty, crude and crafty, but loyal to a fault, even if he is unwilling to admit it to himself. He fights alongside Solly Mont for reasons of his own.

Cain, the son of Adam, represents the forces of chaos. An immortal with even more power than Solly has, Cain yearns for the final death of the last star and the unbridled hunger of the void. He has sold his soul to Solly's enemies and promises to kill Solly.

Shadows-Dancing-On-Wall is a Storyweaver himself, and he is waiting for Solly in the first place Wisdom sends him after he receives his training in magic from Taliesin. Shadow is a shaman of the People; a tribe of humanity that escaped to the Arctic Circle shortly before the Apocalypse. They are a tribe of hunter-gatherers who live according to a strict regimen of laws designed to keep this tiny enclave of humanity alive long enough to repopulate the earth. Shadow tells him the story of Weaver-of-Shadows: a proud father whose beautiful, perfect son—on track to be the next chief—is killed during the ritualistic hunt of manhood. It is Shadow who tells Solly the story of mankind's final end, and it is Shadow who tasks him with the impossible. Solly has to save Shadow's people from extinction at the hands of Weaver's vengeful spirit. If he doesn't, mankind will die.

Tales of the Fallen: Book 2

"I am who I have been since I started, Jack O'Green: Solly Mont - Storyweaver – The Unknown One - The Wanderer - The Soldier. I am Wisdom's Servant, Wisdom's Slave. I am no-one. But I will see humanity shine. I will see them rise above the muck of their lives and take their rightful place in the universe. I will see man sparkle like a handful of diamonds. I will see humanity make the Creator proud. I willl lead them into the light, Jack O'Green, and I will do it again and again until I get it right!"

With these words, Solly hurls his challenge directly into the teeth of eternity as he dares confront time itself in his never-ending battle for the survival of humanity.

Tales of the Fallen: Book 3 – The Lord of Concrete

Return to the fantastic universe of Tales of the Fallen in this third installment by America's most enthusiastic fantasy writer, Nescher Pyscher. In a sewer at the end of the world, Solly Mont, a man older than the universe and the last Storyweaver, watches the world of man burn itself down before the final killing blow. His is the duty of persevering; to renew what remains and preserve a small hope for humanity's future Solly's universe is as thin as an egg, peopled with all the myths, monsters and stories of yore and spread across the entirety of existence from the Big Bang to the Big Crunch.

Not quite human, not quite a god, Solly has to save the light of life from extinction while redeeming his own failures. His quest takes him to the limits of human endurance and beyond, and promises to be a tale told to following generations as both an assurance and a warning.

Tales of the fallen is a saga about perseverance, failure, triumph, love life, laughter, music, magic, family, lies, truth, sex and everything else that makes being human endurable in a cold, unfeeling universe. Through Solly's struggles to understand the powers that beset us, we find the answers to the questions we ask ourselves and the hope that things can only improve

Solly Mont and Jack O'Green have to save the world again, and this time they have a powerful new ally: an eight year old boy named Jonah Fender. They are confronted by ghosts, goblins, demons and willful gods who try to thwart them every step of the way. Behind them lies the first criminal and the Scion of Night, Cain Bloodspiller and behind Cain lies the embodiment of chaos and evil, the Naught Wind.

Can Solly, Jack and Jonathan save the universe? Or will Cain manage to burn it all down? Come find out in Tales of the Fallen, Book 3: The Lord of Concrete.

Dynamic fantasy series
available from
W & B Publishers

www.a-argusbooks.com

www.ingramcontent.com/pod-product-compliance
Lightning Source LLC
Chambersburg PA
CBHW071522260626
47170CB00002B/462